BLUE COLLAR

DELILAH DEVLIN   ELLE JAMES   LAYLA CHASE
ADELE DOWNS   MEGAN MITCHAM   NJ WALTERS
ROBIE MADISON   KALISSA WAYNE   TRAY ELLIS
JENNIFER KACEY   MIA HOPKINS   SUKIE CHAPIN
M MARIE   BELINDA LAPAGE   KRIS NORRIS
SUSAN SAXX

TWISTED PAGE INC

BLUE COLLAR

BOYS BEHAVING BADLY BOOK #2

Edited by
DELILAH DEVLIN

New York Times & USA Today

Bestselling Author

ABOUT THIS BOOK

When it comes to love...Blue Collar is better! It's time to set aside those sexy billionaires and enjoy stories about the everyday, even sexier bad boys you meet in real life. They may have dirty hands and wear tool belts and jeans instead of Rolex watches, but they're earthy alpha males unafraid to get down and dirty when face to face with a woman in need —*whatever her need may be!* ***Just a few of the titillating stories inside...*** In "Elevation" by Megan Mitcham, an always-in-control policewoman trapped in an elevator shaft gets a sexy rescue from the handsome repairman. A single woman ready for adventure drives a thousand miles to meet an oil field roughneck ready for a long night of laying pipe in Mia Hopkins' "We Drill Deep While Others Sleep". Jennifer Kacey shows the lengths to which an enterprising gal will go to get the owner of an oil change shop to check her fluids in "The Boss". And those are just a few of the sexy stories inside this collection about the everyday hero next door. These are men who've built their powerful muscles from hard work rather than a inside any gym, and they sure know how to use their hard-earned skills to pleasure a woman...

In "Elevation" by Megan Mitcham, a policewoman trapped in an elevator shaft gets a sexy rescue from the handsome repairman. A lonely woman drives a thousand miles to meet an oil field roughneck ready for a long night of laying pipe in Mia Hopkins' "We Drill Deep While Others Sleep". Jennifer Kacey shows the lengths to which a woman will go to get the owner of an oil change shop to check her fluids in "The Boss". These are men who've built their muscles from hard work rather than inside any gym, and they know how to use their hard-earned skills to pleasure a woman...

CONTENTS OF BLUE COLLAR

INTRODUCTION

If you're like me, you have an eclectic appetite for book boyfriends. I can just as easily fall in love with a cowboy, a billionaire, a werewolf, or a Navy SEAL. One hero I can't seem to find in abundance is that everyday alpha male—the blue collar working man.

And let's be real. What woman hasn't ogled a sweaty, well-built road construction worker flipping his Stop sign, and haven't you gazed up at a lineman strapped to a telephone pole and thought, *Oh. My . God.?*

Once, I watched a pair of tree-trimmers swinging in the branches of the huge oak in my back yard, like aerialists from Cirque du Soleil, and I thought their act was the sexiest, most beautiful thing I'd ever watched.

So, asking authors to give me their fantasies featuring those every day, *accessible*, hard-working men, seemed like a pretty good idea to me. I hope you agree, because when it comes to love, ***Blue Collar is better!***

Delilah Devlin

WE DRILL DEEP WHILE OTHERS SLEEP

MIA HOPKINS

The highway is a ribbon of blacktop strung across a whole lot of nothing. Hours slide under my tires as I pass another filling station and another rest stop. In between? You guessed it. Nothing. I drive on. One sleepy country radio station bleeds into the next.

The time's nearly noon when I pull into the parking lot of a brand-new motel, no doubt built to accommodate travelers on their way to the oil fields farther north. I spot Seth's beat-up truck with its bumper sticker: *We Drill Deep While Others Sleep.* Oil worker humor. Dirty and punny. I remember him deciding between this one or *Pump Her 'Til She Squirts.* Classy guy, my Seth.

I put the car in park and turn off the engine. I'm exhausted and wired at the same. I take out my phone and text him. *I'm here.*

His response is immediate. *Room 254.*

I check my makeup in the rearview mirror and grab my duffel bag off the passenger seat. It's heavy as I walk upstairs. When I sidle past a housekeeping cart, the young maid flashes me a faint smile.

I knock on the door hung with a *Do Not Disturb* sign. When it opens, Seth fills my vision and blocks out all the light. Six foot two, all muscle and heat. The room is cold, because the windows are wide open. He's always run hot. He's wearing basketball shorts and a white cotton undershirt. The style's called a wifebeater, but if he ever tried to hit me, I'd smash in his skull with a lead pipe.

"You're late." His voice is so deep.

"I know. I had a problem with—"

"I don't want to hear it." He reaches forward, grabs my arms, and pulls me into the room.

The door slams behind me. I drop my duffel bag in surprise as he pushes himself against me, pinning me against the door. "Seth—"

He cuts me off. "You've been driving all night."

A statement, not a question. I nod. He likes me cool. Emotionless, even a little bitchy. But waves of heat rise off his skin. I can smell the clean, soapy sexiness of his body, and I can't possibly act like he doesn't affect me. He shaved. His lips tempt me, dare me, to kiss him. I'm shaking with horniness, and he smiles because he knows it. The bastard.

His green eyes narrow. "Too tired to fuck me?"

I should be tired. I've driven a thousand miles to see him, but I feel as if I have two bodies, one that clocked the miles, and one that rested up to meet him. Just like at home—one body to do the work and take care of the kids, and one body to sit around pining for him, aching in silence for his touch.

"Hailey." He lowers his lips to my ear. "I asked you a question. Are you too tired to fuck me?"

I close my eyes, hot desire dripping from my brainpan down my spine.

"Answer me," he growls.

"No, Seth."

Despite the late autumn weather, I'm in a yellow sundress, a short cotton nothing with spaghetti straps, his favorite. I'm wearing heels, by request. I've done my makeup, and my hair is loose and carefree, the way I wore it before he moved away, in the hot summer when I fell asleep next to him every night and woke up at his side every morning.

"So sexy," he murmurs.

He's never said I look pretty. Never beautiful. But that's Seth's ultimate praise for a woman: sexy. In truth, I look like a whore right now, and with Seth's rough-and-ready fingers reaching under my skirt, I feel like one, too. Sex delivered like pizza, hot and ready. And I am.

He holds me in place with his body. I gasp when his fingertips find my pussy. I'm wet and swollen for him. Two and a half months—I can't believe we've gone this long without each other. I reach up and grab his shoulders. His rock-hard deltoids flex against my touch as he lets out a strangled groan. He's breathing hard. We both are.

"This first one," he whispers, "ain't gonna be pretty."

"I know." I shut my eyes tighter as he swipes from the back of my hot slit to my clit. His fingertip lingers there, grazing tiny circles on me like he's teasing the button to a nuclear bomb.

I open my eyes. "I don't want it to be pretty."

He doesn't even kiss me. Eyes wild, he spins me around and crushes me against the hotel room door. I turn my head to the side as he lifts my skirt. I'm not wearing panties. I hear him slide down his shorts. Blindly, I stare at the laminated motel evacuation plan taped to the door and feel the hot slide of his cock teasing my dripping, ravenous pussy. I groan. Without another word, he rams himself into me, our shared frustration and loneliness focused on the single point where his body enters mine.

His first thrusts are deep and wild. He's pushing me against the door, smashing me with his muscular body. The air escapes my lungs, and I make tiny gasps through my mouth, fire filling my veins. He's barely touched me, but his familiar heat and size hit all my pleasure points, and soon I'm speeding toward climax faster than I ever have before. I shove my hand between my body and the door. A few caresses of my clit, and my poor stretched pussy clamps down on him. I come so hard, I can't see, and when he feels the contractions, he tightens his grip, drilling into me without mercy, grinding out that first wild climax head-on like the beast he is.

"Fuck, I'm coming," he whispers, but he doesn't need to say anything.

I feel him explode inside me.

We clean up in the bathroom, and when I lie down on the bed, stark naked except for what I imagine is a slightly dazed expression, we still don't talk. Since he left for this first hitch, our phone calls have been short and purposeful. We only exchange important information about bills, the kids, his work, documents I need to send him, banking stuff, and news about his mother. He's always been a man of few words, even fewer over the phone.

I'm not a romantic. I feel his love in the practical things, the way he regularly deposits money in our household account, the way he asks after the kids and remembers what's going on in their lives. I'm not a romantic, but I fucking miss him. When he said he'd gotten a job in oil, I had no idea what it would mean for our family, for us as a couple.

Right now he's stripped naked, too, and in the fading sunlight, my gaze drinks him in. We've been together for a long time, but I'm still fixated on his body. His muscles are more prominent. Is he eating enough? He's always lifted weights, but working on the rig has given him absolutely wicked forearms. I know he wears coveralls and a hard hat for protection, but his face is tanned, deep and dark, bringing out his green eyes. I stare at his tattoos, the old ones he'd gotten before I met him and the new ones—the names of our kids over his heart. His tattoos had slowly become invisible to me, the luxury of looking at a body I took for granted. Now my gaze greedily swallows each slate-green swirl, each faded line.

He'd worked as a loader at an oil refinery near our home before the layoffs. After two months on unemployment with no good prospects, he said, "I think I can get work as a roughneck."

The paycheck? More money than I'd ever seen. The tradeoff? Twelve weeks on, two weeks off, thousands of miles apart. He'd be living in the middle of nowhere, drilling wells with a small crew.

I put on a brave face and told him we could do this. I had my own job at the dental office, and his mom would be around to help with the kids. But inside, I was a mess. Life without Seth? Could I be both mom and dad, handyman and disciplinarian, good cop and bad cop? Who would I go to at the end of the day to talk to, fuck senseless, and fall asleep with?

I felt guilty about these anxieties. Military wives did this. Women whose husbands worked overseas did this. And what about single mothers? What relief did they ever have?

When the time came for him to leave, I told Seth I was proud of him and waved him off. As he drove away, the kids wailed in my arms for their father while my heart wailed silently in my chest for my man.

We'd been apart nine weeks when I confessed. That day, Seth's elderly mother had put a foil pie pan in the microwave and blasted it, Benny had gotten in trouble at school for biting, and Lauren was crying in her bedroom as I tried to comb her hair.

"Stop, Mama. Stop!" she screamed, clutching her stuffed lamb like I was torturing her.

"We have to comb your hair, Lauren," I said, frazzled after a long day. "Pretty ladies comb their hair. Don't you want to be a pretty lady?"

"No, I don't want to be a pretty lady. I want to be like you!"

That night I told Seth about this over the phone. He suppressed a laugh.

"It's not funny," I grumbled.

"It is, a little bit."

I didn't say anything. There was no more wine in the house. I had to settle for a juice box. Angrily, I sucked it dry until it collapsed into itself.

"You know you're sexy, right, Hailey?" he said. "Ain't no one sexier than you."

I didn't need my ego stroked. I needed him. For the first time, I said, "I can't do this, Seth. I don't think I can."

He grew quiet. He didn't assure me, didn't try to. "Come see me," he said instead.

"What?"

"Come see me. Between here and home." He told me a date and a place.

"But you've still got three more weeks."

"I get some time between shifts. We'll have a few hours together."

A few hours with Seth. Could we do this? "Your mom will burn down the house."

"If it makes you feel better, take everyone over to my sister's. Her kids are always at our house. Time she returned the favor."

I did as he said. And now here I am, a thousand miles from home, lying stark naked in a hotel room, my nipples hardening under my husband's hot green gaze.

"Hey," he says quietly.

"Hey, yourself."

I stare at him and crack a smile. We weren't young when we got together. He'd been married before. I was almost thirty-five, no great beauty, and long resigned to the idea of spending my life alone. But we fell in love through the clear eyes of adults. We see each other, even our flaws and vulnerabilities, and that's what I need. A man who sees past my bullshit. A man who doesn't think I'm too stupid to see past his.

When it comes at last, the kiss we share is sweet and slow. Everything that was missing from that first hard fuck we give each other now. Gentleness. Affection.

I love kissing him. He tastes sweet, my Seth, and his lips are hot. Still locked in his kiss, I prop myself up on my elbow and lean over him, my hand resting against his hard chest. I stroke his smooth skin, the faint raised etchings of his tattoos, the tender pink tips of his nipples, so vulnerable on top of all that muscle. He shivers when I graze my nails along his side and rest my fingers in the deep groove at the top of his hip.

He's in amazing shape. He knows I have a thing for muscles, so he's never stopped working out, never stopped being a little vain. Honestly, I'd love him even if he were five hundred pounds. But he hasn't decided to go there just yet. So for now, I'll enjoy my beefcake and the sideways glances of admiration he gets whenever we go out.

I don't care. He's mine.

I embrace him, skin on skin. He groans deep in his chest and pulls me close. His kiss grows hungrier, and his tongue slides against mine. He's holding on to my ass, kneading the cheeks in both hands. His cock hardens against my thigh.

He breaks the kiss but holds my gaze. "Did you miss me?"

I nod as I graze my hand over his abs. He shivers again. The smooth, hot skin gives way to sparse golden hair below his belly button, and I follow the happy trail to his searing, rock-hard shaft.

He palms his big balls as he stares at me.

"So, how much did you miss me?" His green eyes narrow.

I grip the base of his cock with both hands and lower my lips. I tease him with my tongue, licking the slick head like an ice cream cone. He tastes clean and familiar. My mouth waters, and my pussy clenches. When my lips slide down to take him deeper, I feel him shudder. His abs flex, and he reaches forward to stroke my hair.

"That's my girl," he says.

I suck him hard, my hands working in rhythm with my mouth. I close my eyes, losing myself in the task. His cock swells and thickens between my lips. A few minutes pass. Even though he's just come, already he's twitching and trembling, ready to shoot off another load.

"Hailey," he warns.

But I don't care. I open my eyes.

He throws back his head on the pillows and lets out a strangled cry.

I tighten my grip, and his cock goes completely rigid in my mouth. When hot come hits the back of my throat, I take him as deep as I can. Now he's pulsing straight down past my tongue. I can only taste hints of that familiar sweetness as I stroke his balls, cradling them, emptying them. The last drops shudder through him as I watch. His chest heaves as he swallows huge lungfuls of air. His nipples are hard and a darker pink than they were before. His skin is flushed. Handfuls of blankets and sheets are crumpled in his enormous fists. I release him gently, and his heavy cock twitches in the cool air. I drop soft kisses along his inner thighs and stroke his rock-hard quads. I look up at him, my big bad roughneck, and the love I feel for him washes over me like a tidal wave.

Seth sets the timer on his phone, and we sleep like the dead for two hours. I wake up to the sound of my duffel bag unzipping. The sky is nearly dark outside. Seth turns on all of the lights in the motel room, even the lights in the bathroom. He turns the T.V. to some shopping channel.

He digs through the bag. "You brought everything I sent you?"

I yawn and rub my eyes. "They're all there."

"You use any of them?"

I'm silent for a second. The first package came three days after he left. One came a week after that, and another the week after that. "Just the silver one."

"That's it?" He looks at me with a scowl. "I told you to try each one."

"They're all really loud. I can't use them in the house. Are you crazy?"

"The glass one's silent." After laying down a towel from the bathroom, he throws all our new toys on the bed next to me. He props up his phone on the nightstand and adjusts the angle.

"Not my face," I whisper.

"I know."

This is for him. He's told me he's tired of porn. I guess I should be flattered he wants to jack it to a video of his wife.

I prop myself up on the pillows.

He puts both hands on my knees and draws them apart slowly. His eyes widen, and his pupils dilate. He's breathing harder.

I can't see his dick, but I'm pretty sure it's hard.

His hands slide down from my knees to my inner thighs. He spreads my legs wide.

Now I'm on view for him and for the tiny lens on the back of his phone.

He lowers his mouth and licks me long and slow.

Soon I'm breathing hard. I reach down and run my hands through his soft hair.

"Yes, baby," I whisper.

It doesn't take much to get me wet. Since the kids arrived, we've perfected the art of the quickie, and my body responds fast. We've rarely had a hotel room and hours to ourselves, and the time apart has sharpened our hunger.

He hardens his tongue and drags the tip through my folds, slowly zigzagging up.

My toes curl when he swirls the tip of his tongue around my clit. I'm so wet I can feel the moisture pooling in my pussy. If he tipped me forward, I'd spill out like a pitcher of cream.

I'm close. When he leans back, I frown.

He smiles and says nothing.

The tiny packets of lube he sent me have long nozzles, like the beaks of hummingbirds. He breaks one and very gently slips the applicator in my ass.

I squirm. We haven't done this much, but Seth loves it. I knew he'd want it today.

He tortures my clit with feather-light licks as he squeezes the tube inside me. The gel is cold, and I clench. When the tube is empty, he pulls it out.

I know what comes next—the glass plug. He coats it in lube and presses its gently pointed end against my ass, working it past my tight muscles. My body resists him, but he's patient, teasing me with his tongue and pulling back until I'm ready again. His tongue is torturously good. When the head of the plug slips past my opening at last, Seth lets go. Like a reflex, my body pulls the plug deep into place.

That's when I hear the hum of the silver bullet vibrator. The egg is tiny in his hand as he runs it up and down my slick pussy lips, lingering in my opening before dragging it back over my clit. I'm so keyed up that I jerk against the mattress.

Seth smiles and presses it into me. He yanks gently on the filament of a cord.

My body grips the vibe, resisting him.

"Fuck," he whispers, eyes on my pussy. "So sexy."

On their own, my hands go to my breasts. I'm breathing hard as I play with them, kneading them and lightly pinching my nipples. The air's so cold in the room. My skin is covered with goose bumps, but I feel like I'm going to combust, blood pounding through my body, and my nervous system over-loaded with sensation.

I watch, half-coherent as Seth lubes up one more toy. An expensive pink silicone thing with multiple speeds. When he presses it to my clit, my body goes rigid, and my head falls back. I shut my eyes and gasp. I've never felt anything like this. Between the vibe and the bullet, the pleasure is so powerful my body can't handle it. I'm on the knife-edge of coming when Seth pops out the silver bullet and withdraws the pink vibrator.

"Nope. Not yet," he says.

I look into his wicked face and grind my teeth in frustra-tion. The angry words slip out before I can stop them. "Everything has to be on your terms, doesn't it?" I hiss.

I immediately regret what I've said. His expression is neutral.

Fuck.

I'm so emotionally charged, a sob escapes my chest. And

now I'm the weirdo with a butt plug up her ass crying in the homemade porno.

Quickly, Seth removes the plug, drops everything, and turns off his phone and the TV.

When he reaches for me with a placating look in his eyes, I slap his hands away. I don't want him to see me like this. Messy and weak.

"No," I say. "Stop."

He tries to wipe my tears, but I turn away. I'm embarrassed, and he knows it.

"Babe—"

"Just give me a minute, okay?"

He leans back. "Okay."

We can't choose when our emotions come to the surface. Now is the worst possible time. I crush the pillow against my chest and let out another sob. I need to get over this.

A minute passes. When he takes the pillow away, I let him. When he looks into my eyes, I feel lost. I agreed to this. I love him with every part of me. So why am I so angry?

I'm struggling with what to say when Seth speaks first.

"I feel it, too." He reaches out a tentative hand. His rough fingers stroke my hairline with the barest touch. He's studying my face but avoiding my eyes. "Give me a year. We'll pay off the credit cards and as much as we can on the house. We'll put something in the kids' college funds. I'm hauling in a lot of money right now, but it's boom and bust, not meant to last. This is *not* forever."

I'm blinking at him, chest imploding with pain. We've talked about this. I nod. "I know. I know it's not forever."

His voice softens as his fingers skim my eyebrows, my cheekbones. "Since the moment I met you, we've never spent more than a week apart. I thought about it yesterday, Hailey. Eleven years."

His touch soothes me. My nerve endings sparkle with pleasure, but my heart is too hurt to enjoy it.

"I miss our house. Our bed. My wife." He pauses. "Life...it's not really life without you."

When he pulls me into his big arms, the warmth and weight of his body settle me. He strokes my head and doesn't say anything when I finally break down and cry. I close my eyes, and my tears soak his chest. I hold on to him.

"Talk to me," he whispers.

Okay. Here goes. Truth time. "I'm angry that you're doing this," I say. "I'm angry that you're gone all the time, and I just have to deal with it."

He points to his phone. "I'll call them right now. Quit. We can go home."

"That's not what I want—"

"We're in this together. I never want to see you hurting."

"No. I'd be hurt more if you did that." As soon as I say it, I know it's true. The issue's not the money. It's his pride. I'm doing this to protect his pride. The kind of pride Seth has— it's not the fragile, egotistic kind. It's the deep-down kind that drives a working man to take care of his family. I can't take this away from him.

When we make eye contact, it's like he can read my thoughts.

"I'm asking a lot of you," he says. "I know that. Thank you, Hailey."

At his words, something happens. Like a sore neck or a stiff shoulder or a cramped leg, the muscle of my heart releases its pain at last. Was that all I needed? An acknowledgement?

I sniffle and wipe my face on the towel.

Seth looks at me.

I know my makeup's smeared. My eyes are puffy and red. I must look like hell.

"Fuck, you're so beautiful," he whispers.

He's always called me sexy, but never beautiful. I smile. "Who are you, and where is my husband?"

"Right here."

The next time we make love, we're face-to-face. No cameras, no noise, no talking. Just me and Seth, doing what we do best. Our lovemaking's deep, slow, and rough. He isn't gentle. I don't want him to be. I feel my heart getting stronger, the pieces welding back together by the heat of our fucking.

When he's close, he looks down with those feral eyes. Drilling into me with that big dick, he pumps me hard until I can't hold back any more. We come together, wet and nasty, and it's so good we're laughing, too happy to keep our joy inside.

When it's time for him to turn on his camera again, I'm ready for my wicked, horny husband. In goes the lube and the plug. His eyes are wide as he makes me come with the silver bullet deep in my pussy and the pink vibrator on my clit. Then he switches the two and makes me come again. By the time he slips the plug out of my ass with a soft pop, I'm aching for him, my body on fire.

His dick is so hard, it's purple. He takes his phone in one hand and his shaft in the other. On all fours, I bury my face in the sweat-soaked sheets and moan when he prods my asshole with the blunt, lube-slicked head of his cock. Between my legs, I'm holding the pink toy in place, its oscillating vibrations bringing my tender clit back to life.

I'm ready for the pain, because I know it also brings pleasure—the deepest kind. Seth gives me both, in bed and in life.

"Don't be gentle," I rasp.

"I won't be," he says.

He isn't.

For the rest of the long, sleepless night, we fuck the way

life has fucked with us—hard. But here, in each other's arms, we're the ones who win.

At dawn, Seth pulls me close and draws the blankets over us. We're sweaty and spent.

"I love you," I whisper.

He gives me a squeeze. "I love you, too."

Closing my eyes, I rest my head on his chest. I fall asleep, lulled by the sound of his heartbeat—strong and steady, just like him.

ELEVATION

MEGAN MITCHAM

*L*aurel shoved through the precinct door and let the heavy thing slam on her partner's cocky face. Tomlin's "oomph" offered little consolation to the irritation that had built over the last ten hours—and three months—she'd been assigned to the flagrant womanizer.

"Come on, Hutton."

The thick glass muffled his pleading. Damn the man, but he pulled the door wide and breezed through with his full Latin lips stretched into a wide smile. He pointed to his crotch with both hands, as though offering the most magical gift in the universe.

"You can't tell me you've never wondered what it would be like."

"Oh, I know what it would be like." She forged ahead, aiming for the shift sergeant's desk.

"Fucking amazing, right? Best moment of your life." He nodded and hurried past her toward the locker room.

"More akin to sucking a sewer pipe. Thanks, though."

His dust-powdered boots screeched to a stop on the worn vinyl floor. He whirled and clutched his heart. After a fake teeter of rubbery knees, he chuckled, shot his finger pistols, and skated for the showers.

Laurel snagged his sleeve before it moved out of reach and reeled him back. "Paperwork, then blow job."

"Blow job!" Someone hollered from rows of desks, perps chained to chairs, and piles of godammed paperwork. "Tomlin, you givin' 'em?"

"Fucking hilarious," her partner shot back.

Her shoulders shook, and lightness seeped slowly past the horrors of the long day, easing their hold on her heart.

Tomlin fist-bumped a fellow officer at the first desk and started running his mouth about their last call.

Thoughts of the suicide attempt dragged her newfound buoyancy to the bottom of the ocean. Teenagers should be playing video games, sports, or dreaming about getting laid, not threatening to throw themselves off the top of an under construction high-rise.

"Hutton, you looking for me?" The sergeant's gruff voice barked from over her shoulder.

She fought the natural instinct to jump or the trained one to turn and attack. Either would be viewed as a sign of weakness. Perceived weakness in any officer could mean the difference between life and death, for themselves and others. A hint of weakness in a female officer and she'd find herself behind a desk faster than Tomlin could find a chick to suck him off.

"Yes, sir." Laurel exhaled smoothly, turned, and offered a thick stack of paper to the paunchy man who made her life as difficult as possible four out of seven days per week. Each detailed report meant another perp wouldn't slide out of court or a troubled kid would get the help he needed to become more in life than a stain on the street.

"Nice work, talking that kid down. Way to end the week."

Sergeant flipped through the pages, carefully eyeing each one.

"Thank you, sir." Laurel nodded stoically, but in her head celebrated with gyrating hips and double fist pumps.

"You're missing a signature." Her superior stomped all over her little victory dance. Before she could ask for clarification, he thrust the offending sheet at her. "Get it, or the kid won't get his psych evaluation."

What? She hadn't missed a dotted "i" on that damn report. The kid struck a cord with her, and most days she couldn't allow that to happen. A reaction incited others to react. To lead in a crisis, she had to display fortitude and nothing more. That kid, Jeremy, had needed a connection. She scoured the page. What Sarge returned wasn't her report, but a witness's account of the event. At the bottom of the page, the elevator installer's signature—the one Tomlin had "gotten"—was missing. She'd sent her partner to get the guy's signature, because she hadn't wanted to deal with the all-American hottie while still so vulnerable from her exchange with Jeremy.

"Yes, sir." Laurel stepped to her desk and dialed the witness's number, a Mr. Nash Briggs. "Tomlin." She barked his name across the room. No one's head turned, not even her partner's. "You were supposed to get the witness's signature."

"I did." He stood from his perch on another officer's desk.

"No, you didn't." She held up the page. The phone line rang in her ear.

"My bad, Hut. I appreciate you covering for me though." Tomlin kissed the first two fingers on each hand, blew her peace signs, and walked backward into the hallway.

When she was about to tell him no way in hell was she covering for his screw-up again, the line came to life. "Hel—o?"

"Hello? Mr. Briggs?" The connection cut in and out with buzzing in the background.

"This is—Briggs."

Shit. His deep gravelly voice rumbled straight to her clit.

Laurel swallowed her gasp, collapsed into her chair, and strived for focus. Hell, she couldn't hear half of what he said anyway. "This is Officer Hutton with the MPD. I need to get your signature on the statement you made tonight."

"I—finish this job—by tomorrow—come Sunday—You—come to the site—all night."

Good lord, if this guy kept talking, butchered by a bad connection or not, she would come all night. A smirk formed on her lips. Maybe Tomlin wouldn't be the only one getting laid. It had been a long damn time.

"I'll be there in thirty." God, had she just said that? Laurel waited for a response. The universe didn't gift her with any more of his voice. She returned the phone to its cradle and set out to get it for herself.

* * *

Nash returned to the job-from-hell with the panel he needed. Silence settled around him, easing the knots in his traps. When the contractors had left more than five hours ago, he'd expected to get a handle on the plagued install. Trouble had started from the first with the delivery of the wrong elevator models and ended—if he worked through the night—by finding a kid trying to toss himself off the roof.

The circus of first responders, complicated by the chaotic mix of teenage hormones and over privilege, had vacated two hours ago, but already the police had called him back about something. What? He had no idea. His phone didn't work in the shafts. When he'd come out and returned the call, the officer had left for the day.

"Good." He set his tool bag by the elevator doors.

The solid grumble of his stomach echoed in the marble foyer. He needed to eat for the first time since breakfast, but replacing the short-circuiting control panels in the main entry's bank of elevators came first. He'd been going non-stop for ten hours already, getting another job underway. The muscles in his forearms throbbed from turning a wrench all day, since the damn battery had gone out in his drill.

A faint noise, almost a whispered sigh, perked his ears. The sound struck him as feminine and damn hot. When he surveilled the large room, no one was there. His dirty thoughts immediately flew to the fine lady cop on scene earlier. Her pouty little mouth had been bowed, and her sandy blonde brows pinched in concern for the kid.

She had to have been the one on the phone earlier. The hard-on the sight of her pouty mouth had given him on the rooftop roared back to life. He hadn't heard much past his last name and the word statement. That jerk-off partner of hers probably screwed up the paperwork. The guy'd been in a rush, his mind on something else. Nash's had been, too. Judging by the withering look the hot cop had given her partner when he'd tried to hurry Jeremy along, the reason for the haste hadn't been the same. Nash had wanted the tough-and-tenderhearted, drop-dead-gorgeous cop. Hell, he still did. Hours later, he had wood thinking about the way her ass filled out her uniform pants and how her long blonde ponytail would feel wrapped around his palm.

Jesus H. Christ, thinking about her conjured the noise again. No, the noise had brought her back into focus. It wasn't consistent like the air or a compressor. It came at different intervals, some louder than others.

Nash eased toward the elevator doors and pressed his ear

to it. Surely, the sound wasn't … but it was. It came from the elevator shaft.

"Holy fuck! Holy mother fuck." If that kid had come back and tossed himself down the shaft, Nash would have to take a vacation, a long one.

"Please don't be Jeremy."

His knees turned rubbery. He dropped the panel, drew a deep breath, grabbed the seam of the doors and pulled, expecting to see the top of his lift dented in and blood seeping from the seams. Instead, he stared into the dark shaft at the empty space where the elevator car should've been. His stomach immediately settled. Curiosity, not so much.

"What the hell?"

When he'd left thirty minutes ago, the thing had been on the ground floor and only working sporadically thanks to the busted panel. He headed for the stairwell, taking the steps two at a time until he reached the freaking thirty-second floor. With several long strides, he arrived at the shiny metal bumper doors he knew so well.

Heavy, labored breaths radiated from the elevator shaft, each laced with sheer terror.

Again, Nash grabbed the seam of the doors and pulled. The car stood between the two floors below. He wedged open the doors with the wrench from his back jeans pocket, sat, grabbed the edge of the shaft, and lowered himself to the car's ceiling. The trap door's latch turned easily under his grip, and he didn't understand why the person wouldn't have unhooked it and climbed out, if he couldn't fit through the space between the main doors.

He pulled it wide. A woman in figure-hugging jeans and a body-molding black tank pressed both palms to the back wall. Breaths wheezed loudly in the small space. Each exhale accentuated the dip of her narrow waist. Straight blonde hair hid her face, cascading over well-defined arms and shoulders.

"Ma'am?"

Her head and hands remained glued to the metal.

Hell, maybe she couldn't hear him over the obvious panic attack happening in her head, or maybe she was high as a weather balloon. After all, they were in downtown DC after hours, and he'd already come across crazier shit tonight.

EACH BREATH OFFERED Laurel less and less oxygen. It siphoned from the cell she'd die inside. The metal box contracted with each passing second. Her lungs refused to expand and rational thought had fled the instant the moving coffin stopped mid lift.

Large fingers wrapped around her bicep, crushing the tiny grip she had on sanity.

She yanked her right arm high and struck with the left. Her palm heel connected to her assailant's jaw. The snap of teeth meeting teeth sounded like a gun shot against the metal walls. The noise tore her through the tumult of panic and planted her firmly in the WTF.

A wide, unforgiving chin wrenched his neck like a flip top. Scuffed leather boots turned toes up. The massive man's grip slipped from her arm and his well-worn jeans hit the elevator floor, jarring the unstable foundation. Squeaks and metal-on-metal scrapes threatened to pull her back under.

His groan anchored her composure. His all-American face—the face she'd been seeking when she'd gotten onto this tin can—incited her humiliation.

"Mr. Briggs?" she croaked. Heat crawled from her extremities, pooling in her cheeks. He took up most of the floor space, but the elevator seemed bigger with him inside it, bigger than the pin hole she'd been trapped inside, alone.

"Well, shit, darlin'." He waggled his jaw with one hand. A day's worth of scruff scraped against it. His broad shoulders teetered along with his handsome chin.

Laurel squatted next to the man and looped a hand under his thick arm. Stunning green eyes rolled back into his head. Dead weight threatened to pull her over. She reached around his back with her other arm and caught him.

The move shifted his body. He slumped toward her.

Momentum knocked her clear off her wedges onto her ass.

"Christ." Her back landed against the narrow end of the elevator. Nash Briggs' wide shoulder smashed her breasts worse than her bulletproof vest had all day. His back pressed between her sprawled legs.

"I'm a lunatic. The kind of crazy I put away." Laurel relaxed her head against the wall and stared through the open ceiling hatch. None of the terror she'd experienced earlier threatened to drown her.

The scent of sweat and faint cologne wafted up her nose, stirring her earlier notions to life. She chuckled and looked down at the expanse of work-hardened muscles she'd knocked unconscious. Like any man's ego would tolerate that.

"Not a chance, Hutton." Her breaths slowed and steadied, matching the movement of the man's chest nuzzled atop hers expand and contract.

His pulse beat against the side of his thick neck.

Laurel pressed her fingers to it, for purely medical purposes, right? Hot skin and pointy little hairs greeted her pads. The contact traveled up her arm, warming her as it went. Several seconds passed, and nothing happened. She relaxed her hand, joining it to his feverish flesh. Sweat clung to his neck, forming a thick layer between them. Small droplets collected on his shirt between the mountains of his pecs.

Laurel's heart beat in her throat, and excitement had nothing to do with being trapped in a small space. With this guy, she didn't mind it so much. When he woke she probably would, but now… She let her hand slide down his neck and over his chest.

Without warning, his hand clamped over hers.

KNOCKED on his ass by a girl. Mark that off his bucket list. Even better, while his marbles settled, her hands roved over him. Nash caught her hand over his heart and held it there, mooring to her while he opened his eyes. A dark circle like a devil's halo clung to his vision for a few throbbing beats, and then slowly receded.

"Pretty, and you pack a punch. I'm in love."

"Mr. Briggs." She tried to lift her hand away.

"Nash," he insisted.

Her struggle stalled. "Nash." She tested his name on her lips.

He sure as fuck liked the way it fit and wanted her to say it again. "That's good… What's your name, slugger?"

"Oh, I'm officer…" She stopped.

The cutest squeaky breath warmed his cheek.

"I'm Laurel."

"Nice to meet you, Laurel."

"I don't know that nice is the right word."

He wiggled back against her soft breasts and the V of her strong legs.

Her hand splayed across his chest, digging into his skin. Her gasp turned to a moan before she cut it off.

"I'm sure." Nash nodded.

She cleared her throat. "I'm so sorry I hit you. I had no idea you were in here. I didn't hear you."

"Nah. It was my bad." His thumb massaged a small circle on the silken skin of her wrist. "You were pretty caught up in your hell."

"Yeah." She groaned.

"What is it?"

"What is it?" She hesitated for a pile of seconds. "I lost my shit. If my partner had been here, if anyone had seen me break down…"

Nash let his head fall to the side. His equilibrium had re-calibrated enough that he could stand—in a minute. "Shhh." He let his lips brush the inside of her forearm. "Seen what?"

"You're nice," she sighed, "but a loss of control like that could put me behind a desk for the rest of my career."

A laugh rumbled in his chest. "Laurel, I'm not nice."

"Oh?"

He lifted her wrist to his mouth and scraped his teeth across the sensitive flesh.

"Oh."

"Nope, because by the end of the night, I'm making you lose control." Nash kissed a trail up her palm to the tip on her index finger and sucked the tip into his mouth.

"Really?" The word became a moan.

"In a much better way." He held onto her hand, stood, and pulled her up to meet his chest. Her soft breasts and unyielding belly pressed against his front. He straightened, lifting her off the floor. She fit pretty damn good in his arms.

"Sure of yourself, aren't you?" Her blonde tresses clung to her striking cheekbones and strong jaw. Incongruous to her challenging words, her strong arms wrapped around his neck.

"Just as sure of me as you are." He didn't offer a wink or anything to take the edge off his intent.

Laurel's full mouth gaped, and then slowly turned into a smile.

"Let's get you out of here." Nash set her on her feet and grabbed her hand.

"Please."

"Up or through?" He directed her gaze to the hatch and double doors. "You'll have about a two-foot gap either way you go. Just a matter of how you want it."

OH LORD. This guy knew all the right buttons, from his voice to his face and god-like-body to the delicate way he treated her. She didn't do casual sex. It wasn't worth the risks involved, but Nash stirred something deep inside that muted her inner police woman. "I want it the way you'll give it to me." He'd given her the courtesy of no BS. Turnabout was only fair.

"Dammit, Laurel. I like you, a lot. I have a feeling I'll like you a lot more, really soon." Nash offered her his cupped hands. "Up you go."

He boosted her, and she pulled herself through the hatch into another world of cables, steel, and concrete. Before she could reach down to help him, Nash was there, closing the hatch and offering her another boost.

She ignored his hands and grazed her fingers over the curve of his face she'd brutally hit. "How's your jaw?"

He leaned into her touch. "You may have to kiss it." A simple grin stretched his hard lips.

Her heart skipped across her chest cavity. Laurel wrapped her hand around his chin and pulled his face to meet hers.

His green eyes sparked with warning. "If you start it, I'm prepared to finish it, right here. Are you?"

"I should have done this sooner." She shoved her fingers

into the waist band of his pants, pulled him close, and pressed her mouth to his.

Nash snarled like an animal unleashed. His fingers bit into her nape, locking her to him. His lips tore at hers—tasting, sucking, biting.

The overwhelming urge to let down every guard and free every part of herself had her relaxing into his hold.

"That's it, Laurel. Let me have you." His mouth trailed over her jaw to her ear. "I've thought about you all night."

"Really?" She sounded like a phone sex operator and didn't care.

"You're fucking amazing and have no clue about it." He smirked, unfastened her pants, and then ate a path down her neck. "When I saw you handle Jeremy—not take his shit and, instead, care for him—you struck me."

He remembered the kid's name. That little nugget nestled its way into her heart more than his compliments.

"You look like the girl next door, but you're more. You're strong and...vulnerable."

His mouth found her nipple through her shirt and clamped down, encompassing it in wet heat. A hiss seeped between her teeth. "Men don't like strong women."

"Pussies don't."

He yanked down her pants and the lacy underwear she'd worn for show to her ankles, without a care for the soft material or the way the color complimented her skin tone. His hot gaze lingered on her skin.

He knelt on the elevator's roof and worked off her shoes and pants. "I'm not a pussy, but I'll enjoy the hell out of eating yours."

The vulgarity of his words empowered her. Before she had a second to contemplate any nuance of the heat and elevation whipping her into a frenzy, his shoulders shoved her legs wide.

"Mmm." His rich voice rumbled over her clit.

Her knees threatened to buckle, and he'd yet to touch her.

"Grab the cables, slugger. Strong or not, you'll need them."

"Damn, you're cocky." She straightened her back and propped her hands on her hips.

"Confident, Laurel. Let me show you the difference."

Nash sucked his middle finger and pinkie into his mouth, and then shoved the middle one inside her.

She smiled…because a single finger wasn't much to brag about.

His blazing green eyes flashed.

Two fingers spread her lips wide.

"Oh God." Her middle hinged forward, and her knees threatened to buckle as his pinkie pressed slowly and insistently against the rim of her anus.

He chuckled, then his closed mouth against her clit.

Laurel's right hand sank into his thick hair, and she tried to shift away from his pinkie.

"Ah-ah. You want it the way I'll give it to you, remember?" Nash's smile eased away from her clit.

Laurel groaned, but stalled her escape and released his hair. The instant her hands touched the metal cable, hot, wet lips suctioned her clit. A moan escaped through her teeth, but she clamped down on the impulse. This guy was good, but he needed to be taken down a notch.

His fingers played her like an aboriginal drum. Every beat reverberated through her. Every stroke incited a cascade of synapses to explode. Every strum threatened to topple her.

"Nash." His name was a sigh on her lips.

"You're so hot, I'm going to come just hearing you scream."

"Scream? I'm not that girl, Mr. Briggs."

"You'll scream."

The pad of his middle finger curled into her pussy wall, massaging her to madness from the inside. His illicit pinkie gently pumped in and out to the tip, whirling a foreign current of ecstasy toward shore. Wet flat strokes of his tongue lapped at her clit in easy licks that built with strength and speed. Jesus, the noises rumbling from his chest and bleeding out of his mouth ratcheted every sensation.

Laurel's belly quivered. Her thighs trembled. She held onto the cables for dear life. Her head canted toward the highest ceiling, other than the sky, she'd ever been under.

A scream, closer to a cry and a mating call, from her tantalized body poured out of her lips and echoed back. The inescapable wave of her orgasm cascaded over her in brilliant explosions of pleasure. Still he didn't stop, pushing her on, higher, wilder.

"Nash. Oh my, fuck. I can't. Oh yes, that feels..." She forgot every notion about taming his ego. The last bit of herself slipped through her open fingers. "Please, Nash. Give me everything."

"That's it, strong Laurel. Let me make you feel." His hands continued to torment her.

"I do. I feel everything."

His hands fell away in an instant. He stood, shucked his shirt and pants—not before snagging a condom from his wallet—dragged her shirt over her head, and hoisted her into his arms. Impossibly, she felt more there—eye to eye, heart to heart—than she had with his fingers shoved knuckles-deep inside her. The light green of his eyes called to her, and she plastered a kiss on his sloppy mouth.

"You taste good, don't you?" He bit her lip and shuffle-walked them backward until her ass cheeks hit a cold metal pole.

Her fingernails sank into his shoulders.

"I've got you, slugger. Safety first." His eyes waggled. He

rolled on a condom onto his thick cock. "Don't you feel safe?"

She shouldn't feel safe hundreds of feet in the air with a man she'd just met, but she hadn't felt so secure in a long time. "I can't believe you work up here." Saying that was easier than admitting the truth.

Nash spread her legs wide and rubbed the tip of his cock around her slick cunt. With each pass, her clit pulsed and drowned in aftershocks. He braced her back and pressed the crown of his cock to her entrance.

"I can't believe I'm inside you up here."

She opened her mouth to explain that he'd yet to enter her. The barely-hinged man plunged deep, stealing her breath and her rejoinder. Laurel arched into him and screamed into the abyss again. "Pretty much, you can be inside me anywhere." Her teeth sank into his shoulder to keep from calling out again.

"I'll take you anywhere you want me to."

The tips of his fingers gripped her hips. He set a break-neck pace straight out of the gate, pounding into her body as though he'd never had the pleasure of a woman before. It was the hottest damn thing she'd ever experienced.

HOLY FUCK, he was going to scare this woman right out of his night—forget about his life—but he couldn't rein in his passion. Her scents, her sounds, her taste drove him to the edge of sanity and launched him into the stratosphere.

"You have me, Nash. You have me." Laurel tossed back her head and rolled her hips in time with his frenzied thrusts.

Her words were almost his undoing. Pressure gathered in his sack, but talk about too soon... "Yes, I do," he rasped.

Unwilling to miss an opportunity to give her another orgasm, he skipped pace for a beat and pulled down the straps of her bra. Small pink areolas centered perky breasts that would fit perfectly in his hands…later. For now, he dragged his fingers over one pointed tip and rolled and pinched it between this thumb and middle finger. Laurel's stunning blue eyes went wide. He tortured her nipple until gasps shot rapid-fire out of her mouth.

Nash slowed his strokes, tamping down his inner beast long enough to enjoy the way her hot, tight pussy hugged his cock. When he shoved deep, her taut little ass met him on one side, while her swollen clit and full lower lips hit him on the other. He hugged her close, clamped a hand on the back of her neck and soldered their mouths together. Her hair danced over his arms. Her heels dug into his ass. She kissed him like she never wanted to stop. He let her for a long minute, until she broke away, mewing for air.

"I WANT to come inside you, Laurel." Fuck it all, he never did bare, but the need to mark her clawed at his spine. He wouldn't. Not tonight, but soon.

"I want to feel you with nothing between us." Her fingers dove into the hair at the base of his neck. Her gaze met his. "Yes, Nash. I want you. All of you."

Her words were all he needed to drive them to the brink, together.

He pounded inside her. Laurel screamed boldly, holding nothing back. Every muscle in his body tensed. The overwhelming white noise of the orgasm that rocketed from his cock drowned out the world for a handful of seconds. When he came down, she was there, clinging. The pillow of her cheek rested on his shoulder, and her lips placed tiny kisses on his neck.

He stroked a hand over her silky hair and down her back, but made no move to disengage their bodies. As far as he was concerned, they could stay that way all night, work be damned.

Minutes passed.

"If you were scared, why'd you get in the elevator?"

She laughed against his neck, tickling him.

"I've never been even a little afraid of elevators, but the building was so deathly quiet, and I couldn't find you."

Something warm and fuzzy wrapped itself around his torso. "You came here looking for me?" He turned his head to read her gaze.

Her swollen bottom lip tucked into her mouth, and she dragged it against her teeth. "I'd noticed you earlier, too." She smiled, but then it faltered.

The fuzzy stalled. Warmth hung on, because her arms clamped tighter around him.

"I needed your signature on a report, so I hopped on the elevator to search the top of the building where you'd been earlier, and then the damn thing stopped. All I could think was I'd be trapped in it for days and die slowly, all alone."

Nash pressed a kiss to her forehead and dragged his lips over her cheek. "You're not alone, Laurel."

Her fingers massaged lazy paths at the base of his neck. "No, I'm not."

"Let me take you to dinner?"

"I'd love…" Laurel bolted upright.

"What's wrong?"

"The paper, I lost it in my freak-out."

She cupped his face and kissed the point of his chin— where he'd have a bruise tomorrow, a bruise he'd proudly don. "It's in the elevator. Can it wait?"

Laurel looked down between their bodies and sighed.

"No, not really. Jeremy needs that paper to get the help he needs." She started to pull away. "I'll get out of your way. I know you were working before…"

Nash held her in place. "I'll get the papers and give you the signature. After we turn them in, we'll go to dinner, and then you'll come home with me." He tried to pull away, but she flipped the script and held tight.

"I'll get the paper with you." A sultry smile spread across her lips. "I want to make a new memory in that tin can."

UPSIDE DOWN LOVE

ADELE DOWNS

*I*t's true what they say about riding a bicycle or having sex. Once you know how, you never forget. Lillian Holmes pedaled along the coastal road while salted-breezes rustled her hair. Sunlight warmed her cheeks and made them tingle. She opened her mouth to taste the air, and the breath filling her lungs made her come alive in ways she could barely recall—either on a bike or in bed.

The wheels glided along the macadam road, free of traffic this time of morning, and she almost…almost…let go of the handlebars to do a silly balancing act like she'd done as a kid. Instead, she held tighter to the grips, aware that skinned knees on mature flesh didn't heal as well or as quickly as they once did. Her T-shirt, Capri pants, and sneakers wouldn't offer much protection from the asphalt. She really should have bought a helmet to go with her bike, but they weren't mandatory in Delaware, and accessories like a basket and horn could wait until another payday.

In the spirit of learning to have *fun* again, Lilly shouted and squealed as she picked up speed. "Whoop, whoop!" Her voice pierced the air and scared the gulls perched near the home construction site on a plum spot facing the bay. The birds took flight, and she called out as they soared overhead. "I'm flying, too!" The seagulls screeched and found new places to land, clearly indifferent to her or her freedom.

Lilly eyed the water, rippling softly at high tide, as blue as a pool of sapphires capped with sunshine. She'd been right to move to this beach town. She had the bay, the ocean, the boardwalk, and her book club to keep her company. Her convertible made driving to work at the bakery a pleasure, and her new bike would offer regular exercise. Who needed a husband of twenty-two years when she could fly?

The birds scattered again when a backhoe rumbled, and Lilly slowed to watch the construction crew lay a foundation. A few of the guys glanced over at her, and the man operating the pile driver smiled. He looked to be her age, mid-forties, with a trim build. She couldn't clearly see his features beneath his ball cap and sunglasses, but his expression was friendly and open and not at all salacious or threatening. For that reason alone, Lilly smiled back.

The simple exchange warmed her from the inside, out. Maybe the divorce hadn't stripped away her sex appeal along with her self-esteem, after all. The idea that she could attract a new man hadn't occurred to her…maybe because she hadn't been paying attention. She let her gaze linger on the man as he continued his work.

The pile driver hung in the air on a heavy cable, ready to plunge foundation holes deep into the soil. Rehoboth Bay rarely caused storm damage, but rising oceans made it necessary to build new homes on stilts as a precaution against unusually high tides.

By the look of the layout, the house under construction would become the centerpiece of the neighborhood. Lilly took a deep breath and blew out her envy on a long exhale. She would never afford a place on the water. The owners of this home would enjoy spectacular views she could only see during her walks or from the seat of her bicycle. Still, she loved her little fixer upper and considered herself lucky to be part of this waterfront community.

Lilly raised a hand to the construction worker, and he waved back, and she continued on her way.

An oncoming car moved toward her, taking more than its share of the narrow throughway. Lilly hugged the shoulder, fighting handlebar wobble, as the tires crunched sand and cinders and the spokes got nipped by foliage.

Just then, an enormous sound erupted from the construction area behind her, shaking the earth and sending tremors through the ground. Startled by the noise, she lost control of the handlebars. The front tire slipped as Lilly lost control, and the bike flipped sideways.

Lilly heard herself scream as her bottom flew off the seat, her knee connected with a handlebar grip, and her shoulder took the brunt of her landing. When the back of her head slammed the blacktop, daytime turned to night.

* * *

SHE DIDN'T KNOW how long she'd been out when her eyes fluttered open. A thousand hammers pounded her skull. Lilly blinked and squinted against the sunshine, and then something moved to block the glare.

She glanced at her arms from her prone position, but couldn't see her legs. She fluttered her fingers then wiggled her toes inside her sneakers. Everything from the chest down seemed to be working okay. She let out a groan of relief.

When Lilly looked up, the bluest eyes she'd ever seen stared back—bluer than the ocean on a perfect summer day, with lashes framing them in darkest ash. The man's short hair was dark, too, though lightly salted around the temples.

He leaned close, and the heat of his body skimmed her arms, raising goosebumps.

She caught her breath, blinked, and blinked again. He had to be a vision, right? An illusion? The blow to her head had dropped her into the path of a man worthy of his own calendar.

"Don't try to get up," Mr. July said. "I've got you."

Even in her fragile state, she could read the concern on his face. He brushed strands of hair off her forehead, causing her to wince—not because he'd hurt her, but because so much time had passed since a man had touched her.

"Sorry." Strong fingers slid away.

Little did he know she would have welcomed his hand against her cheek, or the feel of his breath against the shell of her ear—in theory, if not in practice. A familiar longing surged through her to add to her misery. The wounds to her body were minor compared to the damage her ego had taken, but the combined injuries might never heal.

"Is she all right?" came a voice from somewhere beyond Lilly's range of vision.

Lilly couldn't tell if another man or woman had joined them.

Mister July shook his head. "Not sure. I'm guessing she has a concussion. I called an ambulance."

Concussion. Of course. That would explain the pain in her skull and her inappropriate thoughts.

He stood then, and she watched his fingers lift the hem of his T-shirt above his hard belly. A trail of fine, dark hair disappeared into the waistband of his low-rise cutoffs, and Lilly tracked the vertical contour beneath his zipper. Her glance dipped to his muscular thighs and up again, watching from her place on the ground as he raised his shirt over his torso in a glorious unveiling of bronzed skin. Though her head throbbed and her eyes teared, she couldn't help but stare as he bared his chest.

A body honed by years of physical labor stood before her. White scars crisscrossed his left side in vivid contrast to his tanned flesh. A faded military tattoo covered the pectorals over his heart above a smattering of dark hair. Brown nipples turned hard in the breeze.

The man with the vivid blue eyes pulled the shirt over his head and balled it in one large, work-weary hand. Then he kneeled beside her, folded the shirt, and gently laid it beneath her head. Seagulls captured the scene from above.

Though the morning air and the ground beneath her chilled her flesh, her eyelids grew heavy.

The man took her hand and pressed it to his chest. His heartbeat moved against her palm like steady kisses. "If your brain is bruised, you need to stay awake."

Lilly met his gaze and marveled again at his gorgeous eyes. He smiled down at her, and the skin around those eyes crinkled.

"Give her some water," another voice said. A small crowd had formed.

He looked up then, reached for the bottle of water someone handed him, and helped her take a sip. "Better?"

Her head seemed to clear a bit. "I think I can sit up now." Lilly leaned her elbows against the ground and tried to pull herself up, but her vision swam, and the pain in her head and shoulder thundered. "Ow. Maybe not."

He guided her back to the makeshift pillow. "Help will be here soon." The man with the blue eyes dampened a cloth he pulled from his back pocket. Tenderly, he wiped her brow with cool water.

Sirens drew closer, and soon, she was lifted into a vehicle and swept away.

* * *

A NURSE BUSTLED into the room. "How are you feeling this morning?"

"Not great," Lilly replied, from her bed, "but I'm not complaining. I know I was lucky." She almost managed a smile at the nurse, Jacque, but couldn't quite bring it off. "The headache is gone, thank goodness. Riding my bike without a helmet was really dumb."

Jacque took Lilly's temperature. "Your concussion is grade two. You *were* lucky; any worse and you might have had brain damage." The nurse checked her vital signs on the monitor beside her bed. When she was finished, she said, "Short-term light sensitivity could be an issue. You'll heal with time, but it's also possible confusion and memory loss might reoccur. According to the ER doctor, you were pretty out of it when you arrived."

"I was?" Lilly clutched the edge of the sheet folded over her chest. Had she imagined the bystanders who'd helped her, including the man with blue eyes? "Has anyone called about me in the past twenty-four hours?"

The nurse nodded. "Uh… yes, a woman phoned the nurses' station. She wanted to know if you'd be okay. She said you lost control of your bike after you passed her car, and that she stayed with you until help arrived. We couldn't give her your patient information, of course, but she sounded worried."

"Right. Okay, thanks." Lilly hadn't seen a woman at the scene, but that didn't mean she hadn't been there. She wondered about the man with blue eyes who'd folded his T-shirt for her. Had he been real or a delusion? "No one else checked on me?"

Jacque shook her head. "Not that I know of." Her expression softened. "Were you expecting somebody else? Will someone come by to pick you up?"

"No. I'm new around here." Her daughter Anna lived across the country, and her ex-husband Matthew wouldn't care enough to look after her. He had a new mistress to keep him busy. "I'll call a cab."

Lilly worried she'd imagined Mister July. Maybe the knock on her head had caused her to hallucinate. Maybe she'd been so lonely the past year, and the years before that, when Matthew lost interest in their marriage, that she'd invented the handsome stranger with kindness in his eyes. Maybe her need for comfort had made her pathetic. She closed her eyes and fought back despair.

The nurse turned to leave. "Breakfast will be up in a few minutes. Afterward, the doctor will examine you, and if you're cleared to go home, she'll sign your release papers."

Home. Lilly sighed and let her sadness fade. No matter what, she still had her little house near the bay, the beach and the boardwalk, and her book club. Maybe she'd make new friends in her community. Real friends. The kind who invited you over for coffee and good long chats.

Home is what you made it.

* * *

Two weeks later...

Lilly pulled pans of test-recipe, pineapple upside down cakes from the oven seconds before her doorbell rang. She put aside her pot holders, pulled off her apron, and crossed the house to answer.

A man wearing a ball cap and sunglasses stood on the threshold.

She searched the foggy recesses of her short-term memory to place him but came up blank—until he smiled.

40

Then she recalled her quiet morning on the bay and the construction worker manning a pile driver who'd waved before her accident.

"I hope you don't mind me stopping by," he said. "Lilly, right?"

She couldn't hide her surprise. "How'd you know my name?"

The man pulled off his sunglasses and took off his cap. Then he offered his free hand for a handshake. "I'm Theo Easton."

The instant her gaze met his brilliant blue eyes, Lilly caught her breath. She took his large, rough hand in hers. "It's...*you*." She hadn't imagined him. The man who'd helped her after her fall was the same man who'd smiled from the construction site.

"It took me a while to find you. I had to ask around the neighborhood. I wanted to see for myself that you're okay."

Lilly released his hand, but their fingers brushed before she lowered her arm, coursing sensations through her that made her want to touch him again. "I'm doing well. Thanks. Come in." She led him inside her tiny living room and motioned for him to set his belongings on a side table.

Before Lilly could offer him a seat, Theo spoke again. "I think my pile driver scared you."

"What?" She had no idea what he was talking about. Lilly turned and saw remorse reflected in his eyes.

"Your accident. Indirectly, my fault." He tapped a finger against the back of his opposite hand. "I...*ah*...watched you ride off on your bike after we waved to each other. You looked so beautiful, I couldn't help but stare." He looked down at his feet then, clearly uncomfortable. When he glanced up, he continued. "I saw your bike skid after the pile driver slammed the ground. I've felt bad about that ever since."

No one had called her beautiful in years. And his concern for her wellbeing touched her deeply. Lilly reached out a hand and laid it over his. His skin felt warm over hands strengthened by hard work. "I had an accident. Nothing was your fault. I wanted to thank you for helping me."

They stared at each other for what seemed a long time. Theo seemed larger than she remembered, and even more handsome, if that were possible.

Was it her imagination, or was he leaning toward her the same way she leaned closer to him?

"Something smells good," Theo said, finally, and they grinned at each other from mere inches apart.

"Experiments. I work at a bakery and help the owner develop new recipes. One day, I hope to have my own place."

Theo sniffed. "I think your experiment succeeded."

"And I think I'll make us a pot of coffee to go with the cake. It's upside down."

"Upside down seems to be a habit with you."

He winked at her, and Lilly truly laughed for the first time in a long while.

* * *

THEO DRANK the last of his second cup of coffee and downed the last bite of his second piece of cake an hour later. He wiped his mouth on a napkin and pushed the plate away. "That was great. I hope your customers appreciate you." The smile that touched Lilly's lips made him want to lean over and kiss her. Instead, he cleared their dirty dishes and utensils and carried them to the sink.

Lilly came to her feet. "You're my guest. I'll take care of those." She moved up behind him.

As a widower, he was used to doing everything himself. "Dishwasher?" Without waiting for an answer, he started stacking the plates. Then he grinned over at her. "I want to make sure I get invited back the next time you bake."

Lilly's smile reassured him that he didn't sound like a freak. He hadn't been this close to a woman since Teresa passed. Since she'd been the only woman in his life for twenty years, his flirting skills were as rusty as a bucket of old nails.

Lilly had knocked the wind out of him at first sight. With the breeze blowing her long red hair around her pretty, freckled face, and her tanned legs pedaling her bike, she had that indefinable *wow* factor that made a simple activity something special to watch. Meeting her had made him more hopeful for the future than he'd been in three years...since the world as he'd known it crumbled.

Though surrounded by water, he'd been living in a desert. He turned and met Lilly's gaze. He wanted to get to know her... to be her friend, to hold her... and make love to her, goddammit.

They moved closer in unison, and he grazed the side of her neck with his fingers. He'd almost forgotten how soft a woman's skin could be. He ached for her with a fierceness that brought a groan past his lips. When Lilly closed her eyes and released a sigh, he reached for her.

He thought their first intimate touch might be awkward, or clumsy, but when he took Lilly in his arms, she stared up into his face and eased against him. He pressed his mouth to hers, and she kissed him back with tenderness and longing that quickly turned breathless and hungry. He ran a thumb over the hard tip of her nipple and cupped her breast.

She deepened the kiss and dug her fingers into the hairline at the base of his neck as her tongue touched his. Theo ran his hands along her sides and up her back before pressing her against the counter and adding friction to their embrace. His erection strained against the fly of his jeans, and he grunted with desire as his groin met hers. He raised his hips, slid down, and then repeated the movements.

When Lilly moaned and pulled him closer, he knew he'd found her sweet spot. Her breathing turned ragged, and she pressed her face into the curve of his shoulder. He moved against her again, then again, and she cried out, one hand gripping the edge of the counter as she lost control.

He wanted to lift her skirt and tear off whatever she wore beneath but sensed her coming back to herself and letting him go. She took a side step away and released a quick breath.

Clearly, he'd taken things too far, too soon. So much time had passed—too long—since he'd made love, but he wanted to make love to Lilly when the timing was right.

According to what Lilly had told him over coffee, she'd been crushed by infidelity and emotional abuse. He'd lost his wife to a devastating disease. They might both need physical release, but Theo was sure they needed emotional connection more.

Maturity did that to a person.

He kissed her forehead and took a step back. She tilted her head and smiled up at him. "Wow," she whispered. "Just wow."

"Yeah." He'd never been one for fancy words, but when they finally got together for real, he knew they'd create fireworks. "I'd better go—for now," he said, and then kissed her again. The heat between them flared until he almost lost his will to leave.

"Maybe that's a good idea—for now," she whispered back, pushing her fingers against his chest.

Theo took her hand and held it while she walked him to the door. He grabbed his hat, sunglasses, and cell phone from the side table. They exchanged phone numbers.

"Saturday night," he said. "Let's go on a real date."

"This Saturday?"

"Every Saturday."

Lilly closed the front door, leaned against it, and giggled. *Giggled.* A few hours ago, she'd been baking upside down cake. Minutes ago, she'd been brought to orgasm by a living, breathing male. The first in so long, she wondered if she'd blown dust into her underwear.

Lilly smiled. Mister July, the gorgeous construction worker with blue eyes, had a thing for her. And she *definitely* had a thing for him. Theo had reawakened her feminine self and refueled her dormant desire. It had taken all of her willpower not to satisfy him in every way possible in her kitchen...and her living room...in her bedroom...and anywhere else they could manage. She'd been crazed by him and just barely managed to hang on to her morals and better judgment before she led him to the door.

Well, considering she'd climaxed against him—a veritable stranger, maybe the *morals* and *better judgment* ships had sailed.

Lilly laughed. Who knew a concussion would lead to this?

* * *

One month later...

Theo stepped into Lilly's living room to pick her up for their fourth date—not counting the times he'd gotten cleaned up at his condo after work and driven to her place for drinks on her porch or walks around her community.

He tried to keep his cool under his jacket and tie and hid the gift he held behind his back, though Lilly hadn't made standing still easy. She wore a slinky black dress that bared her cleavage and high-heeled shoes that showed off her sensational legs. She'd pinned up her hair, too, and wore a strand of gold around her neck with a diamond pendant.

Theo couldn't take his gaze off her. "You look beautiful." He meant that she looked sexy as hell, and smoking hot, but "beautiful" sounded better.

Lilly kissed him, and Theo breathed in the scent of her hair and traces of sweet soap on clean skin as he returned the kiss. The gift bumped her hip when he tried to hold her in his arms.

Her soft voice brushed his ear and made his skin prickle. "Got something for me?"

For a split second, he thought she meant his hard-on. He stifled a comeback more suited to a construction site than a dressed-up-for-dinner date and replied, instead, "*Only* for you."

They'd kept their relationship casual since the afternoon in her kitchen, when they'd almost lost control, but Theo's desire had simmered to the boiling point. Tonight, he intended to make his feelings known. He wanted this woman badly, but more than that, he wanted her to stay in his life. Lilly was courageous, strong, and kind. She was beautiful, smart, and had sex appeal to spare.

Could he be falling in love?

He took a step back and held out the gift he'd brought. "I thought the time was right to give you this."

Lilly's eyes widened, and then glistened with apparent pleasure. "Such a big box. No wonder you had trouble hiding it behind your back."

They sat side by side on the couch while she opened the cardboard container wrapped in plain white paper. As she did, she gave him warm sidelong glances that made him feel good about the present he'd chosen. He'd picked it out carefully, wanting to offer her the best possible option.

Then again, what if she hated it? Nothing about the gift

spelled romance. No one in the world would call it sexy. His heartbeat thrummed, and he suddenly wanted a glass of water. What the hell had he been thinking? He should have brought her flowers, or perfume, or tickets to a show.

Then… wouldn't you know…Lilly lifted the bicycle helmet from its box…and burst into tears.

"Shit!" He'd screwed up. Women wanted lingerie and stuff that smelled nice. What had possessed him to buy a fucking bicycle helmet?

He wrapped an arm around her. "Don't cry. I'll take it back and get you something else. I wasn't making fun of your accident. Honest. I suck at gifts." She'd probably break up with him and never speak to him again.

Instead, she leaned over and pressed her mouth to his in an amazing kiss that rushed blood to his ears—and everywhere else.

"This is the kindest, most thoughtful gift anyone's ever given me," she said, at last. She held up the helmet for them to admire. "It's perfect. I love it."

Relief filled him. Though Lilly seemed to understand the significance of his gesture, he wanted to tell her what it meant to him. What *she* meant to him. He lifted her chin with his thumb and met her gaze. "I never, ever want anything to hurt you again. I want you to be safe from harm…and I want you to know…I will never hurt you."

Tears trailed down Lilly's cheeks. She closed her eyes and nodded.

After a moment, Lilly wiped away her tears. "I have to fix my makeup." She gave him a peck on the cheek, laid the helmet on the coffee table, and stood. "Be right back."

Theo wanted to tell her to forget about her makeup and their dinner reservations. He wanted to lead her to bed. But Lilly looked knocked-down gorgeous in her dress and heels, and he didn't want to spoil her evening. She clearly considered their date night special.

His gaze honed on the hallway leading to the master bedroom at the back of the house. He hoped that one day, sooner than later, he'd get to see it.

He relaxed on the couch until the sound of Lilly's heels on the hardwood floor announced her return. Theo stood, ready to go to dinner, but when Lilly entered the room, wearing filmy white lingerie and fancy bedroom slippers, his feet became riveted to the floor. His breath caught, and his pulse pounded. How the hell did he get so lucky?

"You like?" Lilly gave him a sultry smile, followed by a slow pirouette.

Theo drank in the sight of her creamy skin, full breasts, and long bare legs. She'd let down her hair, too, and rinsed the makeup from her face.

"You're spectacular." He couldn't stop staring.

Lilly held out a hand.

Theo tore off his tie, slid out of his sport coat, and tossed them on the couch. He kicked off his shoes then took Lilly's hand. She led him into a bedroom lit with candles where the scent of vanilla filled the air. An open bottle of wine, two glasses, and a box of condoms stood on the table next to a queen-size bed. A comforter had been folded down over crisp blue sheets he intended to rumple like mad.

Theo grinned. "You thought of everything."

Lilly helped him undress. "Dinner wasn't the only thing I had on my mind tonight."

LILLY HAD NEVER BEEN SO TURNED on in her life. After Theo lifted the nightgown from her body and took her in his arms, she trembled so much she could hardly stay on her feet. She guided him onto the bed and lay face to face with him, touching every inch of his skin, between deep, delicious kisses.

She shuddered and sighed as he cupped her buttocks while he rubbed his erection against her sex to make her ready. His fingers kneaded her flesh.

He kissed her again and then slid his tongue inside her mouth before running the tip over her bottom lip. Stifling her moan with his mouth, he nibbled the fullness at the center of her lip and sucked it gently between his teeth. While they kissed, his hand caressed the inside of her thigh where the skin was softest, and then stroked the sensitive mound between her legs.

When she pressed tighter against his palm, he rubbed his thumb over her pleasure center, and supported her spine with his opposite hand. Lilly arched her back, and her breasts lifted, creating an instant mental snapshot of the most erotic moment of her life.

Her breathing turned shallow as his tongue laved the hard tip of one breast while his thumb circled her swollen bud in perfect syncopation. She gasped when he increased the pace and pressure between her legs and moved to her other breast to suck. When Lilly thought she couldn't take another second of stimulation without climaxing, Theo released her. She let out a gasp of protest.

"I'm not near finished, sweetheart." Theo moved lower, ran his tongue over the circle of her navel, and groaned deep in his throat when he tasted her.

Lilly's heartbeat seemed to thrum through the room.

A condom wrapper crinkled, and through the candlelight, Lilly watched as Theo prepared to enter her. She raised her hips and offered herself with total trust. As they moved together, and he gave himself to her, Lilly cried out, too.

An hour later—or maybe two—Lilly poured glasses of wine, and they sat naked on the bed after cleaning up.

Theo offered a toast. "To bike rides and bicycle helmets."

Lilly took a sip of her drink. "Who would have thought a concussion would bring us together?"

"That and upside down cake." Theo gave her a hungry look, reminding her of their first steamy encounter inside her kitchen.

"I heard one of the guys on the job joke about 'upside down.' Turns out, it's more than a cake, it's a sexual position." Theo tasted his wine. "I checked it out on the Internet. Has to be the most uncomfortable looking thing I've ever seen. Who the hell thinks up this shit? We'd break each other in half, but you'd definitely go first."

Lilly laughed so hard she almost spilled the wine on her new sheets. Falling in love with Theo was turning out to be fun. She placed her wineglass on the bedside table, took Theo's glass, and placed it there, too. "I can think of lots of ways to give us pleasure, and none of them hurt." She straddled him and let nature take over.

Theo buried his face in her neck and nibbled his way to her ear. "I think I'll buy a bike so that we can ride around town together."

Lilly leaned back. "Remember to buy a helmet. And maybe a pair of those sexy bike shorts. Checking out your ass will give me extra incentive to add miles to our route."

Theo stroked her shoulder and let his fingers trail her arm. "We'll get you a pair, too." He stared down at their joined hips. "I sure like watching you move."

PLAYS WITH FIRE

ELLE JAMES

*L*ola Engel flipped the sign in the window of her shoe shop to display CLOSED and exited the building, pulling the door shut behind her. She locked it and glanced at her watch.

Damn.

She had only an hour to get home, change, and stage an "accident" before Chance Grayson went off duty at the fire station.

Running in high heels was never good, nor classy. If at all possible, Lola avoided running in public. Scarred as a child by name-calling bullies, she didn't want anyone comparing her to an epileptic giraffe during a grand mal seizure. So, she hurried, skipping along, and then running all out when she verified no one was watching.

For a thirty-nine year-old woman—okay, forty-three, though no one but her doctor knew the truth—she kept her body in top physical condition, with not an ounce of fat on her thighs or belly. Since her husband had passed, she'd had loads of time on her hands. Time she preferred to fill working out or flirting with the best-looking man in Hellfire, Texas.

Chance Grayson. One of the four Grayson brothers, all of whom were incredibly clean-cut, drool-worthy, butt-hugging, jean-clad cowboys and firefighters. They'd struck it rich in the gene pool, and Lola wouldn't mind having some of that gold stretched out in her bed.

Oh, she wasn't looking for long-term commitment or love. She'd already been in love once, and losing someone you cared for as much as she'd cared for Mr. Engel hurt far too much.

No, she'd vowed to enjoy an active sex life with whomever the hell she pleased and screw the tongue-wagging, back-stabbing biddies of the community who thought they were better than anyone else because they were married and settled.

Settled only meant living in a rut. Lola refused to slip into a ring or a rut. Losing her husband had taught her one valuable lesson: life was too damned short. She had to seize it by the balls and hold on to that orgasmic finish line.

Two blocks down, two to go. Why the hell had she walked to work that morning? And why the hell hadn't she worn tennis shoes?

Because you're too goddamn vain and won't let others see you in anything less than the most expensive shoes this side of the Mississippi.

New York City didn't have anything on Hellfire, Texas. Lola made damn sure of that. If she didn't sell many expensive shoes in her brick-and-mortar store, she sold a truckload every week from her online shop.

Just because a person lived in small-town, snail's-paced Texas didn't mean a woman had to deprive herself of the best and sexiest shoes from some of the most fabulous designers this world had to offer.

Slowly, but surely, she'd educated the ranchers' wives on the difference between Jimmy Choos stilettoes and Ariat cowboy boots. Not many of the wives had the kind of money for the more expensive brands, but Lola stocked budget knock-offs to satisfy the locals.

At that moment, she would trade her Jimmy Choos for some running shoes. All because she wanted a shot at seducing Chance Grayson. The younger man had caught her eye the day she'd seen him shirtless hosing down his big, red fire truck.

The day had been a typical hotter-than-Hades summer one in Texas. Sweat glistened on the young man's shoulders, and all Lola could think was how she wanted to run her hands over every part of Chance's body. Then she'd start all over with her tongue.

Who said a woman of thirty-nine had to settle for men her own age? Forty-year-old men dated twenty-somethings all the time. Lola was a heck of a lot better in bed than most of those little girls. She could show Chance Grayson a thing or two. She just had to get his attention.

So far, she was zero for three in her attempts. She'd picked days she knew he was on duty to call 911 for help only the fire station, and his particular truck, would respond to.

Finding a kitten to strand high in a tree had been a challenge. Chance had been the first responder. Lola had dressed in a low-cut, midriff blouse, showing off her tightened breasts and flat belly. She'd worn the strappy, pink Christian Louboutins.

Chance had saved the kitten and left, without giving her a second look.

The worst part had been his partner, Flannigan, who'd frowned, his gaze raking her from top to bottom. But not in a good way. "You'll break an ankle in those," he'd said and left, shaking his head.

The red-haired, tattooed, motorcycle-riding bear of a man hadn't known squat about the pricey shoes she wore.

Lola had been mad enough to throw one of her pricey shoes at the back of the man's head. When she'd leaned against the tree, holding the squirming kitten, a bee stung her in the ass.

That hadn't been the worst part.

She'd jumped way from the tree, came short of launching the kitten into outer space, and stepped in a pile of dog poop. In her Christian Louboutins!

All that trouble, and Chance hadn't given her even a wink. Now she had a ruined pair of very expensive stilettoes and a cat named Flannigan. Yes, she'd named the cat after the asshat Flannigan with the intention of kicking it every time she remembered that day, her failure, and the ruined shoes.

Fortunately for Flannigan, Lola didn't have the heart to hurt the kitten. Hell, she'd never much cared for cats and had refused to get one, afraid she'd be labeled a lonely cat lady. And, to top things off, the darned kitten had taken up residence on her pillow at night, half-lying on her head.

Lola would never tell a soul that she kinda liked the little guy. She sure as hell wouldn't tell Flannigan, the tattooed firefighter. He'd laugh her all the way to the Jimmy Choo shoe factory in the UK.

His obvious derision of her shoes and attempt to capture Chance's attention made her even more determined to snag the Grayson brother. She was older, but far from dead, and in the hormone-humming, sexual prime of her life.

The second attempt had been an equal failure when she'd personally jammed the electronic locks in her old car and called 911, asking for them to bring the Jaws of Life.

Sheriff's Deputy Leamon and the fire truck arrived.

Chance had been there, but he'd stood back while the deputy slipped a flat tool down her window into the door and unlocked it in like two seconds flat.

By the time she'd stepped out of her vehicle in Manolo Blahnik spikes—which should have snapped the man's head around—her efforts had been wasted on Lenny the sweet, but clueless sheriff's deputy, who couldn't have been more than eighteen years old. Okay, maybe twenty.

Burning leaves had been another disaster. Yes, she'd done right by calling the sheriff to tell them she'd be burning. A little while later, she'd called 911 to say her fire was getting out of control, but she'd nearly burned down her garage in the process.

Chance had been one of two firemen who'd gotten there first. Flannigan had been the other, much to Lola's disgust.

While Chance had unrolled the giant fire hose, Flannigan put out the fire with Lola's garden hose. When Chance saw Flannigan had it under control, he'd folded and fitted the giant hose back onto the truck.

Meanwhile, the odious Flannigan, carrying her garden hose, had stopped in front of her. "Why didn't you keep your garden hose handy?"

Disgruntled at the man for ruining her third attempt, she'd glared and said the first thing to come to her mind. "I certainly didn't want to get my shoes wet."

That day she'd been careful to rake the leaves while wearing worn work boots. But when it came time to burn the leaves, she'd changed into a sexy leopard-print, off-the-shoulder shorts romper and her matching Salvatore Ferragamo, lace-up, espadrille wedges.

She'd stomped her wedge-heeled foot. "And why are you always with Chance? Why can't he come alone?"

"Is that what this is all about?" Flannigan-the-Bastard had shaken his head. "Woman, you have to stop calling 911. The sheriff can arrest you for wasting our time." He'd shot a derisive sneer at her feet. "And get some real shoes, if you're burning leaves in your yard." As he'd handed her the garden hose, he'd squeezed the handle, sending a spray of water onto her beautiful shoes.

Lola had squealed, dropped the hose, and hopped away. Unfortunately, the handle jammed in the open position, and the hose twisted and spun like a snake on speed. Before she'd caught the hose, her sexy romper was soaked, the hairstyle she'd spent hours perfecting was equally drenched and lying limp around her face. Her makeup had run in rivulets down her cheeks, but that still hadn't been the worst of it. Her lace-up espadrille wedges were now covered in mud and falling apart.

All because of one tattooed jerk of a firefighter.

Not to mention, Lola had run out of reasons to call the fire department, short of setting her house on fire.

Until today. At lunch, she'd stopped by the station to drop off a batch of cookies for the guys and learned her nemesis, Flannigan, had taken the day off to work on some construction project. Chance had been outside, washing the ladder truck. That's when it hit her. The idea that would give Chance the opportunity to save her, and she'd show him her appreciation in such a way he couldn't resist.

She just had to get home in time to catch Chance before he went off shift.

Lola reached home with twenty minutes to spare. She rushed inside, almost tripped over the kitten, and set her purse on the counter. Quickly changing into a pair of shorts, too short to be legal, and a miniscule button-down top that bared most of her midriff—because the air was hot, and it was Texas. *Uh-huh*. Not to mention, this particular, scoop-necked top was so tight it gave her extra lift and displayed her breasts to their best advantage.

Back out to the garage, she ran, found the ladder that had hung in the same spot since her husband had died more than six years ago, and hurked it off the hooks. Heavier than she expected, it nearly clobbered her. But Lola was determined. This might be her best opportunity to capture the Grayson hunk's attention. And she'd gone a long time without sex. She'd worn out two battery-operated-boyfriends. The time had come to have someone in her bed.

Back to the house, she set up the extension ladder and climbed up to the roof. She was all right, until she looked down. Two stories didn't look like much when your feet were steady on the ground. But looking down…

She swayed, her pulse pounding and her breaths coming in shallow gasps. If she weren't careful, she'd hyperventilate and fall off the roof before Chance could save her.

Hauling in a deep breath, she sat back on the shingles, pressed her ankle-strap Prada sandal against the ladder, and gave it a shove.

It leaned out and came back.

Damn it.

She did it again, giving it a heftier push.

This time the ladder swung away from the roof and teetered between falling toward the roof or away. For a moment, Lola thought it would come back toward her. She held her breath and nearly cheered when the ladder fell away.

Congratulating herself on achieving the first part of the plan, she pulled her cell phone from her back pocket.

Poking her manicured nails at 911, she waited. Even before the first ring, she could hear the blare of sirens. How could already they know she needed help?

Then a terrible thought occurred. The fire department was being deployed to an actual emergency.

Daniel Flannigan stopped by the fire station on his way home from the house where he'd been working for an older woman whose husband had passed away. Her roof had begun to leak, and she couldn't afford to pay a contractor to fix it.

Daniel had heard about her through one of the members of his motorcycle club who lived on the same block. They'd planned a day when they could all be off to do the repairs the woman might need for the near future.

With ten people from his club there, they'd put in a full day's effort and completed all the work they'd set out to do, plus a few other fix-it items they'd discovered along the way.

Feeling good about what they'd accomplished, Daniel stopped by the fire station to see if any of the guys wanted to grab a beer at the Ugly Stick Saloon when they got off shift.

Already the men for the next shift were arriving when Daniel pulled into the parking lot, a ladder and his power tools still in the back of this pickup.

Chance Grayson ran out of the building toward the pumper truck, shrugging into his fire-retardant jacket as he raced across the concrete.

"What's going on?" Daniel called out.

"Old man Ford caught his pavilion on fire with his barbeque grill."

"Got enough men to handle it?"

"Yeah, between the two shifts, we've got it covered."

The fire chief stepped out of building, shaking his head. "Got a minor emergency—woman trapped on her roof with no way to get down." He shook his head. "Hate to tie up anyone when that fire might get out of control." He cast a glance at Daniel. "What are you doing here? I thought you took the day off."

"I did," Daniel said and jerked a thumb over his shoulder. "I've got a ladder. Do you want me to check out the lady on the roof?"

"Would you?" The fire chief handed him a piece of paper. "I want to stick around in case they call for more help with the pavilion fire. I might get out the tanker truck and follow them to Ford's place."

Daniel shook his head. "Go. I can help the woman down."

"Thanks." The chief hurried toward the tanker truck parked at the rear of the station.

So much for a beer with his buddies. Daniel glanced down at the writing on the paper and groaned.

Not again.

He recognized the address, having been there with Chance on three previous occasions over the past six months.

Lola Engel lived there, and she came up with the lamest excuses to call out the fire department.

After the first couple times, Daniel had seen through her *emergencies.* The woman had the hots for his buddy, Chance Grayson. Chance hadn't clued in, probably because Lola wasn't his usual kind of woman. Oh, he treated her with the kindness and respect due an older woman.

Unfortunately for Lola.

But seriously, crying wolf for the fourth time? This bullshit had to end. Since Chance couldn't see what was happening, Daniel would have to take matters into his own hands and tell the woman to stop.

While the fire trucks headed out of town, Daniel drove his pickup to Lola's house a little over two blocks away, thinking of the words he'd use to put the woman in her place. As he pulled into her yard, he almost laughed out loud.

What woman in her right mind climbed onto a roof wearing stilettoes? Only one woman he knew—Lola Engel.

He got out of his truck and started to unload his ladder when he spied an extension ladder lying in the grass.

"Oh mother, please tell me it's not true," she muttered from above.

"What's not true?"

"I call for a real hero, and I get you."

His lips quirked at the corners. He always got a great deal of pleasure out of calling her bluffs. This time would be no different. He glanced up at two slender, well-toned and tanned thighs hanging over the edge of the roof. "Ms. Engel, are you all right up there?"

"Yes, of course I am," she snapped as she peered downward. "I just can't get down. Could you please put up the ladder? That's all I need. Then I can climb down by myself."

His grin stretched at her disgruntled tone. "Toss down those shoes, and I'll think about it."

"Are you out of your mind?" she asked, her eyes wide. "You don't *toss* a pair of Prada onto the ground from two stories up."

He fisted his hands on his hips. "You do if you want to get down off the roof. I'm not giving you the ladder until you lose those ridiculous shoes."

She frowned. "Do you promise to catch them?"

"Hell, no."

"Then I'm not dropping them." She crossed her arms over her chest. Without her hands on the roof, she slipped a few inches. Her eyes widened, and she slapped both palms flat on the shingles. "Okay, okay." With one hand on the roof, she slipped the straps off the backs of her heels. Then she leaned toward the edge and held out her hand with the shoes dangling from her fingertips. "Are the bushes right below my hand?"

"Seriously?" Daniel shook his head. "Yes, the bushes are below your hand. Now, drop the shoes before you fall and break your damn neck."

Lola pouted. "You don't have to be so grumpy. Do you have any idea how much these cost?"

"No," he bit out, his jaw tightening. "But they sure as hell aren't worth your life."

"That's your opinion." She sighed. "Here goes. But if they're damaged, I'm blaming you."

"Blame me. I don't give a rat's ass."

Lola let go of the shoes then released a breath.

No doubt she'd listened for a thunk and had been reassured when her shoes' fall was cushioned by the azalea bushes. Again, he shook his head.

Good for his word, Daniel propped the extension ladder against the eaves and started up.

"What are you doing?" she asked.

Daniel hid a smile. "Saving a damsel in distress."

"I told you, I can climb down on my own."

"You'd deprive a knight in shining armor from doing his duty?" He didn't slow until he reached the top.

Lola snorted and muttered beneath her breath, "Knight, my pearly white ass."

Daniel stopped near the top and took a moment to admire the picture she made in her tiny shorts and top. The woman was flashing more skin than most did on a beach. "Do you want off this roof, or not?"

Lola bit her bottom lip. "Well, since you're here…I guess you can help." She eased to the edge. "Climbing up was a lot easier than getting back down." She chewed on her lip as she scooted her bottom along the shingles to the edge.

"Turn over and lie on your stomach. I'll guide your feet to the first rung."

She frowned. "Are you sure that'll work?"

"Positive." He snapped his fingers, impatiently. "Hurry up. I don't have all day."

"Bossy much?" she groused and did as he said.

With her bottom in the air and her legs within reach, she presented Daniel a different perspective than he was used to. Instantly, he developed a great appreciation for her *pearly white ass.* "You shouldn't climb up ladders without someone to spot you, Ms. Engel." He wrapped a hand around one trim ankle and guided her pretty foot to the rung. "You could fall and break those sexy legs."

"What?" She jerked around and almost slid off the roof, taking him with her.

"Hey, watch what you're doing!" Daniel steadied her with his hands on her silky thighs then eased the other foot onto the ladder in front of him.

"You shouldn't say things like that when you have a woman in such a precarious situation."

"Well, it's true." He wrapped an arm around her and held onto the ladder.

"Which part? The part about falling, or the part about my sexy legs?" she asked, her attention on the rungs in front of her face.

"Both," he said against her hair. "Now, I'll take a step, then you take a step."

One rung at a time, they eased down the ladder. The entire way, Daniel inhaled the scent of honeysuckle. He glanced at the ground, searching for the source, but couldn't find one. That's when he realized what he smelled was Lola.

He inhaled, startled at the lust coiling in his groin. Shit, the woman had to be ten or twelve years older than him.

And probably had a lot of experience in bed.

Daniel shook his head. Forget it. She had a thing for his partner, Chance.

Her tight ass bumped into his belly several times on the way down, causing more discomfort in his tightening jeans.

What the hell? The woman was a nuisance. She liked crying wolf just to catch the attention of a man so much younger. And Chance didn't have a clue, nor would he appreciate a woman like Lola. "Do you work out or something?" Daniel asked, before he could stop himself.

"Every day. Since my husband died, I've taken up yoga and running. Why do you ask?"

"It shows."

"Oh." She paused for a second, and then continued, "Well, thank you."

When they reached the ground, Daniel stepped back, his body hot, his pulse pounding. "Ms. Engel, you've got to stop calling 911. One of these days, you'll have a real emergency, and no one will take you seriously."

She stared up at him, her eyes wide with fake innocence. "I really couldn't get off the roof."

Daniel narrowed his eyes. "I know what you're up to."

"I don't know what you're talking about." She spun away to retrieve her shoes from the bushes.

"Chance Grayson is not that into you," Flannigan pointed out.

Eyes narrowed, Lola lifted her chin. "He will be."

Daniel shook his head. "Why would he be? I mean, you're probably old enough to be his mother."

Lolo spun on Daniel. "You need to take that back, right now. I'd have to have given birth when I was a small child myself. And what's wrong with a younger man dating an older woman?"

"Well..." Daniel rubbed the back of his neck while he looked around for an escape. "It's just that older women aren't as attractive to younger men."

"Is that so?" She stepped up to him, pressing her breasts against his chest. "Are you saying you don't find me attractive?"

"Now, don't go puttin' words in my mouth. I told you that you have sexy legs. I don't say that about just anyone.

Besides, you shouldn't go fishin' for compliments. You might not be happy with what you catch."

"No?" With a catlike smile stretching her lips, Lola walked a finger up his chest and over his chin. "What if I like what I catch?"

He grabbed her finger in his big hand. "You like Grayson. Leave me out of this."

"A woman has a right to change her mind." She pulled the hand he held toward her and pressed it to her chest, running his knuckles across the swells of her breasts. "And just so you know, they're real." She winked up at him and pressed her hips against his.

Damned if his cock didn't rise to the occasion.

Flannigan stared into her gaze, fighting to keep his hands from clasping her thighs and wrapping her sexy legs around his waist. Finally, he settled on grabbing her arms and pushing her to arm's length, away from his growing erection. "Woman, you're really playing with fire, here."

"Oh, I'm not afraid of getting burned." Lola batted her eyes, swept her tongue across her full, luscious lips and tilted her chin in challenge. "Are you?"

Something inside Flannigan snapped. "Fuck no," he muttered. With his hands still on her arms, he slammed her to his chest and crushed his mouth over hers.

At first blaming it on her taunting, his kiss was angry, vengeful, and harsh. But the sweet, minty taste of her mouth and that damned scent of honey-suckle wrapped around his senses. He skimmed the seam of her lips with his tongue.

When she gasped and dropped her shoes, he thrust through, caressing her mouth with thrusts, imitating the age-old motion of mating. His dick responded, growing so hard he could barely breathe.

At first rigid, Lola's body was like a brick against his, her hands pressed flat against his chest. As the kiss continued, she softened, and then leaned into him. She raised her hands, entwining them around his neck to pull him closer.

What had started as a lesson in his ability to control the situation, ended in Flannigan getting schooled by the teacher.

HOLY HOT TAMALES! Lola's body turned traitor. She'd tempted the big firefighter out of a need to prove he was wrong, and that older women could be every bit as sexy as younger women. What she hadn't expected was for him to go along with it. And she certainly hadn't expected to like it.

Once the kiss began, she had every intention of being the one to break it off and laugh in his face. But, *holy guacamole!* Now, she wasn't sure she needed to breathe as much as she needed Flannigan's lips on hers. In fact, she couldn't seem to get close enough to the man. Too many inches were between them, though their bodies were pressed together. No, inches weren't the problem.

Clothes were.

She slid her calf around the back of his and upward until her crotch straddled his thick thigh. Her pussy ached for more, and rubbing against him only increased the heat.

After what felt like a lifetime and yet must have been only a moment, Flannigan lifted his head and stared down into her gaze. His big, rough hands had migrated along her back. His eyes narrowed at the same time his fingers tightened around her ass.

LOLA'S HEAD SPUN, and her lips throbbed. Her breathing was labored as if she'd been running a marathon. Through the fog of her thoughts, one emerged, *Burn, baby burn.*

She swallowed hard and went for bravado. "What's the matter, big guy? Never kiss a *real* woman, before?"

"I've kissed plenty of women," he said. "Some more experienced than you."

"Yeah, did they make you lose control?" she asked, liking the feel of his hands on her buttocks—warm, hard, and strong.

"I'm always in control," he said, his brows dipping.

"Uh-huh." She nodded toward the house across the street. "Do you always prefer an audience when you kiss a woman?"

Flannigan shot a glance over his shoulder at Lola's neighbor.

Mr. Harden was the nosey old man she loved to flash when he spied on her through his binoculars.

Flannigan glared at the man. "What the hell?"

"Mr. Harden's harmless. He just likes to watch." She tilted her head, a smile twitching at the edges of her lips. "Care to come in for a glass of iced tea? It's the least I can offer after you rescued me from the rooftop."

He hesitated, and then shook his head. "I should get going." He stepped back.

Lola resisted the urge to sink her fingernails into his arms. Instead, she stepped back as well and shrugged. "Suit yourself." She turned and glanced over her shoulder. "Is Chance on duty tomorrow?" She knew perfectly well he was, along with Flannigan.

The firefighter frowned. "I meant what I said. You have to stop calling 911 unless it's a real emergency."

Lola stooped to grab the shoes she'd dropped, giving Flannigan and Mr. Harden an extra-sexy glimpse of her bottom beneath the hem of the shorts. Something very much like a growl sounded behind her.

"Damn it, woman." Flannigan said. "Grayson isn't into you."

She turned and raised an eyebrow. "And you are?"

"I didn't say that," he muttered.

"Good, because I don't think you're man enough for a woman like me."

His chest swelled, and his eyes flared. "And what the hell is that supposed to mean?"

Lola raked her gaze over him from the top of his head to his boots, taking in the tattoos, the dirty jeans, and ripped T-shirt stretching impossibly tight over his broad chest.

Her heart thumped hard against her chest, but she forced calm to her face. "Seems like a man with tattoos is covering up something, or compensating for what he lacks in other areas." She shot a meaningful glance at his package.

She had no doubt the man was equipped, based on the impressive bulge beneath the denim. And no doubt he was proud of it, like most men.

When she raised her face to his, she swallowed a gasp.

Anger blazed from his eyes. "My tattoos have nothing to do with compensation."

She shrugged. "So you say." Lola turned and walked away, placing one foot in front of the other for maximum hip action. "Don't let me keep you. I'm sure you have younger women to impress with your…manliness. I'll take my *chances* on a real man."

A more sinister growl sounded behind her, and the next thing Lola knew, a heavy hand yanked her around, and she was flung over a broad shoulder. Strong arms clamped like vices around her thighs.

"Hey! Put me down!" Lola braced her hands on his back and pushed against rock-hard muscles.

Flannigan didn't pause or slow as he marched toward her front door.

With her gut being jounced on his shoulder, Lola could

barely catch her breath. "Let…me…down…you Nean-derthal." She pounded his back.

The beast came to an abrupt halt.

Lola pushed herself farther upright and caught a glimpse of Mr. Harden staring at the couple, wide-eyed.

"Let me down, or I'll scream," Lola said. "Mr. Harden is watching us. He'll call the sheriff and have your ass arrested for molesting me."

"You wish." He shoved open her door, turned and waved at Mr. Harden. "She didn't want to walk barefoot," he called out loud enough for the older man to hear. Then he slapped a heavy palm against Lola's bottom, hard enough to make her jump.

She should have been angry, but the smack had an entirely different effect.

Desire coiled in the pit of her belly, and her thighs burned where his hand and arm held her tightly.

Having a strong, sexy firefighter throw her over his shoulder and carry her away to make mad, passionate love was every woman's dream.

But Flannigan was the wrong firefighter.

He stepped inside and shoved the door closed behind him with his boot. "Apologize," he demanded.

"For what?" Lola wiggled. "You've made your point. You're a caveman. You have muscles." *And a great ass.*

"Is Chance's ass why you're so hot on him?"

Lola bit her lip. "Did I say ass out loud?"

"Yeah, and you still haven't apologized."

"For what? Calling it as I see it?"

His grip tightened. "For bad-mouthing my tattoos."

"Put me down, and I might just give you that apology." Now that Lola had noticed his firm butt in the faded jeans, she couldn't stop staring. Just when she considered lowering her hands down his back to touch him there, he hiked her up in the air and dropped her body to cradle her in his arms.

The movement placed her face so close to his, she only had to turn her head a little and her lips would be within kissing distance.

"The apology?" he prompted.

Lola raised her gaze from his lips and stared into his eyes, her pulse hammering, pushing hot blood through her veins. "What?"

"Apology? Tattoos?"

Flannigan didn't even break a sweat holding her above the ground. Lola shifted her gaze from his eyes to the view of his chest at the V of his neckline. "Why so touchy about the tats?"

"They hold special meaning."

She huffed. "Of your old girlfriends?"

"No, of the men I fought with in the Army. The men who came back in body bags."

Lola looked up, guilt twitching in her gut. "I'm sorry. I didn't know."

He nodded and dropped her feet to the ground, retaining his grip around her waist. "Now, you do."

Lola traced the little bit of tattoo she could see on his chest and neck. "Those men must have meant a lot."

"They were my brothers." He caught her finger and lifted it to his lips. "Promise me you won't call 911 unless you have an emergency." Holding her gaze, he pressed his mouth to the tip of her finger.

Her finger tingled where his lips touched it. A spark flowed from that point all the way south, making her pussy clench. "What are you doing?"

"Oh, this?" He kissed her finger again. "It's best that I focus on your hand."

"As opposed to focusing on what?"

"What I really want to do."

Her heart fluttered then pounded against her ribs. She curled her fingers and dragged her nails down the front of his chest. "Aren't you afraid I'll ravage your body?"

He shook his head. "No, I'm afraid I'll do this." Flannigan scooped her up by the backs of her thighs, wrapped her legs around his waist, and turned to press her against the wall. His mouth crashed down on hers, stealing away her breath.

Who needs to breathe, anyway? Lola wrapped her arms around his neck and clung to him, her tongue meeting his in a duel for supremacy. She locked her legs around his waist and sank lower, rubbing her pussy across the bulge of his cock. She wanted much more than a kiss.

While he kissed her, she grabbed a handful of his T-shirt and dragged it up his body.

Flannigan lifted his head, fisted his shirt in his hand and ripped it over his head, flinging it to the floor.

He worked at the tiny buttons of her shirt.

Frustrated, Lola pushed aside his hands and freed the last button.

The firefighter pushed her shirt off her shoulders then nipped and kissed her collarbone, her chin, and the sensitive area below her ear.

Lola leaned her head to the side, giving him better access, while shrugging out of the shirt. Once free, she inhaled, her chest rising.

Flannigan accepted the invitation and rolled her nipple between his teeth, through the lacy cup of her bra.

A moan rose up in Lola's throat, and she tightened her legs around him.

He pushed one of her bra straps over her shoulder and followed it downward, leaving a trail of kisses and nips.

"What are you doing to me?" she asked, every inch of her body on fire.

A low, warm chuckle rumbled in his chest. "If you don't know by now, you're not the experienced woman you claim to be."

"I'll show you experience," she said, making room between her hips and his. She reached for the button of his jeans and thumbed it open. Then she lowered the zipper halfway and slipped her hand beneath the denim. Her lips twitching, she looked up into his face. "Commando?"

He drew in a sharp breath, leaned closer, and whispered against her neck. "The only way to go." The firefighter tongued the pulse beating at the base of her throat.

"Mmm, yes," she said as she curled her hand around his cock and pushed lower to cup his balls.

He placed his hand over hers. "Don't tease."

She rolled his sac in her fingers, her gaze seeking his dark eyes. "Does this feel like I'm teasing?"

"Some women like to take a man to the edge and leave him hanging."

"Sweetheart, I'm not one of them." She squeezed gently, and then slid her hand up his cock. "I don't start anything I'm not willing to finish."

"Good." He gripped her ass and carried her to the kitchen, swept the salt and pepper shakers off the table with his arm, and set her bottom on the edge. Then he stood back, the motion forcing her to remove her hand from his jeans.

Lola frowned. "Are you teasing me now?"

"No, but I want you to know an experienced woman has nothing on me." His brows descended. "Say no now, and I'll walk away."

"Or?" She parted her legs and rubbed her fingers over her pulsing pussy. God, she was hot. The intensity of Flannigan's expression made her want to strip off the rest of her clothes and jump on his dick.

Sweet Jesus, she'd gone far too long without sex. She lifted her chin and waited for his next move.

"*Or*, I'm going to blow your mind."

"Blow, baby, blow." Lola arched her back and released the catch on her bra. For a moment, she wondered if the slight sag to her breasts would be a turn off to a younger man who'd probably seen more women with perky, young breasts than Lola had seen naked men.

If she hadn't been studying his face, she might have missed the slight flare of his eyes as the bra fell away.

By the expression on his face, the man wasn't turned off. In fact, his zipper had slipped lower and his cock sprang free, jutting straight out—hard, thick and ready.

Flannigan bent over her and pressed his lips to her nipple. He sucked it into his mouth and rolled the tip on his tongue. Then he nipped.

"Ouch!" She laced her fingers into his hair and pulled. "Those are attached."

He moved to the other and licked the nipple into a tight bead. "I noticed." Then he drew it into his mouth and sucked hard.

Lola moaned and clutched the back of his head, urging him to take as much of her breast into his mouth as he could.

He laved, sucked, and nibbled until she squirmed on the tabletop.

Without raising his head, he urged her to lie back on the table. As he blazed a trail over her ribs and down her abdomen with his mouth, his hands worked the button loose on her shorts and slipped the garment down her legs. The shorts fell to the floor, leaving only a lace thong covering her sex.

The firefighter slipped his fingers beneath the elastic band, and he cupped her sex, dipping a finger into her pussy.

Lola moaned and spread her legs.

His hand was hot against her skin. His finger felt so good. But, it wasn't enough. Lola squirmed again, laid a hand over his, and pressed him closer, encouraging him to fit more of his fingers inside her.

He obliged, swirling around the juices.

Lola moaned.

"Like that?" he asked.

"I might," she said, her tone tight, her breathing ragged.

Then he edged her panties lower, parted her folds, and blew a warm stream of air over her clit.

Lola gasped and came up on her elbows. "For Pete's sake, don't tease me!"

"Do you want more?" he asked, his thumbs looping through the straps of her thong.

"Yes!" she managed to say on a rush of air.

He ripped off the panties, wedged himself between her thighs, and dropped to his knees.

Oh, sweet heaven, the man *did* know what a woman wanted.

Lola lay back on the table, grasping the edge, prepared to experience the joys of sex.

Flannigan parted her folds and stroked one long, work-roughened finger across her clit and down to her damp entrance.

Tossing her head, Lola gasped, "Oh, my."

He chuckled. "Hit the spot?"

"Oh, *yesss!*"

The rumble of his laughter was offset a second later by a cool stream of air blown over her heated center.

Lola's breath hitched and held in anticipation of what might come next. She wasn't disappointed when he flicked her clit with his tongue.

Lola arched her back off the table and clung to his hair. "Sweet tea and grits, that's the spot. Oh, yes! That's the spot."

"Thought it might be," he said, his breath warm against her pussy.

With that wonderful tongue, he teased, tapped, and twirled the sensitive nubbin until tingling started at her center and shot out to the farthest reaches of her extremities, sizzling a path of nerves to the point Lola tipped over the edge, her body tense and throbbing with her orgasm.

He didn't let up his ministrations until she lay back against the table, as limp as a dishrag, too spent to move a muscle but not ready for the encounter to be over.

A chuckle rose with Flannigan as he straightened between her legs, his cock jutting forward, hard and thick.

Though movement was a struggle, Lola managed to push herself up onto her elbows. She refused to be outdone by the sassy firefighter. He might have proved he was capable of making her squeal, but she was up to the challenge. "I call your bet and raise the ante." She slipped off the edge of the table, thinking she'd never be able to look at it as purely a place for eating food again. Eating, yes. Food, not so much.

With as much grace as she could muster, she stood, naked and proud, and held out her hand. "Protection?"

Flannigan's brows furrowed then lifted. "Oh, yeah." He pulled his wallet from his pocket and extracted a condom, handing it to her. Then he tossed the wallet on the table.

She held the foil packet in her hand for a moment, and then turned on her bare heel and walked toward her bedroom, giving him her backside, naked from head to toe. She knew her body wasn't a young twenty-something, but she was fit, her muscles were well-defined and tight. She could bounce a quarter off her abs. She knew, because she'd tried it.

She'd taken a total of five steps when a growl sounded behind her, and she was scooped off her feet and carried at a much-quicker pace to the bedroom at the back of the apartment.

She lay an arm over his shoulders and quirked an eyebrow. "You know I can walk like normal people."

"You're not normal, and you walk too slowly," he said, his tone raspy.

His grip on her felt tight to the point of almost painful. A thrill of excitement ripped through Lola. This was a man who knew passion and kept it under control. Her challenge was to shake his control.

Once he passed through her bedroom door, Flannigan tossed her on the bed and stood back. "I have to go."

What the hell? Lola blinked, her only outward reaction to his announcement. From the look of his narrowed eyes, this had been his plan all along. Thinking quickly, she knew she had to use the big guns to make this man stay and service her.

She rolled onto her side and slid the condom package from her hip up to the curve of her breast, then flicking the tip of a nipple with the package. "Sure you won't stay a little longer and put this little gem to use?"

"I have better things to do," he said, though his gaze followed the path of the foil square.

Moving her hand, she brushed the condom across her belly and down to the juncture of her thighs, and then slowly rolled to her back. "Better?" She raised her brows, not that he was looking at her face.

His cock was as hard and straight as a tire iron, ready to jack her up.

Lola eased off the bed. "Let me show you to the door, since you're in a hurry to leave." She stopped in front of him and danced her fingers across his bare chest and downward, skimming over his ribs, past his belly button, following the arrow of hair to the thatch disappearing into his sagging jeans. His cock jerked in anticipation of her touch.

Yeah, he wanted her, but why was he fighting that most natural of urges?

Lola refused to let him leave before she'd had her way with him. Starting with his dick. She wrapped her fingers around it and tugged gently. "Unless you can think of another reason to stay a little longer."

His jaw flexed with tension. "I really need to leave."

She nodded and gave him a fake pout. "I understand. Say hello to Chance." She reached lower and cupped his balls. "No, I'll tell him myself."

Flannigan stood still, his breaths coming in rapid, shallow intakes. He gripped her arms and lowered her to her knees.

Lola didn't fight the commanding movement. This was where she'd planned to be even if he hadn't placed her there.

The thrill of anticipation made her pulse beat faster. She knelt before him, her face in front of his cock. "No going back now." She touched the tip of his shaft with her tongue.

A spot of come slipped out.

Lola licked it off, loving the musky flavor of him. Then she traced the head of his penis at an excruciatingly slow pace, paying him back for giving her a condom, and then threatening to leave without using it.

No effing way.

Her core ached with a need only his hard shaft could satisfy. He wasn't going anywhere until he'd taken her to a whole other point in the stratosphere.

No, sir.

And she wouldn't let him go until she'd rocked his world so completely, he'd wish he was Chance Grayson, the man of her lust-filled dreams.

Lola wrapped her lips around the tip of his cock and

touched her tongue to the tip, swirling around its velvety smoothness. Then she let go.

His chest swelled on his quickly indrawn breath.

Good. He wasn't immune.

She cupped his balls in her palm and rolled them as though they were Chinese baoding balls, handling them gently but firmly.

As she touched him there, she slid her tongue around the rim of his head, making a full circle before she trailed down his length and back up again. At the top, she enclosed him in her mouth.

As if he were trying to fight his own instinct, he raised his hands *slowly* and buried them in her hair. His fingertips dug into her scalp, urging her to take more.

Lola did, taking his full length, all the way to the back of her throat while twisting her tongue around his girth.

Flannigan pulled himself almost all of the way out.

Lola reached out and grabbed his buttocks and brought him back into her.

At first, he moved in and out with an easy rhythm.

Lips stretching, Lola made him go faster, guiding him by flexing her hands and squeezing his tight, sexy ass.

Soon, the firefighter was pumping in and out of her, his head thrown back, his jaw tight.

Yes, this was where she wanted him. Lola willed him to lose all control and come in her mouth.

She brought him close; she could feel it in the way his body tensed. Just a little more, and she'd have him.

At that precise moment, Flannigan pulled free.

Noooo. Lola blinked up at him.

He hooked his hands beneath her arms and stood her on her feet. "You will not make me lose control. Do you hear me?" He gave her arms a little shake.

Her lips curled into a feline smile. "Of course not. You

have complete control." She pressed a hand to his chest. "Don't you want to lie down and let me show you just how much control you have?"

He shook his head, his breaths coming in labored pants, like a dog after a challenging run.

Lola schooled her face to keep a triumphant grin from spreading across her face. She gave him a slight push.

He fell onto the bed, his dick protruding from his jeans, his boots still on his feet.

She straddled his leg backward and bent over, giving him full view of her ass and pussy, while she tugged off a boot. Then she stepped over his other thigh and removed the other.

While she was still bent over, a hand smacked her ass, the sound sharper than the pain.

Mmm. She practically purred. "Yes, spank me. I've been a very bad girl."

He smacked her other cheek, a little harder this time.

She turned and straddled both legs, gripped the waist band of his jeans and pulled them over his slim hips and down his magnificent thighs and calves.

He kicked them away with an impatient flick of his legs. Then he scooted back on the bed. "Come here, woman," he commanded.

"As you wish." Lola crawled up his thickly muscled body like a cat playing with its prey. She bent her elbows, dragging her breasts over his cock, pausing long enough to squeeze his length between them.

She skimmed her nipples over his belly, ribs, and finally to his hard, tattooed chest. "I'm here." She rubbed her sex over the length of his cock before stopping with the tip nudging her entrance. "Your wish is my command."

His eyes narrowed. "Fuck me."

She smiled and leaned back, grabbing the condom where

it lay on the bed beside him. As if she wasn't the one on fire in anticipation of what was to come, she took her time to open the packet, fiddling with the foil until he ripped it from her hands.

In less than a second, he had it open, the condom out and rolled over his enormous dick. By the jerky movements of his hands, his control was unraveling. Then he lifted her by her hips and settled her over his erection. "Now. Fuck me."

She nodded, her quivering body past ready for this final act, the one that would fill the lonely space inside. A place that hadn't been touched since the death of her dearly departed husband of ten beautiful years

Flannigan, the loathsome, cranky, bully of a firefighter, would be her first foray into sex in six years. Six long years without a man to fill that empty space inside.

She sank down. Once she was fully seated, she slowed her breaths to allow her channel time to adjust to his length and girth.

This was what she'd missed. And the conversation and laughter. She missed so much about her husband. But she'd promised him on his deathbed that she'd move on. Just because he'd had cancer and died, she didn't have to die with him.

And now, she needed to be reminded of how alive she was.

Luckily, Flannigan was doing a damned good job of reminding her.

DANIEL COULDN'T BELIEVE how good Lola felt on top of him and how good he felt inside her. Her pussy gripped him, holding him firmly within. The woman had tight thighs and everything else. She didn't look or feel twelve years older than him.

And what did it matter she was that much older than him? She was right. Older women knew more about pleasing a man than the younger, more naïve ones. How could Chance have missed this little gem? How had he so easily dismissed Lola's obvious charms? All because a few lousy years?

He pumped up into her, loving how she tightened her kegels, squeezing his dick like nobody's business.

He had to focus on the wall behind her to keep from prematurely ejaculating. God, she had him wound up so tightly, he couldn't think or see straight. All the hot blood raced to his erection, failing to feed his brain so that he could think.

On the very edge of orgasm, he stopped, lifted her up and off him then pushed to his knees.

He flipped Lola onto her stomach, raised her hips and plunged into her from behind.

"Now you're getting the hang of it," Lola said, wriggling her ass for his pleasure.

He thrust in and out, his hands on her hips, slamming her backward against him.

Sensations exploded in and around him. He thrust one last time, then bent over her and captured her breasts in his hands. He remained buried in her until the pulsing lessened and his heart resumed its flow of blood to his brain cells.

He eased Lola down to the mattress and rolled them onto their sides, maintaining their connection, his cock still thick and hard inside her. He liked the way she felt encasing him, her bottom pressed to his groin and the backs of her thighs resting against the front of his. Being with Lola was as close to heaven as Daniel could recall ever being.

But he'd be damned if he let her know. She was cocky, too sure of her bedroom skills and would use that knowledge against him in one way, shape or form, or another.

He had to make it clear that she should not be calling 911 for non-emergencies. And he needed to make it very clear that Chase Grayson was not the right man for her. His friend didn't even know she existed. Or how good she was in bed, or even how sexy her legs were wrapped around a man's waist. "I need to go."

This time Lola didn't try to delay him. She rolled onto her back and touched herself down there, where he'd been licking, nibbling, and fucking her.

Sweet Jesus, he almost fell getting out of the bed. He had to leave immediately, or risk falling back on top of her and doing it all over again.

After scooping up his clothes, he ran from the room, zipping his jeans. All the way through the house, he could hear Lola chuckle.

She had him, and she knew it.

Well, he'd show her. The next time she called for rescue, he'd ignore the call and let Chance handle it. He would do his job and leave. Grayson wouldn't fall for Lola's sexual innuendos or ridiculous shoes. He'd rescue her from whatever bullshit emergency she cooked up and go on about his business.

Daniel bolted for the front door, still pulling on his boots. When he stepped outside, he straightened, smoothing his hair, and tried to act natural.

Mr. Harden sat on his front porch in a rocking chair. When he spied Daniel, he nodded his head in rhythm with the rocking, a smirk on his face.

Daniel glared. What did the old man know anyway?

He marched to his truck, climbed in, carefully, so as not to hurt his still-hard cock and drove home to a cold shower and an even colder bed. He refused to acknowledge the truth.

Lola Engel had taught him a thing or two about what he really wanted in a woman.

THE FOLLOWING WORK day at the fire station, Daniel was on edge. Every time a cell phone rang or the station phone clanged overhead, he jumped.

"What's wrong with you, man?" Chance Grayson asked after Daniel nearly knocked him over when he'd spun to answer his cell phone.

"Nothing." Daniel shoved a hand through his hair and tried to calm himself. The shift was nearly over, and Lola hadn't called in an emergency. He'd made it through the day without having to face the challenge. He let go of a sigh. "I'm fine. I just didn't sleep well last night."

"Oh, yeah? Why? Did you have a big date?"

Daniel's head snapped up, and he stared at Chance with narrowed eyes. "Why do you ask?"

Grayson held up his hands. "Just a guess. You're really punchy, like you need to get laid or something." He flashed him a smile. "Well, I'm calling it a day. I have dinner at the ranch tonight with my brothers. I'll see you tomorrow."

The intercom crackled. "We have a woman who needs assistance with a barbeque fire at the following address. Should only need a fire extinguisher to put it out." Erma in dispatch listed the address.

Chance shook his head. "That's the Engel woman's address, isn't it?"

Daniel's heart tripped several beats and then raced ahead. "No reason for you to miss your dinner with family. I've got this."

Frowning, Chance held up his hand. "No, no. You took it last time. I'll handle it this time."

"No, really. I've got this." Daniel grabbed a fire extinguisher from the storage unit. "I know just what to do."

Chance walked with him out to his truck. "If you're sure..."

"Positive." Fighting back a grin, he slipped into the driver's seat, adjusted his jeans to a more comfortable position over his growing erection and shifted into drive.

He knew just what the woman needed. And he was the man to give it to her.

ROADSIDE ASSISTANCE

N.J. WALTERS

"No. No. No." Esme Jenson stared in her review mirror at the tow truck that had just pulled in behind her. She couldn't be this unlucky.

But even though the evening was closing in and dark clouds threatened rain, there was no mistaking the lean form of Vincent Durango as he stepped down from the driver's side.

Big and hard and tattooed. She was intimately acquainted with her rescuer. Had dated him during high school. Even back then he'd seemed older, more mature than any other boy she'd known. They'd both gone their separate ways after graduation, her to college and him into the army. For the first year, they'd tried to make it work, but their lives had taken different paths.

Now their paths were about to converge once again. He'd gotten out of the service, settled back in their hometown, and opened his own garage specializing in custom body work and restoration. From what she'd heard, he had clients from all over the country.

He'd always been good with his hands.

He strode up to the side of her car and knocked on the window.

She forced herself to roll it down.

He propped one arm on the hood and leaned down. "Hey, Esme."

She was practically hyperventilating and all he had said was, "Hey, Esme." She forced herself to look at him, hoping to see some gray in his hair or some lines around his eyes. Anything to detract from his rugged good looks. No such luck. His hair was still as inky black as ever. The few fine lines fanning out from the corners of his eyes only made him more appealing.

He was still watching her, waiting for her to speak.

She cleared her throat. "Hey, Vincent."

"Heard you were back in town."

The smile he gave her made her want to squirm in her seat. Even wearing jeans that had seen better days and a plain black T-shirt, the man was lethal to her senses.

She wasn't surprised he knew she was back. That's the way it worked in a small town. Her mother had told a few friends, who told a few friends. It had probably taken less than a day for the entire town of Sorrow Creek to know she was home to stay.

He nodded toward the hood of her car. "Trouble?"

"Yes. I was about to call a tow truck." Her misfortune or fortune—she wasn't quite sure which it was yet—was having him pull in behind her seconds after she'd broken down.

"Now you don't have to. Open the hood, and let me have a quick look before we lose the light."

She did as instructed, taking the extra time to get a grip on herself. Just because she'd compared every man she'd ever dated to Vincent—only to have them come up lacking— didn't mean she was ready to get romantically involved with him or anyone else again. For all she knew, he might be married with three children.

Depressed by the thought, she opened her car door and joined him. "How does it look?"

"Nothing obvious. And in another few minutes, it'll be too dark to see. I'll have to tow it back to the garage and have a look."

"You don't have to do that. I'll call Jimbo." Jimbo Devane had run the local service station since she was a kid.

"Why?" He closed the hood and studied her. "I'm here with the truck." He reached out and ran his thumb along the edge of her jaw.

Chills raced down her body, and her shiver wasn't because it was cold. If anything, it was unseasonably warm for May.

She was being silly. She and Vincent had to come face to face sooner or later. Better to get this encounter over with and put it behind her. Especially since she was home to stay. "Okay. Thanks." She turned and headed back to get her purse before she did something stupid, like tackle him to the ground and kiss him senseless.

Vincent hovered next to her open door while she collected her purse.

On the way back to his truck, she was very conscious of him walking beside him. He opened the door and held it for her. She was wearing a dress, which made things a little awkward, but she managed to climb up and get settled inside.

He shut the door and went around to the driver's side.

He didn't take long to get the tow truck maneuvered into place and her car hooked up. She watched him like a woman watches a chocolate cake on the third day of a diet. She wanted to eat him up.

Time hadn't changed him much, except to maybe make him even more attractive.

He filled the cab with his sheer masculine presence when he rejoined her and began the short drive to his garage. "I'm sorry about your dad," he told her.

"Thank you." The loss was the main reason she'd come home. Her father had passed suddenly, leaving her mother to run the small grocery store her family had owned for generations. Her mother hadn't asked her to come back, but Esme was tired of big-city living, of sixty-hour work weeks for a corporation that didn't care. She missed the sense of community Sorrow Creek offered.

She'd only been back for a day, but she already knew she'd made the right decision. Her mother was happy to have her home. And Esme was glad to be there.

"So how have you been?" God, the conversation was stilted. She and Vincent had been able to talk about anything and everything. They'd spent hours sharing their hopes and dreams with one another. And they'd reached them too. Or at least some of them.

"I'm good. I like being my own boss."

He flashed a sexy grin that made her panties damp.

"You never were much good at taking orders." Which was why him joining the army had surprised her so much.

He chuckled. "I learned, but I still don't like it any better than I ever did." He put on his signal light and turned a corner. "Here we are." He pulled into the well-lit parking lot. The building was big with three garage doors and a smaller door which led to an office.

"Durango's" was written in big, bold red letters on a sign atop the building.

"Give me a second to get the garage door open, and I'll move your car inside."

"You can leave it until tomorrow." It was already past eight. "I'm sure your family is waiting at home."

"No family. Just me." He motioned to the far side of the building, the area with the office. "Besides, I live upstairs."

"You live here? At the garage?" Maybe he wasn't doing as well as she'd heard. She ignored her overwhelming sense of relief at discovering no Mrs. Durango waited at home.

"Yeah, I converted the area over the office and storage area into a two-bedroom apartment. Since I was here most of the time anyway, it made sense. Be right back."

The next few minutes were spent getting her car inside one of the garage bays. When the task was done, he parked the truck in the lot outside.

She hopped out before he could come around to her door to help her.

Vincent led the way inside and closed the garage door behind them.

"Let's have a look." But he wasn't looking at her car. He was staring at her.

She was wearing a dress that buttoned up the front, tucked in at her waist and flared out slightly before ending just above her knees. The design was fun and flirty and something she could never have worn to work at her old job, but she'd bought it on sale because she loved how it made her feel.

"You look real good, Esme." His voice was low and rough.

Heat crept up her cheeks, and she knew she was blushing. "Thanks." She felt more like a teenager than a woman staring thirty in the eye. "You look good, too." That was the biggest understatement of the year. He'd filled out in the shoulders and chest since she'd known him. He'd been a teenager then. Now he was all man.

The silence that settled over them was charged. Neither of them could take their gazes off of the other.

"I was giving you a few days to settle in."

"Were you?" She tilted her head to one side. "And then what were you doing?"

Was that really her flirting so blatantly? She'd barely had a date in the past couple of years. Just hadn't been interested and spending all her time and energy on her career. She'd begun to wonder if something was wrong with her. Obviously, she'd just needed the right man to get her engines revving.

He came toward her, his stride fluid and loose. She instinctively took a step back and came up against the cinderblock wall. Vincent kept coming. He placed his hands on either side of her head and leaned down. She got lost in his deep-set green eyes.

"I intended to do this." Then he kissed her.

VINCENT COULDN'T BELIEVE he was kissing Esme. For years, the memory of the taste of her lips, the feel of her lush curves, and the tight clasp of her hot welcoming heat squeezing his cock when they made love had haunted him.

He'd dated and slept with his share of women, but he'd never gotten close to one, not like he had Esme.

She made a small sound in the back of her throat and came up on her toes to get closer. Her purse fell to the floor with a heavy thunk. They both ignored it.

He nibbled on her bottom lip and then ran his tongue across the center seam, slipping inside her sweet mouth when she gasped. God, she tasted good. Like a twelve-year-old scotch. And like the potent liquor, she went straight to his head.

She fisted her hands in the front of his shirt.

He wasn't sure if she was trying to pull him closer or push

him away. When he lifted his head, they were both gasping for breath.

"What are we doing, Vincent?"

He shook his head. "Damned if I know." But he also wasn't about to stop. He cupped her face in his hands and stared into her deep blue eyes. "I missed you, Esme." He'd never had any trouble keeping an emotional distance with other women, but doing that was impossible with Esme. They shared a past. Knew one another in ways no one else ever had.

But that was long ago.

"You don't have a boyfriend, do you?" She definitely didn't have a husband. He'd have heard about that at the local diner for sure.

She shook her head. "No. No boyfriend."

"Good." He captured her mouth and kissed her. He didn't want to talk. He'd waited years to feel this way again. His chest swelled, and his jeans grew uncomfortably tight. But he was in no hurry. Like a kid at Christmas, he'd been patient, and now the time to come to open his present, to get his reward.

She looked fresh as a spring flower in the dress she wore. The garment was soft yellow and had pretty red flowers splashed over it. Her dark brown hair had been longer when they'd dated. Now it was cut into a short style that emphasized her high cheekbones and golden-brown eyes. She looked classy, but then she always had.

He could clean the grease from under his fingernails and pull on a sport coat when the occasion called for it, but he'd never be at home in a suit. His lack of "class" had never bothered him before. He was comfortable with who he was. But Esme always looked put-together, taking care with her appearance. But for all that, she wasn't the least bit vain.

He went to put his hands on her but pulled them away

and stepped back. "I'll get your dress dirty." He worked hard for a living and loved what he did, but there was no denying it was messy.

She reached out and ran her fingertips down the front of his shirt.

His abs tightened, and his jeans felt as though they'd shrunk a size in the last five seconds.

"I don't mind a little grease."

If he was a better man, maybe he'd walk away. But he was a fighter. Always had been. He wasn't afraid of a challenge, and he went after what he wanted. And what he wanted more than anything else in the world was Esme.

He wrapped one arm around her and yanked her closer. "Be very sure, Esme." His voice was rough with need.

She swallowed, her delicate throat rippling. "I'm sure."

He didn't kiss her. He devoured her. Like a man who'd wandered a desert for a decade who'd finally found water. That's what she was to him. Vital. Necessary.

He knew he should at least take her upstairs to his apartment and his king-size bed, but he couldn't wait. His hands were shaking as he undid the four buttons that held the top of her dress together. When they finally parted, he pulled back so he could see what he'd uncovered.

Her bra was as red as the flowers on her dress. The lacy confection was molded to her soft breasts. He ran his finger along the edge. She shivered at his touch. Her nipples were visible so he brushed his thumbs over them.

"Vincent."

He loved the sound of his name on her lips.

He put his hands on her waist and lifted.

She sighed and immediately wrapped her legs around him.

He buried his face between her breasts and inhaled her sweet scent. She might have changed some in looks, become even more beautiful—if such a thing was even possible—but her scent was still the same. The rich smell of vanilla surrounded him. The scent always reminded him of her to the point where he'd get hard walking into a bakery.

He ran his tongue over her lace-covered nipple, drawing a broken cry. His blood rushed through his body, the pulsing sound a roar in his ears. He had to see her.

Vincent pressed her back against the wall. With her legs wrapped around his waist, her mound rubbed against his erection. He was as hard as the cinder block wall behind her.

He shoved his hands inside the opening of her dress and pushed the colorful material down her arms and off. The top of her dress pooled around her waist. Then he reached around, unhooked her bra, and carefully drew it away, leaving her naked from the waist up.

Her breasts were full and firm. He'd dreamed about them for years, but the reality was far better than memory could ever hope to be. He covered them with his hands and took a deep breath, struggling for some kind of control.

She squirmed against him and then began to tug on his T-shirt. "Take it off," she ordered. Esme seemed determined to blow any semblance of control out of the water.

He leaned back, pressing his cock more snuggly against her mound. "Yes, ma'am." He whipped the shirt over his head and tossed it aside.

She made a small purring sound and ran her hands over his shoulders and down his arms.

He rubbed his chest against hers. Her taut nipples poked against his skin, and the soft mounds of her breasts pillowed against his harder muscles.

Vincent ran his hand up her left thigh and under the skirt of her dress. She wasn't wearing stockings, so all he encountered was warm, smooth skin. The tips of her manicured fingernails dug into his biceps.

He didn't stop but kept going until he encountered her panties. The material felt the same as her bra. He'd bet a week's pay they were the same red color. His cock was on the verge of exploding.

He dipped his fingers beneath the elastic at the top of her thigh and found her wet and ready.

ESME WAS afraid she was going to come, and she didn't want to do that. Not yet. Not until Vincent was inside her. God, she loved his hands. They were strong and calloused and just a little rough when he touched her.

He'd always made her feel like she was the sexiest woman in the world. That hadn't changed. The wall was hard and cool against her back, and he was hard and hot against her front. The contrast was delicious.

She didn't care that they were in a garage, the smell of oil and gasoline permeating the air, and bright industrial lights blazing down on them. All she cared about was Vincent.

She sucked in a breath when he pushed his fingers beneath her panties and stroked her. Her sex clenched so hard it was almost painful. "Vincent." She could hardly believe she was here with him. It had been so long.

He pushed one long, thick finger inside. "You're so fucking hot." He nuzzled her neck before kissing a path up to her ear.

She hunched her shoulders, making him laugh.

"Ears still sensitive, Esme?" he teased.

He knew darn well they were. Most women found pleasure having their breasts stroked. While she enjoyed it, her ears were her big hot spot. And Vincent, the devil, knew it.

He caught the lobe between his teeth and tugged. Her inner muscles clamped down on the finger he had inside her. He laughed, and then used the tip of his tongue to tease the sensitive whorls of her ear. She went wild, bucking against him.

He shoved his hand more fully beneath her panties.

She heard a rip but didn't care, because his hand was covering her mound, and his thumb rubbed her clitoris.

Years had passed since she'd felt like this—alive and passionate. She wanted to savor it, but her body had other ideas.

He withdrew his finger almost all the way before pushing it back inside.

She came in an explosion of passion that rocked her to her very core. Shivering, she shook and clung to Vincent.

She didn't realize she was crying until he kissed her cheek and licked away one of her tears.

"Don't cry, baby. Did I hurt you?"

The concern in his voice made her heart ache. She shook her head. "No, it's just been a while."

He smiled then, a smug male smile that she couldn't even get mad about. He'd made her come faster than a rocket on the Fourth of July. He slipped his hand out of her torn panties, and she immediately missed his touch.

He secured one hand beneath her butt and the other around her back. Then he turned with her held snugly in his arms.

She leaned against him, trusting him not to drop her. She thought he'd carry her upstairs, but he only took a few steps and sat her down on the bonnet of a Dodge Charger. She didn't know much about cars, but she recognized this one.

"Yours?" It seemed unlikely, but it looked a lot like the old secondhand one he'd bought when he was a senior in high school, only a much-better version.

"Yeah. Restored it."

She should feel silly sitting on the hood of a car with her dress around her waist and her bra somewhere on the concrete floor, but this was Vincent. She'd never felt shy around him like she always had with other men.

She took her time and enjoyed the view of his bare chest. His pecs were defined, his abs rippled like corrugated steel. He had a dragon tattooed on one bicep and a military tattoo on the other. She ran her hands up his smooth stomach, not stopping until she linked them around his neck. She pulled him down and kissed him.

What they were doing was crazy, but she didn't care. She had to have him. He leaned over her, planting his hands on either side of her. She let her hands trail down his shoulders. His skin was warm and supple, the muscles beneath hard and firm.

She kept on exploring until she reached the button on his jeans. In a heartbeat, she had it open and the zipper down. He sucked in a breath but didn't do anything to stop her. He pulled back from the kiss and lowered his head, dragging in a huge lungful of air.

She shoved his pants and his underwear out of her way. His cock sprang free and into her waiting hand. She closed her fingers around him, loving the hard throbbing heat. He was long and thick, the broad flared head damp from his arousal. Blue veins pulsed up and down the turgid length.

"Fuck, Esme, that feels good."

He cupped her breasts and teased her nipples with his thumbs.

His touch momentarily distracted her. But she'd waited a long time to touch him again and wasn't about to waste the opportunity.

She pushed her free hand into the opening of his pants and cupped the heavy sac between his legs. It was firm and full.

He gave a rough growl and pressed a kiss to her neck just below her ear. "I'll come if you keep that up," he told her.

She shivered, loving his honesty. Vincent was sexual and earthy, and he brought out that side of her. "I don't mind."

He flicked her ear with the tip of his tongue, and her pussy spasmed. "I mind," he whispered. "I want to be buried balls deep when you come. I want you to squeeze my dick so tight I'll beg for mercy."

She was breathing so hard she was almost hyperventilating. She released him, and then lay back on the gleaming black hood of the car, the same one they'd made love in all those years ago. The metal was cool, and she arched her back against the chill. "What are you waiting for?"

He swore and shoved up the skirt of her dress. Her panties were already torn, but he finished them off, ripping them in his haste to have them gone. Her shoes had already fallen off at some point.

Vincent wrapped his hands around her ankles and slid them upward.

She sucked in a breath when he passed her knees and stopped breathing altogether when he reached the top of her thighs.

He slowly pushed them open, all the while keeping his gaze locked on hers.

She gasped and came up on her elbows, watching as he pressed the flared head of his shaft against her opening.

"I'm clean," he told her. "I always wear a condom."

"Me, too." When he raised his brows, she laughed and added, "I've always made sure condoms were used." She didn't want to talk about past lovers, and from the frown on his face, Vincent didn't want to discuss them either.

He surged forward. The fit was a tight squeeze. He was big, and she hadn't had a lover in quite some time. Her inner muscles rippled around him. He was relentless and didn't stop until his balls were resting against her.

Esme was overwhelmed by all the sensations bombarding

her. And not just the physical ones but the emotional ones as well. This was Vincent, the boy she'd once loved, the man she feared she still did.

"Esme." He placed his hands on the car and leaned over her, forcing her to lay flat again. He was buried deep inside her, pulsing and hot, stretching her to accommodate him.

He grasped her hands in one of his and raised them over her head.

She was pinned to the hood of his car by his big body and throbbing cock. Everything inside her seemed to exhale. This was where she was supposed to be.

She intentionally squeezed her inner muscles.

Vincent swore and narrowed his gaze. Then one corner of his mouth kicked up in a lopsided smile. "Think you're tough, do you?"

She licked her lips. "Tough enough to take you," she teased. God, she hadn't had fun during sex in years. Most men were serious and focused. Either that or they were quick and unemotional. Vincent had always teased her, even as he'd driven her to heights of sexual pleasure. Her first lover had been her best.

"We'll see about that." Keeping her hands pinned above her head, he began to move. She wrapped her legs around his waist, driving him even deeper. He kept his movements slow and easy at first, moving so his entire body stroked over hers. His heavy chest rubbed her nipples, turning them into taut nubs. He ground his pelvis against hers, stimulating her clit.

She couldn't touch him, not with her hands manacled in one of his. All she could do was rock her hips slightly. Vincent was in total control.

She found that hot and liberating. All she had to do was lie there and bask in the sensual pleasure.

He began to move faster. When he thrust inward, he hit

the sweet spot inside her channel. She moaned and tightened her legs around him.

Vincent lost it. He began hammering into her, grinding his pelvis against hers, faster and faster until she thought she'd lose her mind. She cried out, begging him to hurry. She'd already come once, but it was nothing compared to the storm building inside her.

She felt his cock swell inside her, the hot rush as he came. He yelled her name and drove deep again and again. Her pussy clutched him hard, heat flashed through her, and passion exploded.

Every cell in her body seemed to be pulled apart, but Vincent anchored her through the sensual storm. He finally collapsed on top of her, but angled his torso slightly to the side so she wasn't crushed. His cock was still inside her. She found it oddly comforting.

He released her arms, and she lowered them, running her hands over his damp shoulders. They were both breathing hard. Her heart hammered against her chest. She was tired but strangely energized too.

Sex with Vincent was even better than she remembered.

Finally, Vincent raised his head, his green eyes serious. He pushed himself upright. She made a small sound of dismay when he slipped out of her body. He pulled up his pants and tucked himself away.

She quickly shoved down her skirt and fumbled for the top of her dress.

Vincent stopped her. "Don't."

Now that the passion was passing, she felt self-conscious. What had she done? She'd had sex with her ex-boyfriend within minutes of seeing him again. Even though she knew it wasn't smart, she couldn't regret it.

She ignored him and pulled the top of her dress back into

place and buttoned it. "I hope we didn't scratch the car." It was a stupid thing to say, but she was suddenly nervous.

"Screw the car."

That shocked her. Vincent had always been particular about the car, even back when it had been a junker, long before he'd restored it. Then her sense of humor surged to the fore. "I think you already screwed me on the car."

He gave a sharp bark of laughter then scooped her into his arms.

"My shoes. My underwear," she protested. Two scraps of red lace lay on the concrete floor, and her shoes were partly under the Charger.

"They're not going anywhere."

"My purse." It was on the floor by the door.

"It's safe," he promised.

She didn't know whether she should laugh or cry at his heavy-handedness. She decided to relax and enjoy the ride. He carried her through the building to a door at the back. He dug a set of keys out of his pocket and unlocked it, revealing a small foyer and a set of stairs. He started up, never once losing his hold on her.

She was curious about his home. Esme wasn't expecting much but was surprised when he unlocked and opened the door. His home was bright and spacious, the living space and kitchen area open and modern. A big-screen television and a dark brown sofa dominated the living room. She caught a glimpse of stone countertops, hardwood floors, and white Shaker cabinets before he took her down a short hallway and into the bedroom.

He sat on the king-size bed with her still locked in his arms. He held her against his chest and buried his face in the curve of her neck. "This isn't a one-time thing," he told her.

She tensed. "It's not?"

He raised his head and shook it. "No. I've spent the last dozen years missing you. I'm not wasting another second."

Her heart soared, and she threw her arms around him. Then she tossed all caution to the wind. "I love you. I don't think I ever stopped.

He gave her his familiar heart-stopping smile. "I never stopped loving you either." He dropped back onto the bed, making her squeal. He turned so they were both on their sides, facing one another. He held his hands in front of her. "They'll always have grease on them."

She took his hands in hers and squeezed. "A little grease keeps the world moving."

He laughed and rolled her onto her back. Then he kissed her.

A sense of rightness, of wellbeing enveloped Esme. She loved and was loved. She'd come home, and this time she planned to stay.

CABIN FEVER

KRIS NORRIS

"And here I thought we'd made it through this unfortunate reunion unscathed."

Juliet Foster froze as Casey's low voice sounded behind her. She palmed the inn's main counter for balance then glanced over her shoulder. Irritation creased his brow as he stood in the doorway, arms loaded with firewood. His deep-green gaze bored right through her before he shifted his attention to the fireplace on the far side of the room.

He angled toward it, his boots barely making a sound on the old wooden floors. "I realize this place is a home of sorts for you, but... Your department's retreat is over. You really should leave before darkness falls. That road's a bitch once the sun sets."

Anger mixed with pain at his disconnected tone—as if they hadn't spent three years of their lives together. In the eighteen months since he'd walked away, she still hadn't gotten close to being over him—the telltale kick of her pulse and the sudden flush of her skin, case in point—even if he'd moved on. Though, nothing had shocked her more than walking through Bradbury Inn's front door and discovering their new caretaker was her ex-fiancé, Casey Monroe.

Juliet firmed her stance, pushing the riot of butterflies in her stomach as far into her boots as possible. "Trust me. The last thing I want is to spend more time…here."

She cringed at the slight crack in her voice, the lie bitter on her tongue. Truth was, she hadn't really felt as if she belonged since she'd left Fulton Springs behind and moved to Seattle, where she'd worked her way onto the homicide squad. She'd always pictured herself as more of a small-town sheriff. Someone who knew everyone and the community. Somewhere that felt like home instead of leaving her feeling like an outsider looking in.

A voice inside her head whispered that her problem wasn't the city, or the position that wouldn't ever feel right—it was losing Casey.

Losing the best piece of her.

She fisted her hand, using the slight bite of her nails against her palm for strength. "I just want to borrow your landline. I can't get any cell service, and I need to call a tow truck."

Casey stopped repositioning the logs and turned to face her.

And damn if he wasn't as stunning as she remembered. Firm, thick muscles bunched beneath the blue cotton, equally large thighs filling out his denim. One strong hand raked through his sandy-brown hair, tousling the messy locks about his forehead. She'd never seen him with anything other than his regulation crew cut, and she couldn't help but wonder how those silky strands would feel wrapped around her fingers as he worked his way between her thighs.

The thought settled like a rock in her gut. She'd spent far too many nights fantasizing about loving Casey one last time —only to wake in a cold sweat, a painful longing gnawing at her core. She wouldn't give him the satisfaction of seeing her desire written across her face.

Lines crinkled around Casey's eyes before he leaned against the mantel. "A tow truck? Please tell me you didn't slide off the road? Damn, Jules, I noticed you didn't have winter tires on your Jeep. Having grown up around here, you should know better than to chance these roads without chains as backup."

That nickname. No one else had ever called her Jules, though she doubted he'd even realized the slip. And had he really noticed her tires but neglected to say a single word during the three days her unit had been engaged in team-building exercises? Had acted as if they'd never met? Sure, she'd avoided him, too, but…knowing the truth still stung.

She steadied her stance, wincing as pain pulsed through her head. "I didn't swerve off the road. Give me some credit. I chase bad guys for a living, remember?"

"My mistake, *Detective*." He pushed off the mantel. "Unfortunately, I doubt you'll get anyone to come up here now. That storm's moving in faster than predicted, which is why I told your lieutenant to leave early. And with the sun setting…roads will be too dangerous to chance."

"Is that your way of saying I'm stuck here? With you?"

"God forbid." He sighed. "Come on. We'll take my truck. I don't have many tools, but maybe I can get your Jeep running well enough to get you down the mountain in one piece."

"A wrench and some duct tape aren't going to fix her."

He continued toward the door as if he hadn't heard her, stopping once he'd reached the threshold. "I'm pretty damn handy with a wrench, and there're a thousand and one uses for duct tape. Bet I can get that junk heap moving."

"Then you'd best bring a chainsaw, because I doubt even your stubborn determination will move the tree."

"Tree?"

She blinked against another throb of pain before meeting his gaze. "The one that fell across the road…and my hood. I took twenty minutes just to wedge open the door. So, if you'll kindly just call for a tow…or a cab…"

His eyes narrowed before he marched across the room, trapping her between his chest and the counter. He leaned in closer, his breath rustling her collar.

A mix of pine and smoke filled her senses, a hint of cologne weaving through the other aromas.

"A tree fell across your car, and you're just telling me this, now?"

"What does it matter? Ditch or tree, I still need a tow—"

"You're lucky you're in one piece. How far?"

"What?"

"How far did you have to walk?"

"About four miles—"

"Dressed like that? In those boots?"

"What's wrong with my clothes?"

Casey scoffed as he swept his gaze the length of her. "Seriously, Jules? You're wearing jeans and some imitation leather boots."

"You're wearing jeans, too, and they're real leather." She pushed against him, grunting when he didn't move. "What the hell has gotten into you?"

He inhaled, grabbing her chin then tilting her head. "Is that blood?"

She twisted out of his hold, wanting some much-needed distance. Her traitorous heart quickened in response, and she swayed against the counter when the room dipped. "A few branches broke through the windshield. It's only a cut."

"Broke through the windshield?" His nostrils flared as he drew in a few hurried breaths, finally looking down again as he reclaimed his hold on her chin, angling her head to the side. "Blood is caked on your skin, bits of glass are in the laceration, and yet, you think it's nothing. Shit, you probably have a concussion."

She tugged against his hand, huffing when he raised his other and palmed her cheek to keep her in place. "I've had concussions before. I'm fine. And having been shot, this barely registers as anything more than an annoyance."

Color rose high on his cheekbones. "You've been shot? When? Why the hell didn't you tell me?"

Shit. Why had she let that slip? "Six months ago, and why would I tell you? You walked out with some bullshit line about needing to find yourself, when all you really needed was to lose me."

Surprise flashed across his expression, followed by hurt. Casey released his hold then took a substantial step back before grasping her hand. "Come on. We need to clean that wound before it gets infected."

"But…" She stumbled after him as he tugged her down the hall, obviously heading somewhere specific. "What about the tow truck? You said it yourself. It's getting late. I need—"

"To not end up with sepsis because you're too damn stubborn to take care of yourself. You think I haven't noticed that you've lost weight? And you rarely slept these past few days. Saw you wandering around every damn night. What happens when all that insomnia catches up, and you're staring down the wrong end of a rifle?" He stopped short, spinning then trapping her against the wall. "Is that what happened? Why you got shot?"

"I—"

"Hold that thought. Your damn head is still bleeding, and just the sight of it…"

He didn't finish as he eased back then continued down the hallway, his hand still holding hers. He pulled her into a large bedroom, stopping beside a winged chair set off to one side. "Sit. I'll be right back."

He lowered her into it before striking off across the room, disappearing through another door.

She blinked, wondering how she'd lost control so quickly, when he reappeared carrying a red bag.

He moved over to her, placing the bag on a small side table.

The metal rasp of the zipper made her jump, her brain still playing catch up. She opened her mouth to question him when his fingers returned to her chin.

The tight press of his lips softened. "Try to relax. This might sting, but if I don't remove the debris, it won't heal properly."

A smile lifted one corner of his mouth at her silent acceptance before he focused on the wound. He dabbed something wet along her skin, and she inhaled at the fiery sensation that spread across her forehead.

"Damn, it's deeper than I thought. You probably should have stitches, but since that's not really possible, I'll bandage it as best I can." He glanced at her. "I'm sorry this hurts."

"Since when do you care if you hurt me?" She groaned inwardly the moment the words sprang free. She'd always prided herself on her ability to remain impartial, and yet, five minutes alone with him, and she'd cracked.

Casey didn't answer.

But she sensed his unrest in the way he shifted his feet as he cleaned the cut. An uncomfortable silence fell between them, and she dreaded each minute that ticked by—together but miles apart.

His rough exhale drew her attention.

"That should do, though you'll probably have quite the bruise by tomorrow."

"Not my first. Won't be my last." She stood, nearly knocking into him when he didn't give her any additional space. "Thanks. Now that you're done—"

"Done? Sorry to disappoint you, sweetheart, but that was just the first step."

"Say what?"

"A tree fell across your damn Jeep. God knows if you're hurt beyond that crater on your forehead."

She arched a brow, cursing when the small movement stung. "I'm—"

"Fine. Right."

"Casey."

The muscle in his jaw tensed as he got impossibly closer.

"Do you know how many soldiers I watched die overseas all because they insisted they were fine? That the pain in their ribs or their stomach was nothing when it was really internal bleeding?"

"My ribs don't hurt."

"You also said you didn't have a concussion, yet I've seen you stumble twice." He placed his hands on her shoulders. "I know I'm the last person you want to show any weakness in front of, but I'll be damned if I let you put yourself at risk in order to save face." He smoothed her jacket off her shoulders. "A quick body sweep then you can ignore me for the rest of the night."

"The rest of the night?"

"Did I stutter?"

"I can't stay another night. I have a job. Cases."

"All of which pales in comparison to dying, which is a possibility if you're harboring additional injuries, or if you chance that road in the dark with a storm brewing. I'll call your lieutenant, but you're not going anywhere tonight."

"Not going…" Juliet palmed his chest, shoving him out of her way before crossing the room. Heat burned beneath her skin as she turned on Casey, hands fisted at her side, chin held high. "Of all the arrogant… Sorry to disappoint *you*, but you lost the right to make decisions for me when you left. Either call me a damn cab, or I'll simply walk—"

Her words cut off as he covered the scant distance between them then pinned her against the wall.

One hand held her hip while the other palmed the spot beside her head. His face filled her view as he lowered to her level.

"You think I don't know how much of a bastard I was to you? But we're talking about your life being at risk—"

"My life was at risk before. You just refused to see it."

His jaw clenched again. "Fair enough. But I'm doing a body sweep, and you're staying the night. Even if I have to tie you to that chair."

Her breath caught as images of her bound and completely at his mercy ran through her head. Though they'd never done much experimenting, she'd be lying if she said the thought hadn't crossed her mind. Not that this was the time or the place, but she couldn't stop her treacherous body from reacting. Prevent her nipples from hardening against her bra or keep the flush from creeping up her neck and into her cheeks. And there was no mistaking the warm, wet feeling growing between her legs.

"Damn, have you got a fever?" He placed the back of his hand on her forehead before she had the good sense to shake him loose.

"I don't have a fever. Just…do the sweep so I can go back to my room."

He merely nodded, reaching for the hem of her shirt.

She trembled as he lifted the worn cotton over her head, leaving her standing there in jeans and a lace bra. Large, calloused fingers skimmed across her flesh, cascading a rash of goosebumps down her limbs.

"Still sensitive, I see." He stopped near her right hip. "What's this?"

She dropped her gaze to a bluish patch of skin. "Probably just a bruise from the seatbelt. It doesn't really hurt."

"That seems to be your default answer. But just to be safe…"

He thumbed open the button on her jeans, lowering the zipper then shoving the denim gently over her hips.

She snagged her bottom lip, trying not to shake under his perusal as he bent to get a closer look.

He smoothed his fingers around the area. "The skin's bruised, but it doesn't seem too serious. Still won't be pleasant. What about your ribs?" He pushed on the skin above the mark. "Does this hurt?"

She swallowed against the rush of need, doing her best to focus on what he'd asked her. But all that registered was the soft glide of Casey's hand along her flesh, and the warm flutter of anticipation in her stomach. She searched for the anger still seething below the surface, but even it faded beneath the sensuous feel of his fingers along her torso and the firm press of his body against hers as he wrapped one arm around her waist, tugging her close.

Juliet dragged her gaze upward, inhaling at the white-hot desire shading his eyes. His free hand found her hair, his fingertips scraping across her scalp before settling on the back of her head. He glanced at her mouth, smiling when her lips parted in invitation.

Casey closed the distance, his breath feathering across her cheek. "I realize there're a thousand reasons why kissing you is a colossal mistake, but damned if I can think of one. So either tell me to fuck off, or…"

She stared, aware she should say something, when his smile flourished and he slanted his lips over hers. Any objections vanished as he tilted back her head and deepened the kiss.

CASEY MONROE WAS A FOOL. A fool for ever letting Juliet get away, and an even bigger fool for thinking he stood a chance at winning her back. He'd tried to reconnect with her several times already but hadn't figured out how to bridge the distance. How to atone. Having her walk through his door... Her appearance had felt like an act of providence. Until he'd panicked and found ways to avoid her. But now here he was, with Jules wrapped in his arms, her lips damp from their kiss, and all because of some freak accident.

Anger roiled beneath his skin. She could have gotten herself killed, yet she seemed completely indifferent to the fact. And how could she act so nonchalant about being shot? Just the thought of it burned his blood until he had to soothe his unrest with the silky glide of her skin. She gave a low, throaty hum as he nipped his way down her neck before easing back, giving her just enough room to catch her breath. Her eyelids fluttered, revealing glimpses of crystal blue irises amidst pale skin. The light blush on her cheeks added a splash of color, the red tinge fading down her neck and onto her chest.

He held her close, drinking in the floral scent of her perfume. Her rough gasps sounded between them, her lust-filled gaze finally settling on his. She lifted one hand and tunneled it through his hair, as if needing to anchor herself.

He trailed his fingers up her side, tracing the soft curve of her breast. Her nipples pebbled against her bra, the firm tips pressing into his chest. Her lips parted on a low moan, and he dipped down, taking her mouth for a second time.

Juliet's grip tightened, the slight sting urging him on. He'd purposely grown out his hair in an effort to leave that facet of his life behind. Help him blend into civilian life. Though, he hadn't anticipated how fucking hot it would be to have Jules wrap her delicate fingers around the strands as he ate at her mouth.

"God, Casey."

He chuckled at the hushed rasp of his name, kissing his way to the edge of her bra. He sucked at the tight bud through the fabric before tugging down the cup—finally drawing the peak into his mouth. Her skin warmed beneath his touch, and he couldn't wait to rub every inch of their flesh together. He'd chase away the chill she'd gotten walking back to the cabin.

Juliet arched against him, her frantic breathing matching the jerky rise and fall of her chest. A tremble shook through her, and he glanced up at her face. Head tilted back, eyes squeezed shut, she looked ready to fly apart.

Casey licked his way to her chin, nipping at her bottom lip until she gazed at him. "Fuck, you're beautiful. You sure you're up for this? You're not too dizzy? You don't hurt too much from that damn tree?"

Lines creased her forehead.

Her confusion showed clear in her expression.

"I can stop—"

"Stop? I swear to God, Casey, if you stop…leave me like this…I won't be the one handcuffed to the damn chair."

"Oh, sweetheart. I love that you think you could wrestle me into submission. I tell you what. You be a good girl and unravel against my tongue, and I'll consider holding still for you…next time."

As her breath hitched, she moistened her lips. "Damn."

"Oh, we haven't quite gotten to damn, yet. But soon."

He lifted her then spun, covering the short space over to the chair. She squealed as he shoved her onto the cushion. While the bed was just as close, he wanted something hotter. And the way she'd reacted when he'd mentioned tying her to the chair seemed more in line with that, even if he didn't restrain her this time.

He moved away enough to yank off her boots and finish

undressing her, leaving her poised on the chair completely nude. His heart raced as he took her in. The smooth expanse of skin, the flex of her muscles. A scar marred her flesh on her left side, the telltale pucker reigniting his anger.

He tsked as he traced the welt. "You're lucky you didn't die."

Something flashed in her eyes, but it faded quickly. "I'm not the only one with scars. Now are you fucking me or just talking?"

"Are you sassing me? Dangerous, sweetheart, especially with your body so eager to come."

Her gaze dropped to where his cock pressed against his fly. "I'm not the only one."

"Fucking right." He dropped to his knees, draping her thighs over his shoulders. "But I can wait. You, on the other hand, are dripping down your thighs."

"Must you be so smug...*yes*."

Her words hissed into a moan as he swiped his tongue along her cleft, her sweet flavor bursting in his mouth. Damn, he'd missed this. Missed her. The way her entire body reacted to his touch. The flex of her fingers against his scalp, or how she murmured his name as if it were a prayer. And he knew he wouldn't have the strength to lose her again.

Casey pushed aside the thoughts. He could figure that out later. Right now, all that mattered was having her drench his tongue. Pulse around his fingers as he sank two inside her pussy, crooking them in order to rub her G-spot.

"Damn, I'm not going to last."

He gently nipped at her clit, smiling when she arched against his face. "Fight it, Jules. I need more time. More you."

She tensed at his words then surrendered, tilting her hips in an effort to take him deeper.

A new rush of moisture slicked her flesh, drowning his

senses with her earthy musk as he lapped at her folds, avoiding her clit just enough to keep her poised on the edge.

Casey urged her closer, and she ground her cleft against his mouth as his other hand smoothed up her ribs and cupped her breast. He pinched the tight bud, moaning at the ragged shout of his name. This is how he wanted her. Raw. Vulnerable. Completely his. Her breathing quickened, her muscles flexing beneath him before she broke, contracting around his fingers as her release flooded his tongue.

He hummed, wishing he could lick her through another orgasm. Instead, he yanked off his shirt and shoved his jeans over his hips, grabbing his wallet before it thunked to the floor. He removed a condom, hoping it hadn't expired, then sheathed himself as he kicked free of his boots and pants. Jules watched him, eyes still lust-glazed, chest heaving. She reached for his cock, but he batted away her hand, scooping her up then switching their positions. She inhaled as he draped her legs over the armrests, leaning forward so she could wrap her fingers around his neck.

"Damn it, Casey. I want a turn."

"As much as I'd love to have your mouth all over me, I won't last. I…"

He couldn't finish. How did he say he needed to feel her surround him—watch her give herself to him again—more than he needed his own release? Her eyes narrowed then rolled back as he snugged his shaft at her pussy.

Her fingers dug into his shoulders as she rocked her hips, taking him all the way inside.

Casey drew her forward until their foreheads touched, keeping them locked together as he helped her ride his cock. "That's it. Take me deep. Fuck yourself on me. I want to feel you come all over me. We can go slower next time."

Shit, those words again. Next time. When had this single encounter turned into needing her back in his life? He groaned inwardly. Simple. Since the moment he'd walked out.

Juliet scratched at his skin, snapping him back. Her harsh breathing raked across his cheek as her body shuddered within his grasp. He claimed her mouth, swallowing the raspy moans escaping her lips as she stiffened within his arms, a series of ripples running along the length of his shaft.

"Fuck, yeah. Now, sweetheart."

He wrapped one arm around her waist, holding her still as he pounded into her from beneath, the slick slide of his cock sounding around them.

Her mouth fell to his shoulder, her teeth sinking into his muscle.

The pressure set him off as his release shot along his spine, gathering in his balls until he thought they'd explode. Juliet shook in his arms then came, flooding his shaft with warm, wet fluid.

Casey surrendered, no longer fighting the crushing pressure in his sac. His cock emptied into the condom as he shuddered through his orgasm. He tightened his hold around Jules as the room faded into the hot press of her skin against his and the gentle caress of her breath on his shoulder. Several minutes passed before he was able to open his eyes and assess the situation.

Juliet's head rested on his shoulder, one hand drawing patterns across his chest. He tried to judge her reaction by the shift of her body, but it was useless. All he could focus on was whether she'd give him a second chance or walk out the door as he'd done to her.

He thumbed her cheek, waiting until she met his gaze. "You okay?"

She shrugged, balancing against the chair when he helped her stand.

The heady scent of sex infused the air, and Casey had to

fight not to toss her on the bed for another round. They needed to talk. Hell, he needed to apologize.

Juliet reached for her clothes.

But he shook his head, handing her his shirt before disposing of the condom and tugging on his jeans. He turned to face her once he was ready, admiring the way his top matched the blue in her eyes. Her chin quivered when their gazes clashed before she drew herself up, the detective back in place.

"Jules—"

"Don't. I knew what I was agreeing to, and…I'll just go to my room."

"What?" He snagged her wrist before she could dart past him. "Did you honestly think I was brushing you off?"

"You made it clear before that I wasn't part of your future."

"I know. And I was wrong." He carded his hand through his hair. "I've spent the past eighteen months lying to myself. Pretending I was learning to adapt, when all I was doing was hiding. From the memories. From you."

She toyed with the hem of the shirt before crossing her arms over her chest. "Why are you up here? I thought you were joining the family business. Helping your dad at his garage."

"I tried, but… Turns out having your mechanic dive for cover every time a car backfires isn't great for business. Thankfully, Russel had an opening at the inn, and… I like it here. Working with my hands. The quiet. And it's not that far driving into town, so…"

"God, Casey, why didn't you tell me you were having flashbacks? Shit, all those nights—you were having nightmares, weren't you? Is that why you pushed me away? Did you think I wouldn't understand?"

He lunged, sandwiching their hands together. "The

reason I left...it wasn't you. I knew you'd stand by me. I just... I couldn't drag you down into that hell. I thought I was doing what was best for the woman I loved, but it turns out...I was being a coward."

Tears gathered in her eyes. "Why tell me all of this now? Is it to make this one-off seem less cheap?"

He chuckled. God, he'd missed her. "You haven't changed a bit. Still all teeth and claws."

"Casey—"

"Ignoring the fact that I owed you far more than just an explanation..." He took a deep breath, knowing he had to put it all on the line or forever live with the regret. "I can make a life. Learn to deal with my past, but without you...it'll be empty at best." He smiled as her eyes rounded and her mouth hinged open. "I'm asking for a second chance. To do things right. I know it'll take time to earn back your trust, but I promise...I won't let you down, again."

Some of the tears slipped down her cheek before she swallowed, cocking her eyebrow. "A second chance, huh?"

"To start fresh. Or pick up from before. I don't care as long as I have you." He reached forward and tucked a few golden strands of hair behind her ear. "I love you, Jules. Never stopped."

She quirked her lips. "Then, I guess it's lucky that I bumped into Sheriff Johnson on my way up here. Seems he's retiring, and he thinks Fulton Springs could use someone like me at the helm."

Hope blossomed in Casey's chest. "Is that right? But what about Seattle? I don't want you to give up your dream for me. I can find a way to cope—"

"You need to do more than cope. You said it yourself." She feathered her fingers against his jaw. "You like it here."

"I love you more." Her smile dropped his stomach.

"I never wanted to leave this place. Not really. Besides, I

might have told the sheriff I'd send him my resume. See if he could pull a few strings. It's time I came home."

"Is that your subtle way of saying yes to giving us another chance?"

"I'm thinking it wasn't so subtle, but yeah. I never stopped loving you, either." She palmed his chest when he tried to scoop her up. "But...if we're to make this work, no more secrets. I don't expect you to forget your time in Afghanistan. To adjust without a few bumps. I just need you to trust me to have your back."

"Deal." He winked. "Which means I have a promise to keep." He moved over to the chair and reached backward, wrapping his arms around the back as he lowered onto the cushion. "I believe I promised I'd hold still. Those handcuffs of yours handy?"

"I don't need handcuffs to bind you, but since you asked... they're in my jacket pocket." She retrieved them, grinning as the cold metal closed around his wrists. "Don't think this means you're completely forgiven. You have a long road of groveling ahead."

"If that includes having you grind yourself on my face again, I'll take my punishment like a man. Now...are you fucking me or just talking?"

SHEAR PASSION

BELINDA LAPAGE

Sam was exuberant. Her first day as a shearer. Her first *real* day. She was ready. All she needed was Band-Aids. Dad's mantra for farming was the Seven P's—prior proper preparation prevents piss-poor performance—and she'd die before she tapped out with a blister.

She pulled up her quad-bike at the Mudgiboora general store beside a shiny orange V8 Hilux with roll bars, spoilers, and about a hundred B&S ball decals on the back window. Bogan farmer obviously, but judging by the Queensland plates, not a local.

The shop's fly screen door banged open, and a dusty set of elastic-sided work boots stepped out.

Oh my.

Bogan farmer? Holy smokes, did I ever get that wrong.

Stained work pants, blue singlet—you *might* mistake him for a bogan farmer. If you were blind. Or stupid. Because it was difficult to miss the chiselled vee of his shoulders, chest, and abs, and the clean, dark blond hair. Sam noticed all these things and several more besides.

Quick, Sammy, think of something witty. "Hi," she said,

tilting her head to one side in an unconscious gesture of interest.

He looked her up and down and offered a dimpled smile. "Nice bike," he said, not looking at her quad-bike at all. "You don't look much like a farmer."

"You don't look much like a bogan." *Oh God, what's wrong with me?*

His face clouded for a moment then he burst out laughing. "Bogan!" he cried, slapping his thigh. He looked from Sam to the hot Hilux. "Yeah, nah, I deserve that. So hey, you live in town?"

"Just out of town." Sam gestured vaguely over her shoulder without breaking eye contact, flattered and hypnotised by the searchlight attention of his gaze. "With my family."

"Shit out of luck. Makes sense, though. Gorgeous sheilas don't stay single in the sticks."

He thinks I'm gorgeous. Wait...crap, he thinks I'm married. "No," she blurted. "I meant, with my parents. Not a...you know...a *family* kind of family." *Oh, really smooth, Sam.*

"Huh." He seemed to consider this as potentially useful but only mildly interesting information, like "petrol is cheapest on a Wednesday". "So, a nice single girl in Mudgiboora..."

He paused, looking for positive feedback, which Sam provided in spades with a beaming smile and almost neurotic blinking.

"Where might a fella find her on a Friday night if he was looking? In the pub?"

Today's Friday. Is he asking me out? Sam planned on soaking in the bathtub after shearing.

"The pub? Sure." Apparently, her mouth had other ideas. "Will you be there?"

"I reckon," he said with a smile. Then he gestured at his clothes. "Do you mind a bloke who smells like sheep?"

"I love the smell of sheep." The smell was of long gone summer afternoons playing beneath the shearing shed, running the gauntlet under the pens, and dodging the inevitable rain of droppings from above. In a flash, she knew exactly who the handsome stranger was. She'd taken over Dad's accounting and was accruing his wages just last night. "You'd better hustle," she said, touching a finger to his chest. "Old man Robinson will spit bullets if you're late."

Patrick looked at his watch. "Shit, you're right." Then he did a double-take. "Wait, what? How did you—?"

But Sam had already turned on her heel and run into the store. She leaned back out the door and called, "See you soon, Patrick."

* * *

Sam approached the shearing shed with butterflies in her stomach.

"Hey, Dad. What's up, Danger." She climbed the ladder to floor level. Dad was there with her baby brother Will, who was roustabout today, collecting fleeces and sweeping the boards. Patrick had his back turned and hadn't seen her yet.

"Pat, meet your new partner."

Sam tried not to beam. She'd only seen him ten minutes ago, and already she was hungry to feast again on those long, smooth biceps.

"Pleased to meet—" Pat broke off when he recognised her. "Hey. It's you."

"Hi, Patrick," she said, losing the battle not to grin like a schoolgirl. "I'm Sam. Robinson." *Surprise, I'm the boss's daughter.* She turned to Dad. "We met at the shop."

Pat frowned. "What are you doing—?"

"Shearing," Dad said. "Same as you."

"But…" Patrick looked dubious. "But she's a sheila."

Sam felt an unexpected spark of anger.

"I think you mean 'shearer'," Dad said, with a note of warning. "I'm not leaving forty ewes in the pens all weekend, so Sam's helping to finish them today."

"Geez, Reg, forty? Can she even shear?"

"I'm standing right here, Pat." How quickly the tides turned. She'd mooned over him just a minute ago, and now she breathed fire. "I sheared my own mob last summer. Fifty lambs."

"Lambs."

She felt a chill of doubt when she realised his point. Ewes were bigger, they had a full year of wool, and not least of all, they were niggly as a cut snake. They took twice as long to shear—and, goddammit, she *knew* that—but when Dad had asked if she could finish forty-odd ewes, like an idiot she'd said yes.

Dad stepped in before she could make a worse fool of herself. "Four an hour, Sam. Give me thirty-two, and Pat can pick up the rest, right, Pat?"

Pat just blinked. "You're the boss, Boss." Then he walked off to the shearing stands, leaving Sam to follow like a…well, a lost sheep.

So, this was it. Not what she'd expected, precisely, but still she was ready. She took off her jacket and hung it on a peg. As she stepped to the catching pen for the first time, she caught Pat admiring the way she filled out her blue work singlet.

"When you've finished sight-seeing," she said. "Maybe we can shear some sheep."

* * *

Sam chose her first ewe and dragged it back to the stand.

"Phew," Pat said. "You got a ripe one first drop."

She looked down at the sheep, and then at the trail of shit and maggots leading back to the pen. *Oh, great. Fly-struck.* She almost visibly deflated. The urge to give up right then was strong, but no way was she fading out before even starting her shears.

She yanked the old and knotted cord, and the handpiece buzzed to life in her fist. *Here goes nothing.* She lifted one hoof up to the ewe's chest and gagged at the beshitted, maggot-ridden, raw flesh underneath. This was not the most disgusting thing she'd ever do as a grazier, but at her age, it was a new personal best.

"Hold still, darlin'," she said, jamming the hoof into the ewe's belly. "Sammy's going to make it all better."

She shaved the shit-caked fuzz all the way down to the flayed, bleeding flesh around the stump of its tail, earning herself a tortured bleat. *Poor thing must be in agony.* The work was slow and disgusting, and Pat had finished three before she finally started on the clean wool.

The ewe was beyond frightened, and every time it kicked, Sam jerked back the handpiece, thinking she'd nicked its skin. The ewe's behavior threw her confidence, and the fleece came off slowly in short, narrow blows that left her stand littered in shavings.

By the time she'd finished and treated the flayed, fly-struck skin with antiseptic, the shearing had taken her forty minutes. But the effort was worth it. Your first fly-struck sheep was like a rite of passage as a shearer, and although she hadn't nailed it, she hadn't failed it either. Pat didn't say anything. She suspected he was secretly impressed she had stuck it out.

She glanced over, not intentionally, but his body naturally drew the eye. He had a nice sheen of sweat on his neck and shoulders, and the smooth curves of his biceps and triceps bulged handsomely from the heavy upper body work.

Mmm, I could use some heavy upper body work.

Maybe he felt her gaze, because he looked up mid-blow and offered her a wink. Sam smiled back, but he was already looking back down at his hands.

Don't be stupid, Sam. He's just eye candy. Pretty to look at, right up to the point he opens his frigging mouth about sheilas in the shearing shed.

* * *

SAM BLINKED BACK THE SWEAT. Her ewe bleated miserably—the last one before smoko. "Yeah, I know," she sighed. "Me, too." Her back ached, and she felt like she was shearing in a pool of molasses. When Pat snapped off his shears, she was still in position two with at least ten minutes' work remaining.

"Go get a cuppa," Pat said as Will cleaned his stand. "Grab Sam's fleece after smoko."

When they were alone, Pat stepped close and switched off her shears.

"Give me the handpiece, Sam."

Intimidated by his muscular good looks, Sam didn't think about it. She couldn't. So she did as he asked, and Pat dropped down beside her and sheared her ewe.

What just happened?

The handpiece, that felt so tentative in her own fist, made long, confident blows, and Sam could see the colour change where he cut so much closer to the pink skin. She could only stand there, empty-handed, bereft and purposeless—a woman with no place in the shearing shed. Not even at her own stand.

"Your comb's a bit dull." Pat darted a glance and

completely missed the boiling volcano of humiliation. "Grab one of mine after smoko." He sat up the ewe, finished the last half-dozen blows down its rump, then sent it scampering down the chute, half pink and half creamy white. "Let's get a cuppa. You look like you could use one."

That was it. The proverbial straw. Sam jabbed a finger into his chest. "Don't you *ever* touch my shears again." She had one more good sentence in her before the tears, and it came out in a low growl. "I don't need you to shear for me, Pat Caldwell."

"Sam, I was only trying to—"

She turned and left him. If she didn't look, maybe she could stop from crying. She had twelve minutes to get her shit back together. Tea would help.

* * *

SAM FELT A PRESENCE BEHIND HER. She took another sip from her steaming mug and kept tightening the screws on the new comb. "What do you want, Pat?" The anger had waned nearly as fast as it flared.

"I'm not sure what I did wrong, but I want to say I'm sorry."

She turned around. Holding the handpiece gave her confidence—at the very least she could brain him with it. "I'm not some princess you can save, Pat. I'll do my own share of the work."

"I was a first-timer, once."

He was standing close, and Sam could smell him. Not the smell of sheep—that was everywhere—but the smell of a man at work, and against her better judgement the tang sent a shiver of lust down her spine.

He touched her hand. "It's hard. There's no shame in asking for help."

"But I didn't ask." She craned her neck to look up into his eyes. "You just took over."

"I get it." He seemed to consider her words carefully. "I should've asked. I'm sorry."

That right there, that was the real apology, and she felt a weight lift. "Thank you." She brandished the handpiece and offered him a grin. "We should get back to it. They won't shear themselves, you know."

Pat smiled, and his eyes darted down to her lips.

Oh Jesus, is he going to kiss me?

"C'mon, you two," Dad grunted, walking past the door. "Crochet circle is over. Let's shear some sheep.

"Coming." Then Pat was gone. And so was the tantalizing moment.

* * *

THE SECOND SESSION went heaps better, and at lunch, Pat left a space on the bale next to him.

Sam took the hint with a secret smile. She selected a handful of sandwiches and accidentally-on-purpose settled back with her arm touching Pat's. His sweat had dried already, but his flesh was hard and rough, prickling with dark blond hairs. Her own skin was soft and velvety, and the contrast made his touch feel even more manly—if that was possible.

Having Dad right there while she explored the edges of a new romance made her feel like a teenager again. She stared at her hands, rubbing absently at the reddened skin on her index finger from gripping the shears.

"Blister?" Pat cradled her fingers to inspect for himself.

"Not yet." She thrilled to the gentle touch of his thick, callused hands. "I brought Band-Aids, though. Prior proper preparation, right, Dad?"

Dad rewarded her with a rare smile. "They didn't teach you that at school, hey?"

"Band-Aids won't work," Pat said. "Need to tape it. There's tape in the first-aid, right, Boss?"

"Believe there is." Dad's eyes darted between them on their shared wool bale.

He knows exactly what's going on. "Pat, will you show me?" Sam asked sweetly.

Pat seemed to consider the offer for a moment, perhaps weighing the wisdom of sneaking off with the boss's daughter. "Yeah," he said finally. "I reckon I might."

The first-aid kit was a rusty metal box behind the shearing stands that had probably been white in the 1970s. It might have even had a red cross on the front. Pat found the Elastoplast tape and brandished a little pair of scissors that looked funny in his big hand.

Sam held up her finger, making it clear she expected him to treat her. That made him smile again, and Sam decided she quite liked watching him smile. When he was done, she turned her finger left and right to inspect his work. "Mum used to kiss it better when she finished."

He didn't lunge, he simply cupped Sam's nape in his palm and kissed her. Between that hand and his lips, she was trapped—trapped in the sweetest, heart-thuddingest way imaginable. The kiss laid bare a whole new vista of unsuspected desire—the desire to be with a powerful, attractive man who knew exactly what he wanted. And then took it.

"I meant my finger," she whispered.

"No, you didn't."

"No," she admitted. "I didn't." She kissed back. She wasn't sure whether she'd done so the first time. Getting her breath was hard. *Meh, breathing's overrated.* She stole another. "You taste nice," she said, unsure now where to take the conversation.

"Sheepy?"

Sam laughed. "Shearers are just crass." She relaxed her body against his, her soft curves brushing delightfully against his hard muscles. "If I'd known you were so awful, I never would have come."

"Yes, you would have."

"Yes," she said. Her lips closed in again. "I would."

* * *

SAM'S RESILIENCE faded after lunch, but looking up now and again at the clockwork perfection of Pat's long, muscular body made the effort worthwhile. How did he do it? Every part of her ached.

C'mon, darlin', you're the last one. Be nice for Sammy, huh?

Position one, belly and crutch. Position two, chest, neck, and foreleg. *Nearly half way.* Rolling down into position three, her back gave an agonised cramp that unhinged her knees. She used the sheep for balance, holding the dangerous shears up off the skin.

And then the animal kicked.

With Sam's weight balanced so precariously, the ewe bucked like a wrestler pinned in the first round, and the shears slipped and tore a long rent in its belly.

"Oh, you niggly old bitch!" Sexist profanity just seemed to come naturally in the shearing shed. "Serves you right!"

"Um, Sam," said Will. "You're getting blood on the wool."

"Oh crap! What have I done?"

The ewe bleated miserably.

Blood ran everywhere, staining the wool stubble around the wound, running down the ewe's teats. Sam pressed her hand over the wound, and blood seeped through her fingers. "Dad!"

"Dad's gone to town," Will said. "He left me in charge of the branding."

Did he leave you in charge of dying sheep, too?

As the panic rose, time fractured and broke all her perceptions into fragments, leaving her looking impotently at her red-soaked hand, and Will staring with wide-eyed dismay.

The tears that threatened earlier finally came and transformed the shed into a streaky blur. She heard Pat's shears go silent. "Pat, help!"

"Fuck a duck, Sam. You want some mint sauce with that? Stitch her up before she bleeds out."

"I don't know how!" she shrieked. "Help me, or she's going to fucking die!"

"I am, see?"

Somehow he was already there, needle and thread ready. *How did he do that?*

"They don't teach first-aid at uni, huh?"

"Not with the blood," she whispered. "They don't do it with the blood."

Pat sewed up the wound, and with each stitch he pulled tight, the bleeding slowed, and the weight lifted from Sam's chest.

"There. Now she's got a nice scar and a story to tell." He peeled off his singlet and used it to wipe up the blood. "Finish her off, and let's get out of here."

Shearing? Maybe—if she could take her eyes off Pat's naked torso. Was he beautiful before? Now, he was magnificent. Eight hours of work had left his pants stiff with lanolin and his hard body drenched with sweat.

"See something funny?"

Sam realised she was smiling. "Just contemplating the new dress code."

"Dress code, huh?" he said. "So when exactly does that kick in for the other shearers?" His gaze darted to Will.

"Hey, Danger," she said. "Why don't you get onto the branding? I'll look after things in here."

Will smiled at the sexual innuendo as only a fifteen-year-old boy can. "You better." He propped his broom against the wall and took the short cut through the chute, then they were alone. Except for the sheep.

"C'mon, slacker." Pat helped Sam to her feet, and holding her from behind in a light embrace, he slipped his callused fingers beneath her singlet and over her stomach.

She felt sure he would cup her breasts—she ached for it—but he skipped around them and lifted the singlet over her head. "Pick up your handpiece, shearer."

Sam shivered. Standing with her small body spooned into his, she'd never felt so vulnerable, so sexy—*so alive*. She reached for her shears, and the movement pressed the cleft of her backside into his groin.

If I was wearing heels, he could fuck me while I sheared.

Pat stroked down her forearm and clasped his hand loosely over hers. "Let's shear."

And guiding her blows, together they finished the final ewe.

"It's like a dance. She wants to know you're in charge, so let her feel it."

With his big left hand cupping her bare midriff just below her breasts, Sam knew exactly how she felt. The self-assured, independent woman inside could reassert later, but for now, she was completely and utterly his. When she snapped off the shears and sent her most beautifully close-shorn ewe down the chute, her body was hot with desire and thrumming with desperate want.

She turned and laced her fingers behind his neck, trembling at the erotic skin-on-skin contact. Pat kissed her and took one breast in his hand, letting her know he was there. Letting her know he was in charge. In the subtlest movement, she offered her body, and he lifted her off the floor.

"The classing room," she whispered, breaking their kiss only for the moment needed to announce where he would have her for the first time.

Pat walked—the same laconic, unhurried movement she'd witnessed when she'd first seen him that morning. Yes, he wanted her, but rushing would make the moment no sweeter. Still kissing, he sat her on the edge of the classing table and unsnapped her bra in just three fumbling attempts, which Sam found charming.

His hands found her bare breasts. They didn't just hold this time, they stroked and teased and discovered all of the things that made Sam squirm with lust, and then used them to drive her into a lather of womanly want.

Exhibiting her own inexpert seductive talents, she fumbled his pants undone, leaving only a pair of trunks between her and the object of her desire. She could feel his shape underneath, thick with excitement and heaving with every touch. She dipped inside and closed around his impressive girth with an urgency that made them both gasp. The ensuing fight against her own pants was frenzied but mercifully brief, leaving her gloriously naked, spread and vulnerable with her glistening sex open and pink before his rearing shaft.

"I don't have a—"

"I'm safe." Sam may have been in a drought, but she was still on the pill. Prior proper preparation, and all that shit.

"You mean you want me to pull out?"

"No." She drew him into a kiss. "I don't." Sam touched his cockhead to her soft inner lips.

Pat pushed slowly forwards.

She felt her entrance stretching, yielding, but then at the

last moment, he angled so that it slipped free, skating the full length over her clitoris. Sam groaned in what felt like a very unwomanly fashion. Her clit sang with pleasure, but her aching pussy clenched, expecting to close wetly around his thick manhood and coming up empty instead. Her nostrils flared. "Pat Caldwell, screw me right now."

Pat repositioned, and then after a short moment for them both to mentally snapshot the erotic perfection of their almost-coupling, he slid firmly into her burning core. In a single slow thrust, the thick, dangerous slab of man-meat squeezed past her entrance into the silky cauldron of her vagina.

Sam gasped. There was some pain, but only for a moment; she was so wet, so ready. Deliciously filled by that first stroke, she wrongly imagined that she had it all, and her twitching pussy muscles adjusting to his girth made it feel farther in, perhaps, than it really was. The second, deeper thrust knocked the breath from her, and when on the third, Pat drove it all the way home, Sam exploded in a shower of ecstatic sparks. "Oh fuck, I'm coming already." The words came as a squeak through her pursed lips. "Hold me."

"It's all right," Pat closed his arms around her trembling body and whispered his reassurance. "I've got you."

Sam clung to his hips, forcing him deeper and riding that over-stuffed wave of climactic passion. Whimpering with each peak, she pumped her hips spasmodically, grinding her soft pussy lips against his root. The orgasmic waves of plea-sure crested and finally ebbed, and her hips slowed to gentle circles, stirring, swirling his length inside her. "Holy smokes." She squeezed with her core muscles. "That's never happened so quickly. Was I awful?"

"You were incredible." He stroked her hair back from one temple and kissed her there. "Do you want to keep going?"

"Hell, yes."

Pat cradled her in his arms and kissed the curve of her neck. While moving his cock with Sam's heels locked behind his back was hard, he lifted her body, fucking her slowly up and down on his rampant shaft like an oversized sex toy.

Wanting more, Sam loosened her hold, and Pat sat her back onto the table, using the new freedom to pump her in long, luxurious strokes.

"Oh. God. Yes." Each word was a euphoric cry, driven physically from her chest by the heavy shaft pounding from below. Sam's tortured labia bulged out around his root. It felt like not just his cock, but his balls as well, were squeezing through her opening. Thighs quivering, breasts lolling against his chest, she had never been so thoroughly reamed. She wanted to give some back, to drive herself down onto Pat's rampant dick, but she had all she could do to simply cling on and take what she was given.

With Pat's words of encouragement in her ear—"That's it, lift your legs. God yes!"—Sam felt another climax building. Arching like a gymnast, she just needed a little... just a...

"Please," she husked, pressing her lips into his ear. "I want to feel you come."

Pat ploughed his big, swollen cock all the way home, lifting her backside off the table. Faster and harder, he pistoned upwards into Sam's yearning cunt, making her cry out in one long, plaintive syllable. And then he was there. Jerking abruptly, he buried his dick inside her and ground against her clitoris. With the cords in his neck taut and his lips peeled back from his teeth, he uttered a final, stuttering, *"F-f-f-fuck."*

Sam worked for her reward, circling her hips and tightening her sex, anticipating the moment from his rising gasps. His balls were snugged up close, and she felt them nestle even tighter in her cleft, preparing to deliver their creamy load. His cockhead swelled prodigiously, and then exquisite heat bloomed inside—white, liquid fire erupted in powerful sprays, straight to her most intimate core.

The sensation was beyond anything in Sam's safe-sex experience. So hot, so vital—to be connected with such elemental perfection. Their bond was complete. The work, the emotional conflict, the exhaustion, they all fell away and showed her the truth hidden underneath. The truth was she was falling in love, and with that realisation, Sam herself finally melted into an ecstatic, searing orgasm.

* * *

NIGHT FOLLOWED DAY, as it is wont to do. A nighttime of talking and dreaming and sweet lovemaking in Pat's caravan. Their first night. Maybe their last.

Following his Hilux back to the caravan park, those Queensland numberplates burned an image on Sam's retinas. Spring shearing was done, and no more shearing meant no more shearers. Pat would be off to follow the work, and she wouldn't see him again until after Christmas, assuming Dad hired him back for the lambs.

She woke with her naked body folded into Pat's.

"What do you want to do today?" he asked.

She craned her neck to kiss him without breaking body contact. "You mean you don't want to just stay in bed?" Sam could think of worse ways to spend the day.

"Let's go out," he said. "I've only seen you shear and make love—you're really good at one of those, by the way—"

Sam smiled.

"—but I want to see you…"

"See me, what?"

Pat craned to see her face, perhaps to check if she was making fun of him. "I want to see you in the sunshine," he said. "If I don't see you ag—" He swallowed audibly. "—for a while, then I want to remember you with sunshine in your hair, not with sleep in your eyes and morning breath."

"That's not morning on my breath." Sam pinched him on the thigh, down near where her face had been earlier.

"Touché."

One more day. "Let's go back to the farm. I'll show you around. And I can pick up my toothbrush."

Pat laughed. "Oh, so you're staying another night?"

"Try to stop me."

* * *

THAT INTERLUDE WAS two months ago. They talked most evenings, and sent photos, but Sam preferred the ones they took that day. In those, they were together.

She was outside putting up Christmas lights around the veranda when she heard the V8 turn onto the long farmhouse driveway. "Mum, Dad. It's Pat!" She dropped the fairy lights and bolted for the front yard, almost getting herself run over as Pat aimed for the shade of the cypress grove. She tore open the driver's door and pulled him out by the lapels. "Come here," she ordered, dragging him close for a kiss. "You're supposed to be in Griffith."

"Finished a day early," Pat said. "The cocky got this flash lady shearer in yesterday to show us how it's done."

Sam kissed him again with the ferocity of a slap in the face. "You're a terrible liar, Pat Caldwell."

"You're one of a kind, Sam Robinson."

She hugged him around the waist. "Sun's over the yard arm. Fancy a beer?"

"Yeah, grab two. And one for yourself if you're thirsty." He plopped into an old sofa on the porch.

Sam floated inside into the kitchen on a cushion of air.

"Pat's here, is he?" Mum said. She was hiding a big smile.

"Are you making fun of me, Mum?"

"Never in a million years, love. I'm happy for you."

Sam went back outside and sat next to Pat. They held hands and took the first mouthful of beer in silence, looking out on the winding driveway where the dust was still settling from Pat's arrival.

He looked down at her hand, their fingers intertwined. "Can't stay long," he said. "Got to head back to Toowoomba to see some solicitors."

"The law finally caught up with you, huh?"

Pat didn't rise to the joke. "Nah. I'm selling the house. I need the money for a business I'm looking at."

He seemed serious, sober, and his grip on Sam's hand was tight. This was it, then. Goodbye? Falling in love with a shearer was bad enough, but at least the work took him all the way up and down the country, sometimes to Mudgi-boora, and sometimes just close enough for a visit. Sam felt sick. "So, what's this new business?"

"Shearing supplies. My numbers guy reckons it's a goer. Reckons I could convert it to a drop-ship and triple my margins."

"That's nice." Sam couldn't swallow. Her mouth had gone dry, and the beer tasted bitter and stale.

"Yeah. It's right near the Pioneer Settlement. The guy who owns it now does shearing demos in there for the tourists at lunchtimes. He reckons he could get me the same gig."

Pioneer Settlement? Sam had been to Toowoomba a couple of times. "Do you mean the Cobb and Co. Museum?"

"No. You know, the Pioneer Settlement," Pat said, as though everybody knew it. "Swan Hill."

Swan Hill.

She turned her head slowly to look at him, not quite ready to believe her ears. Pat was buying a business … *just an hour away.*

"Swan Hill is close," she said, her eyes filming. "Close enough for a day trip."

"Geez, I hope so." Pat was obviously enjoying having surprised her. "'Specially if I have to do it every day...living in Mudgiboora, that is."

Sam didn't know what to say. Her lips were shaking, so maybe whatever she wanted to say wouldn't have come out properly anyway.

Pat was scratching her between the knuckles with a sharp fingernail, drawing her attention to their clasped hands. Except it wasn't a fingernail, it was a ring. And it wasn't just sharp, it was a diamond point.

Where did he pull that from? "Pat, what is this?"

"Did he ask you yet?"

Dad was looking out through the fly-screen door.

"Go away, Dad."

"What did she say? Has he asked her?" Now Mum was crowding behind him, looking over his shoulder.

"Fella can undress a hundred and sixty ewes in a day. Reckon he'd be done with this one a bit sooner."

Sam rolled her eyes. "Will you two please, *for the love of God*, go back inside."

Pat squeezed her hands. "Sam?" he said, drawing her attention back where it belonged.

"Pat?"

"You haven't known me long, but I'm not the kind of bloke who mucks about when making a decision."

"Uh-huh."

"That doesn't mean I make bad ones. I work out what I want, then I go do it, instead of just *thinking* about doing it."

"Yes."

"When I first saw you outside the shop, I decided I'd talk to you. That was just 'cause you were pretty, but..."

"Yes, Pat?"

"Then when you showed up at the shed, I thought you were...geez, I don't know, like some kid playing farmer—"

"I see."

"But when you crutched that fly-struck ewe without chundering, and you ripped me a new one for shearing your sheep, I reckon I knew everything I needed to."

Did you really? Sam hadn't warmed up to him until after that—after he'd apologized.

"I fell in love with you in the shearing shed, Sam. I only needed to work next to you for a morning to know I wanted you beside me for the rest of my life."

Excitement made her belly quiver. "Yes."

"I want to move to Mudgiboora. I want to work in Swan Hill, and you can stay here on the farm. Working, that is. Not living in this house. I want you to live with me. Will you marry me, Sam?"

"Fuck's sake, Pat. Girl said 'Yes' half a dozen times already."

"Dad!"

Dad came outside with Mum holding a short, galvanised rod with a small horseshoe attached to the end. It had a red bow tied around the middle, and it was obviously a gift, whatever it was.

"Sam?" Pat was trying to get her attention back, and the sparkly ring he was holding didn't hurt his cause one bit. "Will you?"

Sam kissed him loudly on the lips. "You bet I will." She offered her left hand, fingers waggling, eager beyond description to see what the ring looked like on her finger.

Pat slipped it on.

Mum came for a closer look, taking brief ownership of Sam's hand while she tried to get it in the sweet spot of her vision. "Ooh, it's lovely, Pat."

"How did you two know about this? And why am I the last to find out?"

"Pat asked for our blessing," Dad said. "I told him he didn't need it, but if it made any difference then he ought to know we were both thrilled."

Sam took her gaze off the ring long enough to look at Pat. "You're a sneak." *What a sweetie. Who would have thought he was so old fashioned?* Pat was maybe getting some dust in his eye, so Sam shifted back to Dad to give him a moment to wipe it clear. "What is that thing, Dad?"

Dad held up the little horseshoe stick. "This? It's your new paint brand, you goose. You'll need to re-brand your own mob of ewes next spring, assuming you can find a decent shearer, of course."

Sam tilted her head to the side. *Ohhh.* It was a letter C, for branding sheep.

Mrs. Samantha Robinson-C-for-Caldwell.

Pfft, yeah, right.

Sam Caldwell.

"Thanks, Dad." Sam took the gift. She couldn't remember ever being this happy. She was literally giddy. She pretended to brand Pat's chest. "You're mine."

They kissed again, and when Sam came up for air, Mum and Dad had gone back inside. She stood and pulled Pat to his feet as well, handing him the paint brand. "Let's take this up to the shearing shed. You get the car started."

"Where are you going?"

"Changing into a dress," she said, giving him a wink. "You took the whole day to get my pants off last time. I'm not making that mistake again."

Sam ran inside. She couldn't take her gaze off that ring, and she knew she'd still be looking at it when Pat sent her to heaven again—and again—on the classing table.

Roll on the summer shearing season. Roll on.

THE TRAFFIC STOP

KALISSA WAYNE

Sarah flew down the empty road, heedless of the speed limit. Darkness encroached on the country road, but the headlights on her Jeep were on bright, dispelling the shadows, at least to the edges of the road. The full moon cast a soft glow over the vast pastures and fields as she flew by. Stars twinkled and mocked her bad mood.

Freakin' City Council meetings, she thought as she shifted gears. She hated attending, because they were nothing but small-town ego maniacs griping about petty differences and what should be done to draw more money to the county. Nothing ever got done, because no one would agree with anyone else. Why she ever agreed to take the position of arbiter she'd never know. She sighed, letting the wind whip over her from the open top. She just wanted to get home, take a nice long soak in the hot tub and go to bed.

She knew she'd jinxed herself when, in her rear-view mirror, red lights flashed, and she heard a siren strobe a couple times. Sarah debated whether to pull over or just keep going, but the siren turned on and stayed on. Taking a deep breath, she pulled off onto the side of the empty county road, put her Jeep in Park and cut the engine.

She closed her eyes and mentally counted to ten, then twenty, as the siren suddenly went quiet. Listening to the silence of the night and the radio traffic coming from the Sheriff's SUV behind her, she decided to just keep counting.

She heard the *snick* of a door opening then closing, followed by the soft tread of boots on the blacktop, loud even above the night sounds that were returning to normal. *At least he turned off the siren.* When the footsteps stopped, she cracked open her left eye and looked sideways.

A massive chest covered in a black bulletproof vest filled her vision, the uniform's short sleeves straining to contain equally massive biceps. Opening both eyes, and turning her head, she followed the impressive chest as it continued down into snug, form-fitting uniform pants interrupted only by a utility belt around his waist. Between all the gadget pockets, a radio and a Glock 45, the belt added some inches to his waistline, but it still looked narrower than his massive chest.

"Registration and ID please, ma'am."

The deep baritone sent shivers down her spine. "Seriously? This is how you're going to play this? You…"

"Ma'am. I need to see your registration and ID. I clocked you doing 75 in a 50 miles per hour speed zone. Even though I know who you are, I must do my duty." The big officer leaned over, looking into the Jeep.

For the first time, Sarah wished she'd left her doors on the Jeep instead of taking them off for the summer.

The man was drop-dead handsome. Short, black curly hair peeked out from under his Stetson. Eyes so dark they looked black gazed from under the black hat brim. Under his eyes, a straight nose led down to a wide mouth. She tried not to stare, but his lips, even firmed up, as they were now, looked soft and kissable.

"Ms. Smith, if you don't produce your identification and registration immediately, I'll be forced to arrest you not only for excessive speed, but also for operating a vehicle without a license and possible possession of stolen property."

Sarah's jaw dropped, and she just stared into the dark eyes of the sheriff.

"Sheriff Carson, with all due respect, you can kiss my ass. You've known me for how many years? And you know I own this vehicle! *Eeeep!*"

Even before she finished the bleated word, the sheriff reached in and unlatched her seatbelt. As she tried to fight off his hands, he pulled her from the seat and turned her to face the Jeep.

"Put your hands on the roll bar now." Even as he made the statement, his big hands shackled her wrists and moved her hands toward the bar.

As she started cussing him, she gripped the bar. "You are an asshole! You know damn well..." Sarah started to turn her head.

"Face forward!" he barked. When she faced back into the Jeep, he ran his hands down her arms to begin patting her down. "If you say one more word, I'll have to read you your rights and charge you with verbal abuse of a peace officer."

Sarah silently fumed as he continued running his hands down over her shoulders, then along her sides. She tried to ignore the fact that he was feeling his way around her body, and tried to ignore that her girly parts were starting to tingle.

His chest bumped against her back and hips as he leaned down to check her legs.

She was glad she had extra padding in that area, because his vest was not the least bit soft.

Her breath hitched when his hands encircled her ankles and forced her legs to spread open. Her skirt, ending just below her knees, allowed for a little movement. As the sheriff ran his hands up the insides of her legs, he forced the skirt higher.

A cool evening breeze drifted up her bare legs and teased the edges of the skirt.

The sheriff stood before his hands hit higher than mid-thigh. He ran his hands up her back.

A shiver worked up her spine when she realized his spread hands stretched from one side to the other. His thumbs ran up her spine as his pinkies rubbed the outside of her rib cage, and she wasn't a small woman. His hands were huge, and it made her girly parts do more than tingle.

His hands skimmed across her shoulders and checked the collar of her shirt before running down her shoulder blades and under her arms.

She twitched a little as his fingers ran over her arm pits. Geez, she hated that she was ticklish. All thoughts of laughing died as he palmed her breasts and gently squeezed. Her brain froze as her breath halted in her chest.

"Carson..." Sarah tried to object, but his name came out as a breathless whisper. She actually whimpered when his fingers tightened around her nipples, pulling on them even through her shirt and bra.

"I have to tell you your rights now. You have the right to remain silent." His hands squeezed a little harder, pressing upward on her breasts. One hand loosened and began unfastening her button-down shirt.

"What are you..."

"Hands on the bar!" he snapped, pressing his chest against her back.

He had to be looking down her cleavage from over her shoulder, even with her five-feet-eight frame and three-inch heels,

"You will stand still unless otherwise instructed, for your

safety as well as mine. If you fail to comply, I will handcuff you while I continue this search."

She stilled and gripped the roll bar tighter. Both of his hands now dipped inside her bra and, running under her breasts, felt for something. Probably weapons, which was ridiculous.

Her shirt had been pulled out of the front waistband of her skirt and was completely open by now.

He gently pulled her breasts from her bra cups. His fingers were calloused and slightly rough as they glided over her breasts, causing her breath to catch as the fingertips brushed against her nipples before moving on. He started to lower his hands along her ribs.

"What the hell…." Sarah reached down to cover back up when his fingers wrapped around her wrists like steel. Once she was still, he slipped both of her wrists to one hand.

"I told you to stand still, ma'am. Now I'm going to have to cuff you."

When she heard the *snick* of his handcuffs opening, she struggled in earnest. She reared back against his chest and attempted to stomp on his foot. "You can't do this! I've got—" Once again Sarah tried to argue, but the damn sheriff just pushed his weight against her back, forcing her to bend over the seat of her Jeep.

"Ma'am, I've asked you repeatedly to hold still and remain quiet. I'm placing these handcuffs on you for your own protection. Please cooperate."

She felt the cool metal of the handcuffs around one wrist before she heard it *snick* closed.

He wrapped one arm around her, brought her upright, and then grabbed her wrists. Slipping her left arm through the steering wheel, he handcuffed her other wrist.

When Sarah looked down, she saw that she was hand-cuffed through the steering wheel with her hands on the seat.

"Really? You think I'm such a danger that you need to do this?" She gave an experimental tug on the cuffs, already knowing it was futile. She also refused to admit her panties were now soaked through. No matter her thoughts on how the sheriff was handling this stop, he was a hot eyeful of male. Another shiver worked its way down her spine, and her nipples tightened even more as she thought of the bulge she'd felt against her butt when he'd forced her down onto the seat.

"You are being an uncooperative suspect. I have the right to protect myself and others. Now, where was I?" Carson hummed before continuing. Running his hands over her head, he investigated the bun she had tucked her hair into for the meeting. Pulling off the elastic band and throwing it in the floor mat, he released her bun, and her long brown hair fell around her shoulders creating a curtain around her face.

"You have the right to remain silent. I suggest you take that advice. You never know who might be around." He was running his fingers through her hair and massaging her scalp.

She closed her eyes in bliss; she always hated putting up her hair. The weight of it always caused her mild headaches.

She groaned involuntarily as the sheriff pushed his hips tight against her butt. A thick ridge rubbed against the crease of her ass, letting her know just what she would have to do to get out of this traffic stop.

"Does that mean you give up the right to remain silent? Because I must warn you that anything you say can and will be used against you in a court of law."

Sarah bit her lip and pushed back against the rigid pole that strained his uniform pants.

Sheriff Carson once again ran his hands down her back and, taking a half step back, continued down over her buttocks. Very slowly his hands each grabbed a cheek and

more, resting her forehead on the seat. Sarah felt her muscles clamp down on his fingers as a mini-orgasm shot through her system. Before she could come down from that little high, another sharp smack sounded, and pain shot through her butt again. This time, the pain morphed into a shot of lust and went straight to her clit.

She realized his fingers were gone, and he was rubbing them over the place he'd just smacked. "You will learn to listen, or you will be doing community service for a long, long time. Ms. Smith, I'm still not quite sure if you have something hidden or not, so I'll have to use other means to determine my safety." His hand released her hair, and his weight temporarily left her hips.

Before she could look over her shoulder, his weight was back. His hands tightened on her hips and pulled up, forcing her to stand on tiptoe, even in her heels. His uniform pants still scratched her thighs and hips, but his hot naked flesh probed at her pussy. His cock felt too big to fit, but he continued to probe and push for entry. One hand left her hip and guided the head of his cock into her opening. Even with just the head inside her, she could tell he would stretch her to the limit—he was that big.

When his hand returned to her hip, his fingers tightened down even harder, and he pulled her hips backwards as his hips snapped forward.

With a ragged groan, Sarah dropped her head onto the seat of the Jeep and tried to catch her breath. He was only in her part of the way, and she didn't know if she could take any more.

"Carson…" she started to say something, whether to beg him to stop or keep going she didn't know.

Carson pulled his hips back a little then snapped them forward while jerking her back again. This time, he didn't stop until his hips were snug against her buttocks.

Sarah let out a small ragged moan even as the sheriff groaned deep in his chest.

"You are so tight, Ms. Smith. I don't see how you could hide anything here, but I need to make sure."

With those words, he set up a pounding rhythm that caused her to see stars behind her eyelids with every stroke in.

The uniform pants were a scratchy rub against her thighs and buttocks while the leather of his belt scraped against the top of her butt cheeks when he swiveled his hips. In, out, in, swivel. In, out, in, out, in, out, swivel. He varied his pace and his rhythm but always kept the strokes forceful and his fingers clenching on her hips. She'd have bruises there later, but his forceful grip felt so good. She heard him moan softly as he edged just a bit deeper on one stroke.

Her chest was heaving as she tried to rock backwards toward the sheriff. Her breath stopped completely when he slapped her right hip.

"You need to stay still, ma'am."

He kicked her feet farther apart, reached down and pulled up her right leg until her foot was on the step-bar. This opened her farther for him, and he started powering in and out, dragging his hard cock through her folds.

Her muscles quivered, trying to hold him inside as an orgasm built higher and higher. The sensation was like a spring tightening down, ready to snap at a moment's notice. She knew when that tension released, she'd probably pass out.

His cock was hard and bottomed out on each stroke. The head bumped against her cervix on every stroke, a tingle of pain adding to the pleasure he gave her. He uttered a small grunt as he surged in, sweat drops falling onto her arm from his exertion.

"So tight. Need to…" He grunted again as he leaned over

her back, pressing her chest into the seat leather. One arm curved under hers, and his hand gripped her shoulder while he wound the fingers of his other hand into her hair.

His strokes became shorter and, impossibly, more forceful as he strove to bring her to orgasm. She felt the seat giving under their combined weight as he pulled back on her hair.

"You've been a bad, bad girl, Ms. Smith. A very bad girl."

Her nerves tightened as her nipples rubbed back and forth on the leather seat. They had gotten hard and distended from hanging in the night air without his attention. Now his every move made them scratch against the leather, teasing them and making her groan.

He pulled her hair just a tad harder, forcing up her head. "You need to come for me, Ms. Smith. You need to come now."

As he said *now*, his other hand reached around, and his thumb and finger clamped down on her clit, releasing the spring inside.

Sarah screamed, the orgasm releasing tension she didn't even know she had. Her pussy clamped down on Carson's cock as he pushed himself as deep as he could. She felt his cock twitch as he groaned into her ear. His Stetson fell into the floor board.

Sarah felt as if she were floating down from the starlit sky as she became aware of reality again. The sheriff was slumped over her back and from the sounds she heard, his breathing was as ragged as hers. His chest pumped like billows against her back, and his hot breath stirred the cotton of her shirt.

As she caught her breath, the sheriff took one big deep gulp and stood, still buried inside her.

He placed a palm in the center of her back and told her to stay put.

She didn't know where she would go, between being handcuffed to the steering wheel and having just had the mother of all orgasms. She tried to drum up her anger from earlier, about how he was handling the traffic stop, but she just couldn't find it. She snorted in her mind. He had fucked her mad away.

Carson groaned as he gently pulled out.

Sarah shivered as another tremble wracked her body. He had felt so good, had filled her up, and now she felt empty. She felt a tug and realized the sheriff was tearing off her underwear.

But then he gently cleaned her pussy, placing a kiss on her left buttock and asked in a low, gentle tone, "Did I hurt you?"

"No, Sir," she whispered.

The sheriff gently bit her butt cheek before pulling down her skirt.

She heard a rustle of fabric, and then felt his hands take hold of her wrists.

The handcuffs snapped open, and he drew them away prior to rubbing her wrists.

Then he pulled her into an upright position still facing the Jeep. "We will consider this your community service, and you did an excellent job. You will not speak to anyone of this matter. Otherwise, next time, I will be much harsher on you. Do you understand, Ms. Smith?"

Even as he spoke gruffly, he gently placed her breasts back into her bra, buttoning the buttons back up and setting her clothes correctly.

"No, Sir. I mean, yes, Sir. I do understand." Sarah climbed into the Jeep on wobbly legs, glad to have somewhere to sit after that mind-blowing orgasm.

The sheriff reached in and buckled her seat belt for her. "Are you okay to drive the rest of the way home, ma'am?"

"Yes, Sir."

"Good, then drive safely and stay under the speed limit. Good night, ma'am." He grinned as he tucked her panties behind his bulletproof vest then stepped back.

Sarah cranked the Jeep. As she put it in gear, she flipped the sheriff the bird and spun gravel as she pulled back onto the black top. While the sex had been awesome, she didn't like the fact she had been standing on the side of the road exposed to God only knew who while the sheriff got his jollies.

The lights and siren came on behind her, but she just floored the Jeep, shifting gears.

Five miles down the road, she pulled into a driveway and parked. As she turned off the ignition, she noticed the sheriff's hat in the opposite floor board and wondered how it had kept from flying out. She leaned over, picked it up and placed it on her head.

At that moment, the Sheriff's SUV pulled in just behind her vehicle.

She grabbed her purse and stepped out of the Jeep.

The Sheriff turned off the lights and sirens before he climbed out. "Ms. Smith. I see you didn't learn your lesson. Now, you can deal with the District Attorney. By the way, I see you took my hat. I'll add stealing to your list of crimes."

Damn his black eyes and deep voice. Her girly parts were tingling again as he swaggered toward her. "Sheriff Carson, I still maintain my innocence. I think I should take my chances with the DA."

Sheriff Able Carson's eyes twinkled even as his lips turned down in a frown. "Ma'am, you cannot verbally abuse an officer of the law. I'll have to take you to the DA's home office and see what can be done about that." As he spoke, he reached up and keyed his radio's mike. "Unit 1 to Base. Unit 1 is 10-7 for lunch. Will advise when 10-8."

"Roger that, Sheriff."

Just as Sarah put her hands on her hips to complain, the front door of the house behind her opened, and District Attorney Cain Carson stepped out on the porch. "Hey, Able. What's going on?"

"DA Carson, Ms. Smith was caught speeding, resisting law enforcement, verbal assault on an officer, attempted assault on an officer, theft of personal property, and refusal to perform community service."

At that, Sarah gasped and started to say something.

"Ma'am, I've warned you before. You have the right to remain silent. Keep whatever you have to say for the DA." The sheriff gripped her arm and hustled her towards the man on the porch. "She had this contraband on her person." The sheriff held out her torn panties to the DA.

Sarah looked up at the exact replica of the sheriff, only he had on dress slacks and a white dress shirt.

His arms were crossed over the same broad chest, and he was looking at her with a gleam in his eyes. "Ms. Smith, did you do what Sheriff Carson said?"

"He made it all up, DA Carson. I'm innocent." Sarah actually felt her girly parts dripping again.

"Well then, I believe I'll need to question you prior to seeing if you will perform some clerical work for your community service. My legal briefs are in a bind and need straightening out."

Sarah Smith-Carson walked into her house, following Cain and being followed by Able. A woman could only be lucky enough to have two husbands who understood her the way hers did...

SPECIAL DELIVERY

SUSAN SAXX

*a*lex Jordan groaned.

She'd delivered the wrong part. The wrong fucking part. So much for building up her business, Intimate Deliveries, by single-handedly capturing the biggest account in the downtown core.

Damn. She needed this account.

Nothing else on earth would have led her to abandon safety and traverse the length of the never-ending, dark industrial unit late at night, with a man she didn't know, in a commercial shop closed up against the late December snow.

On New Year's Eve, no less.

And now she and this dude, Rand Peters, were at the very back, in an enclosed room holding a bunch of lathes. He'd had to try to fit the part she'd brought to the machine they'd ordered it for and found it was the wrong part. Hell.

Now, here they were, waiting for the replacement. Alone. Together.

No one else around.

She adjusted her stance for the umpteenth time as Duane yammered on in the cell phone at her ear, the trendy low

153

boot that was part of her self-imposed uniform pinching. The day had been a long one, and she was so ready to get out of the uniform, party with her bffs, and forget the last year had ever happened.

Instead, she was here with a stranger.

This isn't me. This isn't my life.

She was used to being taken care of, used to being driven in chauffeur-driven limousines. She'd never had to go into any situation she didn't deem one hundred percent safe, unless, hell, she wanted to. A few raves, some upscale night clubs—those had been her *choice*. But things had changed.

Oh boy, had they changed.

The stark reality was, if she could deliver that fucking part, the account was hers. She could eat again. Maybe not escargot and the fancy shit that used to be her fare in the past, but food. And feed her mother, too—the woman who still didn't want to believe what had happened had really happened.

Rand Peters wasn't hard to look at, that was for sure. Over the last year, she'd caught him eyeing her every time she'd popped in. Rand was built. She'd tried to discount his fluid, yet powerful, movements as he hefted parts, that blue uniform masking all the interesting bits underneath.

And the glances he'd tossed her way. Fervent. Those deep, intense blue eyes focused on her, the sensuality and barely concealed intentions…um…barely concealed.

He stood there now, leaning against a workbench littered with tools and metal. "You may be on your cell for a while," he said softy, while he scrutinized her with his gaze. "Your lifeline."

Fiery tingles of lust radiated through her at his voice, especially in that low, intense tone. Even though no one else was there, a dozen people could have been in the room and she would've known his words were meant only for her.

Hell.

The sexual chemistry, or whatever it was, pinged between them. Taunting her with *no, you can't.*

Madness.

And what the hell did he know about her business life? As long as metal met metal *he* was fine. Sure, he was right—her whole life was in her cell—and yeah, she was never separated from it. Ever. A person had to have goals and had to work hard to reach them.

But apparently, he hadn't heard her unspoken diatribe, because he came toward her, a wad of clean rags in his fist. She caught his scent, that of the cold when they'd opened the door, mingled with grease and hard-working male.

Her toes curled.

Seductive. Carnal. He placed the rags on a dirty office chair, pulled it over and positioned it close to her ass, deliberately not looking, though he was close. He patted the seat with that big hand and gave her a pointed look. "Rest."

So, he'd noticed.

He straightened, impaled her again with that *I know who you are* gaze. And her pussy tightened.

The dude would be a bad, bad career move. He was one world. She was clawing her way back to another.

And then there was Luc. Luc—whom, with a few more nudges, might be her official boyfriend. His type, the uber-rich, were so careful regarding status. "Girlfriend" was only a checkmark away from fiancé then spouse.

That he'd rather be with his stuffy parents on New Year's Eve in the Hamptons than with her burned.

Other things, hard to overlook of late, had happened, like the wham-bam-thank-you-ma'am way he'd fucked her the last few months.

And Rand was watching her again. Noting every flicker of sensation on her face, it seemed.

Too much time had passed since anyone had looked at her with such desire.

A dangerous combination. A man who sure wanted a helping and who had wanted it for a solid year.

She checked her text messages, while Duane droned on. Halley, Kelley, Tish… Nothing from Luc. Fuck. Her boyfriend, for all intents and purposes. *Nothing* from him.

Mercifully, Duane was done explaining.

She clicked off the cell with a flourish then caught Rand's blue eyes as he watched her lay it on the table, and something in her halted.

Yes? No?

She gave it a spin.

"You're putting it down?" The incredulity hung in the semi-darkness.

So, he'd noticed that too.

Well, no time like the present to make a change.

Turning to him and raising her eyebrows, she nodded. "I may be slow, but…" She slid her gaze over him, and her tummy burned. The erect stance, the prominent muscles, solid. Relaxed yet taut. At the ready. Everything about this dude was ready. And willing. "When I make a decision, I'm *all* over it."

His jaw tightened, and his breath hitched. His fingers coiled around the rag he held, the knuckles going pale.

She strode to the bank of light switches on the side wall, aware that he followed her with his gaze. Maybe it was too late now to back down. She didn't want to be a cock-tease, but she did pick who she did the nasty with.

And up until now, that guy had been Luc. Only Luc.

Should she do this?

At the wall, she reached up to flick off the first light at the far left of the off-white panel, dirty with greasy fingerprints. She felt a curious thrill when the main overhead light switched off and a yellow emergency light immediately kicked in. She flicked off the next one, deliberately. Another light dimmed. The next one. Somewhere out in back another area went to black.

The tiny machine shop, the little room at the back of the industrial unit, was now bathed in a half-glow amber.

Seductive. Dark. She'd made her decision.

She strode back in the eerie light and stood before him, one eyebrow raised. She was aware she was mocking him—or was that issuing a challenge? "So, Peters. You were saying?" Propping one hand on her hip, she tipped up her chin, waiting for a reaction.

No response, just that dark stare.

Disappointment lodged in her chest. So. Another guy—all talk, no action?

What*ever. Whatever possessed me to—*

"How much do you like this blouse?"

Her gaze skimmed his face, and *oh yes.* Something discordant danced behind those brown eyes. "Why don't you find out?"

Hooking his index finger in the open neckline, he pulled sharply.

She was revealed.

In one swift movement, he bent to her chest, pushed aside her favorite fuchsia lace bra with his grimy fingers, and suddenly, seamlessly, his mouth was on her breast.

Her heart pounded in her throat as the man inhaled her nipple, making it the center of his universe. *Fuck.*

He pulled on it, drew it into his mouth.

She stumbled back a step, her ass connecting with the edge of the roughhewn worktable. Her fingertips curled over the edge, grasping at it as he laved her. His stubble stabbed at her sensitive flesh, and she became aware of his tongue... tasting her. Tasting *her,* as if he never wanted to forget her.

Sucking her to extreme sensitivity. She moaned, the tugs of his mouth a symphony jolting burning sensations to her core.

He moaned, and his head bobbed as he worked in the confines of the small space, pleasuring her.

And whatever the man was doing, he gave his focused attention. She was vaguely aware of his calloused hand moving to circle her, and her bra was unhooked then slid away. She groaned as his index finger and thumb positioned her breast for his pleasure.

And hers. *Oh my God.*

Holy hell, the man could pleasure women for a living. What the hell was he doing working here?

His hand snaked to her ass and connected with the work-table edge pushing into her. A grunt, and he stopped abruptly.

Blinking, confusion swirled through her.

"Sorry. Where were we?" He fixed an intent look on her.

She was struck with the deep cobalt of his eyes as he planted his hands on her waist. The consuming hunger in them overwhelmed her, and her legs trembled.

She clutched at his back, feeling the almost silky flow of his shirt. Perspiration beaded her brow. He was starting to push down her pants and panties. She could barely wait until...

Her cell phone trilled.

"I have to... I need to..." She felt the heaviness of his hands as they curved intimately on her shoulder.

He pivoted her toward the device. "Take your time. I'll do you wherever and however long you want, don't worry. I've got nowhere else to be, other than in your sweet pussy."

His deep voice rasped along her skin. A strange, tentative warmth stole over her.

"Everywhere. Every bloody inch of this plant will have your come on it."

Focus. Focus. You can do this. She reached across the work-table, aware of his hand resting possessively on her ass, while she stretched her arm and bent deep to get the phone, her erect nipple skimming the rough surface, raking it ever so gently.

Flicking open the silver phone, she forced her voice to remaine even. "Did you find it, Duane?"

Eager to report on his progress, Duane launched into another story. But she listened for the key piece of info then did what was suddenly very necessary. "Whatever you say. Take care of it. Gotta go." And she flicked shut the phone like a silver clam.

Nervous energy raced through her. She palmed the phone then sent it skittering away, rattling over the wood surface until it was far out of reach, amidst rusty cans and paper-work...buried.

Her old life. Flying away.

"Ok. Let's go," came Rand's husky voice

She shut her eyes tight for a second and nodded. She wanted to savor this moment.

For so long, Luc had been her only lover. Not just in her bed, but in her view-screen. If he'd been a Viking, his name would have been Luc the Unattainable. "I'm—"

Rand didn't give her a chance to finish. He whirled her to him and took her mouth with a savage groan.

The action knocked the breath out of her lungs. The man kissed her like she was his own private harlot, claiming her lips and driving open her mouth.

The euphoria of being taken so abruptly spun out of control. She hadn't expected this, the sensation of being singularly devoured like this, and it made her spirit soar.

Luc never kisses me like this. The disloyal thought ratcheted through her. And the next second, all thoughts of Luc evaporated as her heart sped and the scalding demand of her body shot through her.

Heat poured from him as he molded his fingers down her muscles, teasing the sinews. His other hand hooked around the small of her back as he pulled her ass greedily against his hardened cock.

A shudder raced through her, and she ground her core toward him.

He groaned as his bulge fit against her, molding to her. He filled the space between her legs, eliminating room for anything to come between them.

He was stiff. Glorious. Good and hard. Hard and good. *Yes.* She wanted intimate knowledge of him. The delicious length and breadth of him spreading her into submission and into the deepest pleasure.

And then he jerked her away from the worktable at dizzying speed, and she found herself against the wall. Slammed abruptly against it.

The thud forced out her breath. His cheek was flush against hers, and his scent was everywhere, erotic and demanding. His lips caressed her ear, his hot breath sensitizing the small hairs, sending shivers through her body to her pussy.

"Here. Right here. I've seen you, just like this, in my dreams, Alex."

The first time he'd said her name.

Then his thumbs were at her temples, his hands cupping her face, drawing her to him, as the fierce whisper erupted from him, "Naked. Open—to me. Your fucking sexy got-to-have-it-in-my-hands ass *in my hands,* or I'll fucking burst. Hitching you up. Getting you in position. For me. For my cock." His hands rose to her shoulders, and then they were all over her blouse.

Yeah, it *had* been white. Not so much now. Creeping under the collar against her skin, he drew it off her shoulders. She felt it fall down her back onto the greasy floor at her feet.

Rough hands palmed her breasts as she gasped, molding the firm globes for his pleasure. "Oh, baby."

"As good as Miss August over there?" She could barely talk, but she had to say something. Root herself into reality.

He groaned. "Better than a fucking thousand of them."

Elation flew through her. *Now.* She wanted him. Her fingers groped the front of his uniform to slide open the buttons, revealing his chest as he tackled the waist of her cargo pants, fumbling to release them from her quaking body.

She caught a glimpse of herself reflected in the glass panel of the wall opposite them. Head thrust back, neck arched and exposed. Propped against a wall. Eyes half shuttered, rounded, naked breasts. A lathe operator's hands shoving down her pants.

She was just a piece of hot ass for this guy she'd just met. A Christmas bonus. That was the start and end of it.

But…he was just a hot piece of ass for her too, and the knowledge made her smile. He was willing. He wanted to. And hell. He'd lit something inside her, and she was damn well going to enjoy him.

If he did everything as well as he kissed…

By god, what he could do with those hands. That mouth. And she damn well intended to enjoy every second.

She moaned as he crouched low, skimming his tongue across the top of her lacey panties. Her fingers splayed against the cold concrete wall. "Rand. God."

He laughed, his hot breath fanning her pussy. "Oh, baby, we're just getting started." He inserted his thumbs under the edges of the fabric framing her crotch.

Damn. If he would just rip them from her body, she'd be good. All naked and glistening for Rand Peters to pillage. She tried to give him better access, but the pants around her work-boots got in the way. She tried to wiggle to get them off, to no avail. "Get rid of my pants, okay?"

He tugged them lower and started to pull them off, but her work-boots and the thick rubber soles stalled any efforts.

Irritation flared through her. "Get them off me!"

She felt his hot breath on her thighs, pleasure just out of reach and driving her out of her mind. Her fingertips clawed into the gritty concrete. And her half-shed pants were still hindering her movement.

But instead of helping her, he moved in close, with an exhalation akin to laughter.

Oh, he'd heard her. But something else was on his mind.

"Don't like being obstructed, pretty girl? Bound?"

Suddenly, he rose while she was still struggling, and his mouth framed hers. His tongue assaulted her, and it knocked the breath out of her. He was forceful. Determined.

She fought him after the first few unexpected seconds, her mouth open to him, her tongue warring with his. Jousting.

The lip battle went on for minutes. Lost in a world of their own making, time stretched and became elastic, eternal. All she knew was his rough breathing, his mouth on hers, their breath and essence entwined in the emptiness of the machine shop. Hearts beating hard, like drums being slapped and forced to make noise.

And her spirit ascended, even as he held out her arms, pressed her naked chest to his broad one, and took her in that magnificent knockout of a kiss.

When they slid toward a timeout together, she remembered where she was. Murphy's Manufacturing. Way in the back. Among the silhouettes of hulking machinery in the semi-dark.

And with who. How could she forget when he finally broke the kiss, allowing them both to come up for air. He pressed his lips to her ear and laughed hoarsely, still holding her arms stretched. "Alex. That was fucking fantastic."

Shivers flew up and down her. Fuck, yeah. It'd been fantastic. "It was. Rand…"

His words vibrated against her ear. "No, Alex. You've got it wrong. I'm not Rand. I'm your Master."

Her core gushed again. She probably had a flood down there by now. Pouring all over the concrete, until he fucked her.

And that was what she wanted now.

She'd never played that way, but this was no longer play, but necessity. For her. "Master," she breathed. Anything to give her relief.

He laughed throatily, and she felt his heart pounding against her chest as he squashed her breasts mercilessly. "I like this new person I'm dealing with, Alex."

Good god. Conversation. When all she wanted was to be fucked with that big dick he still hadn't uncovered.

"Ah, don't be mad, sweetness, there's so much more fun to be had. So many more boundaries to be pushed." He trailed his lips from her temple, slick with sweat, down to her cheek. "You like pushing boundaries, don't you? Seeing how far you can go?" He thrust his tongue inside her lips, forcing them open. Then followed up with quick little jabs, wet and firm.

Demanding. And he didn't need to know it was fucking turning her on. Which actually, pissed her off. *She* ran the show. Or had, most of her life.

Irritation swelled within her. He thought he was in charge, holding her like this. A perfect hold she couldn't break out of, and he knew it. She snarled. "Pushy, aren't you?"

"I'm being me. Not that you know who that is yet. But you're learning quickly."

As he gave her nipple another swipe of his tongue, she watched the top of his blond head bobbing at her chest.

"But we haven't picked a safe word yet." His teeth held her nipple oh so softly, and then he bit.

An arc of brutal pleasure shocked her.

He moved her wet breast aside momentarily. "Suggestions?" Then he was back at her nipple.

His tongue rasped against the sore flesh. His lips latched and pulled hard. Just hard enough. A maddening flame licked through her pussy, and she thrust against him, wetness pooling inside her and need. "God. Fuck me already, you bastard."

He raised his gaze from her breast to look up at her, the moisture shining on his lips. His mouth quirked in a smile. "Uh...not sure you're understanding the concept of safe words, honey."

She scowled. She knew she was giving him her nasty look. She'd never been good with unfulfilled expectations. Which was why she worked so all-out at whatever she did. She wanted what she wanted. Was that so wrong?

He gave her a wet, sloppy kiss on her pouting lips. "You are *so* delicious. But I digress."

The look in his eyes softened for a second. As if his heart was out on his sleeve. For her? He had the most maddening way of switching from sex-crazed to heartfelt. The shift was really quite a whirlwind. Which Rand Peters was he?

This was what she'd wanted with Luc. *This*. This unalterable need for her. For her only.

Hell. If *this* guy was genuine, he could really do some bat-shit crazy stuff to her heart.

"But until we decide a safe word, we're not moving from here."

"Fine. Elephant crap." She had the satisfaction of seeing that cocksure expression on his face jolt.

"Excuse me?"

"You wanted a safe word. You've got it. I doubt either one of us will scream that in the throes of passion. And if we do, it's a bigger problem than either of us can solve." She shuttered her eyes briefly. "Now, for the love of god, *can we get on with it?*"

"Ok, Alex. Use it if you want me to stop. Otherwise, babe, the rollercoaster's now officially at the top." His eyes darkened to a stormy blue. "Get ready for the drop."

Finally.

"But first, I have a surprise for you." Pulling her arms above her head, he reached high, and she saw in the reflection a wide elastic strap, which he pulled down. "Used this a while back for some exercise shit I was into. Never dreamed it would come in so handy." For a moment, he searched her eyes, all movement at a standstill. With a lowered voice, he murmured. "Elephant crap, right? If anything…you know." His eyes went liquid for a second. "Anything at all, Alex."

She swallowed, aware of his brawny strength, his chest against hers. Everything would stall if she so decreed. A big sigh sailed out from deep within her. Then she put on her cheekiest expression. "So. How do you propose to….surprise me?"

His look transitioned.

And she shivered. If she hadn't seen it with her own eyes, she would have sworn he'd worn this expression the whole time. Dangerous. Unrelenting. Hedonistic with a capital H.

Clamping the strap around her wrists, he pushed on it to restrain her. "God, I love Velcro." Leaning back with his groin still fastened to her, he spoke. "Tug on it. See how much give it has."

She pulled sharply. The elastic was firm, permitting only a bit of movement, and excitement quickened her breath. No way was she going anywhere unless Rand, er... *Master* unclasped her. "There's no give." She narrowed her eyes and pouted.

"Good. We're ready." He brushed yet another wet kiss on her lips, and she thrust forward to avail herself of another, but he shifted out of reach. "Sorry. I call the shots now."

"Bastard."

He laughed. "Not the only time you'll say that." Lowering himself to her belly button, he was back at her creamed panties. Hitching a finger in them, he swept them down onto her crumpled cargo pants.

He took a moment, investigating her. His carnal scrutiny tortured her, as did the delighted rumble ensuing from his chest. Her nipples hardened to diamonds.

Then he flicked his tongue into her pussy ravenously, in the general direction of her clit.

She screamed, jerking at the restraints, but they held.

As she thrashed, he placed his hands on either side of her cunt then used his thumbs to spread her farther apart. "Tsk-tsk, Miss Jordan. What a sight. You're wetter than a flood down here. Didn't anyone ever teach you manners?"

She was desperate to splay her legs and allow him entry.

"Oh, baby, you're impatient, yes? All in good time. Master's going to enjoy himself now and teach you a thing or two while he's at it. You need to learn." He reached up to tease at the underside of her breast, while he started to tongue her pussy greedily.

The man was feasting on her like she was a five-course gourmet dinner. She shuttered her eyes, realizing this moment had been a long time coming, this dream—rough, hot, groping sex...two people who *couldn't wait* to do each other.

How had Rand Peters gotten her into this position in a short twenty minutes? A guy she'd barely even known existed?

She'd do anything to get his cock inside her.

Anything.

And then he was sucking her. Doing things with that skillful mouth that should be illegal.

She bucked her hips, thrashed. Ground her pussy into his face. No matter. He was relentless.

Fuck. She levered her hips, angling herself into just the right position, anything to have his mouth give her needed release. And just when she couldn't stand it any longer—

He left her to the hit of cool air and straightened, breathing raspily. "I wanted to paint a bit of grease on those pretty breasts, but later. You're ready. It's time."

She watched, eyes wide, as he shoved down his pants, along with his black briefs, his cock springing free and jutting toward her.

He didn't even look at her. His gaze was glued to his cock as he fisted it at its base, and then directed its thick length at her wet pussy.

The velvet tip was so soft, she wouldn't have known it was there except for the unyielding iron behind it, but oh boy, that was unmistakable. A solid rod of hard, sexual muscle at her entrance.

The ache in her pussy and the desire to spread herself open to him was atrocious. Making her crazy.

Then he nudged forward.

Alex gasped. Sweat cascaded down her as he grunted then thrust. Shallowly. An inch of him was in her cunt. A solid inch. God, it felt so amazing. *More,* she wanted to scream, but knew it wouldn't hurry him.

Then another inch came inside. She gritted her teeth and flicked a glance into the mirror. Rand's taut ass cheeks strained as he bore slowly but steadily into her, impaling her mercilessly on his hard dick. She thought she'd died and gone to heaven. Tears ran down her cheeks.

"Almost there."

Typical male to report on the progress of his dick. But oh, she cared. The sensation was absolutely to die for. The sensation beat all other sensations.

And this time she wasn't dreaming, but getting crammed slowly, inch by inch, full of dick.

New reality. Finally. His hard rod entering her vagina. Cold concrete at her back. He bounced her naked ass against it, ground her into it, as he tormented her sexually.

Rand's face was now against her cheek, and they were both wet, slipping and sliding against each other, heat mingling with their sweat.

She arched her pussy forward, eager to close around him. Her erect nipples squashed against the steel of his toned chest.

"A fucking dream," he murmured, his voice reaching her through the delirious haze.

Alex slipped her face from his, and his head slid forward, his forehead leaning against the wall. She shot a quick glance at him, but his eyes were shuttered and his face lax.

He groaned. "I'm going to fuck the *hell* out of you now."

She flexed her core forward and closed tightly around him. She couldn't think anymore.

And then he started. Rhythmically pulling out while she arched forward, desperate to keep him lodged tight in her. Deep.

Then he rammed back in, pinning her and flattening her cheeks against the cold wall.

God. He was doing it. Fucking her. *Yes.* Masterfully.

"Like that. Just like that." He groaned, his words applauding her. "You're a natural."

An arc of joy spun in her.

"Fuck. Alex. *Fuck*." His movements, his unhinged slams, now reverberated with feral passion. His hands gripped her sweaty face, fumbling. "*Alex*."

The unfulfilled fire mounted in her as she gave herself over to the sensation of being…

And it hit her chest like a ten-ton anvil.

Worshipped. Fucking *worshipped*. This encounter was no longer just fucking. It was…

When he finally slammed into her with an agonizing cry, she thought her insides would dissolve. She flew high, to reaches she'd never been before. When she felt the breathless moment before his release, the earth stopped its spinning through space, and all creation waited with bated breath.

And he came. Hard. His power reverberated through her.

Just for her.

He pumped his seed into her, and she held still and took it. Craved it. His essence, raw and bare.

For her, damn it.

When he collapsed onto her shoulder, she knew something big had happened.

A melding of souls.

Forget they'd been fantasizing about each other…about this…for a year. Him openly—had she been waiting, too, the whole year? Just to see what would happen…*if?*

Well, 'if' was no longer 'if'. Hell no. The fucking was a fait accompli, a done deal.

So done. She'd been done to the hilt. Rapturously.

She glanced at the grimy clock on the grease-smeared wall as it ticked closer to midnight. To the start of a New Year.

As she felt him shudder oxygen into his lungs, she wondered what lay ahead.

His words barely made it to her, they were so soft. More like a groan. "We're not done. Take two coming up. Got that? Elephant crap me now, babe, or the ride's starting again."

She grinned and shook her head. Sometimes a girl knew when to keep her lips clamped tight. *Until they were pressed into service again...*

Rand lifted his head, searched her face, then rewarded her with a slow, sexy smile. An intimate grin, showing her he was very pleased.

Something deep inside her leapt.

He reached high above her, undid the restraints, and pushed her slowly onto her knees to meet his cock.

THE BOSS

JENNIFER KACEY

With his oil-covered hands clamped onto the open front chassis of his cherry red GT350 Mustang, Falco hung his head and finally took a deep breath.

Talk about one long-ass Saturday.

He tried to take off Saturdays and leave it to his guys to run his two oil change facilities.

Tried, quite a few times—fell a bit short.

This Saturday had begun at the crack of dawn when two of his managers called in with the flu. More likely a real bad case of hangoveritis. So instead of sleeping in and working on his car at home, he'd had to come into work and cover their shifts.

All day.

Which had turned into a more than ten-hour day.

Reaching in, he adjusted a valve on the new 5.2L 526 horsepower V8 engine block. Anticipation of feeling that much power beneath him on the way home made his dick hard.

One more tweak, and he was ready to head out.

All the rest of the guys had clocked out and beat feet more than an hour ago.

Falco closed the hood and stood back to admire his beauty.

Her name was Shelby, of course.

Grabbing a rag from his back pocket, he headed to the front to kill the lights so he could head out. He'd had too long of a day already. Anything else could wait until Monday.

A shower and a nice cold beer were in his future, and not in that order. He'd told a friend of his he'd meet him and his wife at a club for drinks, but he was gonna pass. Being pretty certain he was being suckered into a blind date didn't give him any incentive to go.

A *ding-ding* sounded from the front room, and Falco cursed.

That sound was nothing good. It either meant one of his guys had forgotten something, namely to ask for money before payday the following Monday. Or they'd forgotten to lock the door when they left and—

"Hello? Is anyone here?" A distinct female voice bounced off the dirty concrete floor until it reached his ears.

"Dammit." He didn't employ any women at this location so that sure wasn't one of his guys. He tried wiping some of the grease off his hands as he rounded the corner into the front office, more than ready to be the bearer of bad news. "Sorry, miss, but we're closed for…the…"

Holy. Shit.

If he'd ordered a girl straight out of his wet dreams, this would be her.

Holy hot damn.

Mid-length brown hair bounced loose around her shoulders. Perfect for burying his hands in. Pretty smile with crimson red lipstick. Which would look hot around the base of his dick. Green eyes that absolutely looked like trouble.

Yep. He gave her a once-over. And then again, because certainly he was seeing things.

Her off-the-shoulder shirt pictured a unicorn, which matched her short plaid pink-and-black skirt, knee-high white socks and pink four-inch fuck-me heels.

Every inch of him stood up and took notice, especially his cock who was more than ready to clock in and be put to work. She didn't look a day over twenty-something so he told his cock to take a hike.

"I can't imagine you're here to apply for a job, and I most certainly don't have a date with a gorgeous girl on my calendar, so what can I do for you?" *Or to you?* He kept the second part to himself. Barely.

"I'm going to The Library actually," she said it with a mischievous grin that matched her eyes.

He cocked an eyebrow at her.

Twisting her upper body around, she pointed at the window. And the bright fucking neon sign still blinking open. "I was hoping that wasn't a mistake, and you were open late. But the likelihood of you still being open at..." She glanced at her watch and wrinkled her nose. "Five to ten is slim to none."

Correct. We're closed.

I'm out the door.

Are you wearing panties beneath that skirt?

All things he thought of saying, but he went with the chivalrous, "Need some help?" instead. To keep from staring more, he moved around her and turned off the damn sign.

Fuck, she smelled good.

As if he really needed to know that.

"My Check Engine light came on a little bit ago. The cruise control shut off at the same time. Scared me. I'd love to say I'm a car person, and I just stopped in to borrow a wrench to fix the mmrfmugit..." She rubbed her fingertips over her lips, messing up the word with a smile. "But I'd be lying. Was hoping someone could look at it and figure out what happened so I can make sure it's okay to drive. Getting stranded tonight didn't sound like a great plan."

He grinned, despite his desire to be done for the day. Glancing out the front window, he nodded at the vehicle right outside. "Your Forester?"

"Yes, that's mine."

"Pull it around back and into the far bay. I'll have the door open by the time you get around there. I'll get it inside, and we'll see what we can find." He held the door open for her.

Might have been just so she had to brush past him.

Might. Have. Been.

"Thank you so much. I promise I'll be super quick, and if it's more complicated than an easy fix, I can always come back Monday."

Fuck. She smelled really good.

Then she stopped right in front of him. Her gaze locked with his.

She stood close enough he could feel her breath on his mouth.

"Oh. Am I keeping you from plans? Date? Anything?" Her voice got quieter on each question.

"Single actually. No plans tonight, other than a beer with a buddy. You? You mentioned something about the library. Meeting? Date?"

She smiled again. "Not dating anyone. A beer sounds nice. Sounds like I might owe you one." She moved past him, and her hip brushed his fly.

Hot and flirty. His kind of girl. Minus the at least ten-year age gap. Watching her walk away with that tiny skirt of hers flitting with the tiny curve of her ass.

Too bad there wasn't any wind tonight.

And too bad she probably wouldn't be into the kind of sex he needed.

Hard. Dirty.

Tucking the rag into his back pocket, he caught sight of his reflection in the glass windows. Ruffled hair, dirty shirt and jeans. Grease stains in quite a few places. He worked for a living and was damn proud of it. Being a bit rough around the edges came with the package. He'd help her and get her on her way. Quickly.

Closing the front door, he didn't lock it until she was in her SUV with the engine started and the lights on. Less than two minutes later, she pulled into his bay, and he closed the big bay door behind her. Her window was down so he peeked inside. Sure enough the check engine light was on.

As she cut the engine, she opened her car door to get out.

"Go ahead and pop the hood for me while you're still in there. And the fuel door latch, though I think we'll only really need the second." The hood cracked open when she lifted the latch and stepped around her door.

Just. Damn.

Talk about tasty.

"What do you think the issue is?"

Seemed she gave him a once-over as she moved closer. And he stared back at her legs that went on for miles.

Focus.

He had cameras all over the shop for surveillance. Inside. Outside. Even one focused right where they now stood.

Nothing in the world could protect him from the likes of her. Damn, she was hot. But hot normally meant trouble. And he'd outgrown that years ago. He tried focusing past the need to bend her over the hood of his Mustang and sink inside her sweet ass. "Something to do with your fuel cap. I've seen it before. Loses the seal and all sorts of other issues crop up."

"I did get gas as soon as I left the house tonight."

He nodded and stepped around the vehicle, heading to the fuel door. Pulling it open, he took off the fuel cap, which was still factory.

"Could I have just not closed it right?"

He shook his head, holding up the cap at a different angle in the light. "Nope. Come here. The rubber is just worn down. See?" He turned it to her.

She touched his arm to hold it steady.

She might as well have goosed him with a live wire.

"That looks jagged." She looked up into his eyes, and her breath hitched a tiny bit in her chest.

Fuck. Beautiful.

Her touch was like lightning, and his cock jerked beneath his fly.

Then she looked at his mouth and licked her lips.

He cleared his throat, trying to convince himself not to lift her up and fuck her against the concrete pillar in the middle of the shop. Maybe he *should* let his friends fix him up. At least they knew what kind of sex he needed. "It happens. I'm sure I have another one. Won't be factory, but it should get you by for a few more months until you get back to the dealership to get a factory replacement." He snagged another one off the shelf behind him, put it in place and closed the tiny door. "Now go crank it again while I listen to your engine, and we'll see if the light goes off."

Yes, he did watch her walk away.

No, he didn't think she had on panties.

Fuck, he wanted to find out.

Lifting the hood was the only reason he broke eye contact.

She cranked the engine, and it turned over immediately.

Everything looked fine to him. Sounded fine, too.

"The light's still on. No, wait…it went off. Oh my gosh, it went off. You're a genius!"

He grinned, unable to help himself. "Does your oil need to be changed, too? Or are you good?" He closed her hood and moved to the side to stare at her.

She killed the engine and stepped out of the vehicle.

The silence of the shop expanded all around them. The air turned intimate, charged as she moved closer.

Unable for another second to keep from touching her, he held out his hand. "I don't think I ever caught your name. It is?" He waited for her to move closer. Feeling like the big bad wolf staring down little red riding hood made his cock kick behind his dirty jeans. The nibble she gave her bottom lip made him want to growl.

Her slim fingers slid against his palm, and then he pumped her hand slowly.

Just as slowly as he'd want her to pump his shaft.

Just.

As.

Slowly.

"Kellee," she breathed out. "My name is Kellee."

She never dropped her gaze even though nervousness rolled off of her. For some reason that really did it for him. It was a challenge. And he wanted to see exactly what he'd have to do to get her eyelids down as she screamed in pleasure.

"And you are?" she questioned, with a tiny lick of her bottom lip.

"First name is Falco, but my friends call me Eagle." He waited for some kind of flirty laugh or joke about his name. He'd heard them all. Including the jokes about his business name. Eagle Oil and Lube.

Lube.

Yeah.

He'd heard them all.

Instead, she glanced between them where he smoothed the pad of his thumb across the back of her hand. They just stood there, both unwilling to break the delicious connection between them. "So, what should I call you?" she asked.

Falco had no commitments. No relationship to speak of. She had no ring on her finger either. He'd looked. And he was horny. Not just horny, but horny for this girl. So he decided to see how far she wanted to take it. "Sir. You can call me, Sir."

She didn't yank back her hand and storm out.

Nor did she threaten him with sexual harassment.

Nothing like that.

What did she do?

She grinned, her lips lifting on the corners as she nibbled her bottom lip again.

Fuck. Better than a wet dream.

"So…Sir…what kind of barter can we work out for the part and labor? It seems I've left my money at home."

No clue if she really had or not. Didn't matter. He wanted to play. He pulled her a half step closer, using his size to his advantage. Never letting go of her hand, he tipped her up chin with the side of his knuckle. "I'm quite certain we can *come* to some kind of arrangement." Yes, he did stress the four-letter word in his statement. Then he let his lips do more talking but of a very different nature. Her hand still in his grasp, he wrapped around her back, using it as leverage to pull her tight into his body. His other hand dug into her hair, lifting her up to her tip toes as he kissed her.

Not just a simple meeting of lips.

No.

He dove in, nipped at her bottom lip until she gasped, and then got a true taste of her sweet mouth.

Angling her head to the side, he licked past her teeth, and she moaned. Her relaxing against him and the slide of her tongue against his jacked his need to take her even higher. After one more taste, he pulled back. "I have cameras all around the shop. They watch everything. Including the spot we're standing in right now. You need to know we'll be recorded if we go any further." He couldn't continue without telling her the truth, but he held his breath until she spoke.

"And you should know I have condoms in my purse. You need to know you'll be wearing one when you're ready to take me." And then she smiled.

HIS EYES. She'd just thought they looked wicked before.

And his mouth?

Damn, his mouth.

Strong, capable, seductive.

Not to mention the strong grip he had on her hair and the way he drew her into his body.

Her pussy had been wet from the moment he walked around the corner with his short-cropped hair showing a little bit of grey on the sides.

Now?

Now moisture slid along her pussy lips due to his dominant hold. The way he touched her. The way he looked at her.

He pushed all the right buttons, and she wanted to feel more of him. With her hands on his waist to steady her, she brushed against him. Her nipples peaked beneath her little shirt, but she wanted to feel all of him.

She'd been on her way to The Library. Not a place where people borrowed books. Oh no. A place where *members only* could go to live out their sexual fantasies. She'd been planning on watching a scene between a married couple in hopes of joining in. Playing with David and Angel was awesome, especially after she'd been an accidental voyeur to a private scene at their house a couple months prior.

They hadn't meant to share the scene, she hadn't meant to see it, but it had happened none the less. Watching them that day with her hands in her panties, she came so hard.

But tonight, she wanted something different.

Then they'd hinted about introducing her to someone. She'd pass.

But who knew she wanted to get down and dirty with a grease monkey at an oil change place?

The kinky gods apparently knew.

She moaned as Falco tightened his fist in her hair and devoured her mouth again.

And she was more than happy to show her thanks for his help in a very fitting way.

A shiver raced up her spine as he bit her lip and licked away the sting. His fist loosened in her hair, and his rough fingertips skated across the bare skin of her thigh beneath her skirt.

"You're gorgeous. Seems a shame to get your outfit dirty."

Staring at him, she told the truth. "Dirty is sexy on you. Very sexy," she whispered the last two words as she looked up into his piercing blue eyes.

"I'd have to scrub my hands for twenty minutes to get them clean enough to slide into that sweet pussy of yours. Walking away is not something I'm able to do at the moment. So I'm gonna need your help."

She swallowed, her mouth had suddenly gone dry. "What kind of help?"

"Are you wet, Kellee?" he said, answering her question with another question.

Hesitation only lasted for a second. "Yes. I'm sure I shouldn't be. I'm damn sure I shouldn't tell you I am, but I am. So wet." She'd messaged her friends when she stopped in case they had to come rescue her from a broken-down car.

But she wanted the thrill of a no-strings one-night stand. Why not?

"How would I know if you're wet?"

Nibbling her bottom lip, she reached beneath her skirt and gathered pussy juice on two of her fingers. Holding up her slick fingers, she waited.

"What a dirty girl? No panties beneath that schoolgirl skirt?"

"Nope."

"Good girl." He grabbed her wrist and sucked her fingers clean.

His dirty hands latched onto her wrist totally did it for her. "Mmm," slipped out as more moisture coated the lips of her sex.

"Fuck it."

She eeped as he reached between her legs, hooked her knees over his forearms and lifted her up as if she weighed nothing.

Holding the back of his head, she was pressed against the side of a concrete pillar in the middle of the garage with her thighs over his shoulders. Her eyelids fluttered closed as he licked her straight up the middle. "Oh God. Your tongue..." She shivered. "Delicious."

"Yes, you are," he breathed against the flesh of her pussy. His tongue slid beside her clit and then circled the tiny bundle of nerves. The muscles in her slit shivered as he lapped at her wetness. "Pull at the top of your pussy. I'm gonna suck your clit into my mouth, and I'm not stopping until you come all over my face."

A whimper slipped free at his words. With one hand still on the back of his head, she pushed aside the skirt and tugged at the top of her mound.

His gaze met hers as he latched onto her clit.

A breath hitched in her chest.

The tip of his tongue flicked her quivering clit again and again.

"I'm gonna come," she said the words almost more for her own benefit. The color of his eyes changed. They grew darker, more intense, as the pressure on her hips intensified where he held her up.

Something caught her eye on the ceiling as the orgasm shimmied down her spine.

A camera.

A surveillance camera.

Pointed right at them.

"*Fuuccckkkkk...*" she breathed as she came. Being manhandled, videoed, dirtied. Every one of her buttons. Delicious. The muscles in her sex spasmed, and her legs tightened as she groaned. Her hips jolted each time his tongue swiped her sensitive nubbin.

"Hold on," he grunted against her wet flesh. Whipping her down, he helped her stand beside the post.

Unable to help herself, she stood on her tiptoes to lick her slick juices from his lips.

"Jesus. I need your mouth on me." He undid his belt, button, and slid down his zipper on his grease-stained jeans.

Her gaze stayed glued to him the whole time. He backed her up until her ass touched the concrete post. Panting his palms on the edges of the post behind her, he caged her in.

She shoved down his pants, and his dick popped free. Thick. The perfect length to gag on. "Can I have a taste, Sir?"

"You're gonna get more than a taste, little girl."

Sinking to her knees on the hard concrete, she wrapped her fist around his cock, and he groaned. The end wept with a tiny drop of pre-cum at the tip. Lapping it up did nothing but whet her appetite for more as her pussy contracted again from her orgasm mere seconds after he put his mouth on her.

Squeezing his shaft from root to tip, she watched his balls pull up tight to his body. "You're so hard." She swiped her thumb beneath the sensitive head of his cock and then licked the tip again. A sigh slipped out and hummed against his flesh as she sucked him in deep, bobbing up and down on his thick pole.

"Fuck. Me."

Digging her nails into his hip where she held on kept her steady as she sucked him deep. Popping his cock out of her mouth, she pressed his stiff length to his belly and stared up at him. Licking his balls turned her on to the point she was going to drip onto his concrete. One at a time, she gently sucked his balls into her mouth, and his jaw clenched over and over again.

He widened his stance a second before he grabbed a handful of her hair with one hand and grabbed the base of his shaft with the other. "Both hands on my hips. Keep them there." As soon as she complied, he ordered, "Stick out your tongue, little girl."

As soon as her tongue was out, he thwacked his cock against it. A moan slipped past her vocal cords as he fed his cock into her mouth one delicious inch at a time.

"Keep that tongue out. I want in your throat before I fuck your juicy pussy. I can smell how wet you are. Can taste you still. So hot."

She licked his shaft, and her mouth watered at the musky taste of him as he pushed in deep. He withdrew and pushed in again. Retreated and pressed in farther.

Controlled.

That's what he was as she spun out of control.

Risking some kind of punishment, she released his hip on one side and brushed the tips of her fingers across his tight sack.

A growl broke free as he exhaled, then he sucked in a deep breath as he pushed all the way into her throat.

She couldn't breathe as he face-fucked her. Couldn't move, couldn't focus on anything but him.

The sensation was perfect.

One more time he retreated and pushed in deep. He held her in place until she lost count, and she yanked her head away to suck in oxygen.

"So fucking hot," he growled and yanked her off his cock and to her feet.

She almost lost her balance, but he picked her up and moved her to the hood of a gorgeous Mustang. Setting her on her feet again, he swiveled her around and shoved her top half down onto the hood as he flipped up her skirt.

"Hold your tiny ass cheeks open. I want to see the holes I'm about to fuck."

Her abdomen clenched on his words, and she held her cheeks open wide.

"Fuck, that's a very wet pussy you have there, Kellee. Liked choking on my cock, did you?"

"Loved it," she mumbled as he pushed his cock along the wetness of her slit. Too quickly, he was gone. "Loved it so much. Oh God…" she gasped as he tongued the tight rosette of her ass.

"Your taste. So hot."

The crinkle of a condom wrapper barely registered in her mind as he pushed his tongue into her back entrance. "I'm gonna come again. I'm so close."

"Not until I get inside. Then you can come. Again and again." He stood and in the next breath his cock pushed against the entrance to her sex. "I love seeing your little asshole clench as I push inside. As your pussy sucks me in. So hot."

"So hot," they said at the same time.

"Put one of your hands between your legs. Gather up some of that wetness on the tips of your fingers."

At the top of her thighs, she ran her fingertips along her clit and up around where he filled her sex. "So wet," she whispered as she focused on her clit again, more than ready to come.

Before she could get there, he reached between the car and her, grabbing her wrist and pulling it behind her.

"But I thought you said I could—"

"Get up on your other elbow so you can twist your upper body towards me a bit." He helped her up and then grabbed her wrist again. "Which fingers did you get wet, little girl?" He pumped in and out of her. Shallow, deep, quick, slow. She couldn't anticipate his rhythm which pushed her closer and closer to release.

Kellee bit her lip and held up the two she'd coated in her slick pussy juice.

"Good. Now…" Looking down, Falco spit and it landed in the crack of her ass.

Her mouth fell open with the sheer filth of the gesture.

"Spread my spit all over your ass. Yeah. Just like that. Dip one of your fingers into your tight hole. A tiny bit, and out, and back in again. More. More."

Delicious pleasure shivered over Kellee's entire body as Falco grabbed onto her hand and pushed her finger farther into her ass.

He pulled her finger free and licked the two digits she'd originally gotten wet, getting them even slicker. Then they lined them back up to her ass again and pushed them both in, stretching her tight hole as he fucked her pussy.

So.

Fucking.

Dirty.

"I need to come, Sir. Please, please, I need to come so bad."

"Don't stop fucking that little asshole for me. In and out, scissor your tiny fingers so it burns just a bit."

Kellee did what he told her to. So close to coming, but she just couldn't get there without something on her clit.

Then he pulled free.

She almost screamed.

Why would he stop then?

Why would he quit right when she was so—

An orgasm nearly bowled her over as Falco knelt behind her and sucked her clit into his mouth. His tongue pushed her over the edge as she fucked her ass for him, and he flicked her clit again and again. "Sir!" she screamed in pleasure when he pushed back into her spasming pussy and grabbed her wrist to shove her fingers farther into her clenching ass.

"Come. Come for me. With me." He latched onto her shoulders and fucked into her so deep she saw stars.

The pleasure became so complete she had no idea where she ended and he began.

Sensation rolled into another wave as he buried himself balls-deep in her pussy, trapping her fingers still in her ass.

The pain and exquisite pleasure rolled into one as he twitched against her.

"*Fuuucckkkk*," he groaned as his cock jerked inside her.

Even with the condom on, she could feel each spurt of cum as he came again and again.

Satisfaction rolled through her as she finally pulled her fingers free of her ass. "Oh, God," she whispered again.

Planting her lower arms on the hood of the car, she closed her eyes and floated in the warm darkness as he pumped into her several more times.

"Don't go anywhere, gorgeous." He pulled free, and they both groaned.

He walked somewhere, and she heard water running. Then a warm tongue licked her clean between her legs.

Falco gently lifted her off the hood and held her tight for long minutes.

When she glanced up at him, he wore a roguish grin as he bent to kiss her. "Will I ever see you again?" she asked as he stepped her over to her vehicle and helped her inside.

"I have a feeling our paths will cross again. I only consider that round one." That smile appeared again.

Perplexed, she buckled her seatbelt and started the engine while he opened the bay door. He didn't have her number so how would he contact her?

She pulled forward and braked next to him. "Thank you again for your help."

Leaning inside the car, he cupped her cheeks. "Thank you for the payment." His mouth on hers...damn. "Now drive careful."

Determined not to be "that girl" she pulled out of the bay with a smile and waved goodbye. His face stayed with her as she drove to The Library.

She flashed her card at the entrance, and Jackson let her in. She parked in the members' garage and went inside. Kinky people were everywhere, but she found Davis and Angel at the bar.

They both stood and hugged her.

Without preamble, Angel held her at arm's length. "We have a friend coming to join us tonight." She bobbed her eyebrows up and down. "Someone we've known for years and finally convinced to become a member here."

Ugh. Just what Kellee suspected and the last thing she wanted to deal with after her time with Falco. "That's great, but I think I'll pass. I just came to tell you I'd talk to you later. I had car trouble earlier and—"

"Car trouble, little girl? I know the owner of a place down the road. I could put in a good word for you."

The man's voice behind her cut her off, and her heart jumped into her throat. Kellee whipped around, staring at the sexy man as he approached. The sexy man with clean hands. "Sir?"

"Wait. You guys know each other?" Davis asked.

"You could say that," Falco offered up with a handshake before he faced Kellee again. "Told you we'd meet again." He lifted her into his arms, and she automatically wrapped her legs around his waist.

"You knew? You knew before I left that we were supposed to meet tonight?"

He nodded. "I figured it out somewhere along the way. Mmm… Still no panties on." His fingers slid in the wetness gathering on the lips of her sex. "You know what that means, don't you?"

She groaned as he started walking toward the dungeon. "What?" Awareness raced along her flesh as he pushed a finger into her slick core.

"Time for round two."

CHALLENGES MET

LAYLA CHASE

Sweat beaded along Javiero Paz's eyebrows, and after lifting his hat, he swiped the heel of his palm over his forehead. Summer in south Texas often felt like living on the edge of a blast furnace. The heat intensified the earthy scents of dried hay and fresh manure—smells that had always been part of his world. Growing up the son of a horse trainer meant barns served as his playground. Since his discharge from the military, burying himself in his work with animals soothed his battle-weary spirit. The last tour— and the loss of his best friend—had pushed him close to the breaking point.

"Easy now, girl." He shifted his stance and readjusted the horse's leg on his thigh then scraped the file over the hoof. Three strokes in one direction then three in the other. Check for smoothness. Repeat. Might not be the most exciting work, but it beat riding in an armored vehicle into desert villages uncertain of the troop's reception or always looking over his shoulder and waiting for the whine of a sniper's bullet.

Galloping hoof beats broke the silence of the early afternoon, accompanied by a high-pitched whinny.

At the sudden sound, the mare shied.

Javi tensed before he straightened, patting a hand along the roan's shoulders. "Whoa. You're all right, girl."

A blonde with hair that matched the coat of her palomino horse burst into the center aisle of the Wellington Acres barn. "Well, look who's here. Javiero Paz."

"Hello, Mandy." Manners drilled into him since childhood made him lift a finger to the brim of his Stetson. He grabbed for the reins she tossed in his direction. The automatic action flashed him back at least a decade. His grip tightened, and he walked the sweaty, panting horse away from the mare he was shoeing. Bitter memories of being treated like a servant rose into his thoughts. Javi tied off the reins to a post and turned.

"I heard you were back." She sauntered to the open tool box on a stand against the closest stall gate and idly picked up a pick and a file.

News had a way of being spread in a small town like Duketon. "Two months now." A fire-engine red tank accented her full breasts and tucked into a hand-tooled belt cinching her narrow waist. Tight jeans clung to her long legs. The intervening years had been kind to this spoiled rancher's daughter—if her trim figure and the sparkling gems on her fingers and in her ears were any indication. The same grapevine of gossip informing her of his return had supplied the information that Mandy remained single.

"Got that soldiering gig out of your system?" She ran the file over the tips of her manicured nails then speared him with a wide stare of her blue eyes. Her lips formed a pout as she ducked her chin.

Intriguing cornflower blue eyes used to haunt him in the wee hours of the night when his teen-aged hormones needed release however he could get it. Steeling himself from falling back into old habits, he approached the mare and ran a hand over her back. "Serving three tours was hardly a 'gig.'" Military service had been his ticket out of this town, offering a kid from working-class parents the chance to earn enough money to attend farrier school, acquire his certification, and set up his business. Soon as he built up a solid clientele, he could start saving for the ranch he wanted to own one day.

Maybe if he didn't make eye contact again, he could focus on the task at hand. Instead of thinking about how her body might respond to his demanding touch. Which would do nothing but jeopardize keeping her father as one of his accounts. Easing the mare's hoof back onto his thigh, he returned to the hoof trim.

"I can't believe you chose to work with horses."

From the corner of his eye, he spotted the tips of her embellished red leather boots that probably cost her father a couple grand. The disparaging note in her voice set his teeth on edge. But he kept his expression impassive. Her sarcasm had always been razor-sharp. Somehow, he'd thought she'd have outgrown the rebel-child attitude. "The horse business has been good for your family. Certainly has provided you with a comfortable life. Surprised you don't see that." *Or appreciate it.* He ran his fingers over the hoof, satisfied with the smooth surface.

"Why be satisfied with being a big fish in a little pond? I want to see the world."

He straightened to find her only a few inches away. Close enough her scent—an intoxicating blend of exotic musk and warm woman—filled his nose. Crap, how much willpower did he have to display? "Careful what you wish for." He thought of how this pampered, protected woman would fare in a big city where opportunists would pounce once they learned the size of her daddy's holdings.

"You know nothing about my wishes." Her gaze roamed his chest and dipped lower before slowly climbing to his face.

Holding himself in check, he watched as her eyes widened and her nostrils flared after registering how his shirt clung to his pecs and biceps. He'd left home as a slender but wiry teen and returned a hard-muscled man. Now, if she didn't suck the fullness of her lower lip into her— Shit. His cock twitched. "What do you want, Mandy? I have a job to finish." Frustration added a growl to his tone.

"What I've always wanted." She tilted her head and glanced from under her lowered lashes. "A taste of the forbidden."

Lectures of staying away from the boss's daughter and dating only within his ethnic community ran through his mind as he registered her words. Was she really asking for what he'd desired so many years ago? Tired of dancing around the sexual teasing, he stepped forward, invading her space, and glared into her clear blue eyes. "Meaning what?" Satisfaction rose as he watched her pupils dilate.

She tossed her head, flipping a strand of wavy hair across her face. "Well, if you don't know."

Two could play the flirting game. "Don't I?" He reached out a hand and eased the silky strand back over her shoulder, dragging a finger along the ridge. In a flash, the simple touch wasn't enough. Cupping his hand at the nape of her neck, he yanked her close and lowered his head to capture her mouth. Just one taste, he promised himself. Working his lips over hers, he pressed hard, eating at whatever fruity lipstick she wore. His tongue dipped inside, seeking a deeper connection. He anchored his free hand on her hip, so he could hold her in place while he plundered the softness of her cheeks and dueled with her responsive tongue. Blood pounded in his ears, ramping up his lust.

She whimpered and splayed her hands over his chest

before wrapping them around his neck, pulling him closer. A needy moan sounded, and Mandy rubbed her breasts against his chest.

Her moan vibrating into his mouth somehow brought him back to their exposed location. Easing his hold, he moved backward to separate them and jammed his hands on his hips, huffing out a breath. Now he had to goad her into being the one who abandoned this sex play. "Satisfied with your forbidden taste?"

"Hardly." Her gaze riveted on the bulge straining the fly of his jeans. "My guess is neither are you."

"Yeah, well, ma'am, can't help that." He forced a lazy Texas drawl into his words. "I'm just a working man, and the job's not done."

"How about the fact that *I'm* not done?" Glaring, she crossed her arms over her chest.

Fighting every urge to see if her stance revealed more of her shapely assets, he kept his gaze locked on hers. If she stayed mad, he could get past this gigantic lapse in judgment. Then she did that lip-sucking action again, and he had to turn away so he wouldn't haul her back into his arms. "We can't all have what we want."

A gasp sounded. "You want me?"

Javi sorted through his farrier tools just to keep his hands occupied while he thought about his next response. He was not done discovering what Mandy tasted like. Hell, they were both adults. What would a one-night-stand hurt? "Can't do anything now. Or here."

"How will I find where you live?"

He snorted at that inane question. "You'll figure it out. Besides, anticipation is a great aphrodisiac." Only by sheer force of will did he keep himself from looking over his shoulder to watch her fine ass disappear from sight.

* * *

MANDY'S EXIT from the barn was on shakier legs than she would have imagined a single kiss could cause. Maybe her reaction was because she's finally heard Javi admit what she'd hoped for all those years ago. Since coming into her female curves as a teenager, she'd wanted to see appreciation in Javi's dark brown gaze. Instead, he'd always presented an attitude of perfect manners and cool politeness. Being thwarted only served to let her bitchy tongue run wild. Finally, tonight she'd satisfy her curiosity, and then maybe she wouldn't compare every guy she'd dated to the brooding dark-haired guy.

Her pulse still raced from the rough way he'd grabbed her hip and held her in place. Like his grip had branded her as his. A feverish shiver ran over her body. She lifted the damp hair from her neck, letting the movement of her strides toward the ranch house run air over her flushed skin. Her mind raced as she considered the contents of her closet. Tonight's outfit needed to be sexy, not slutty. Suggestive, but not one that labeled her as easy.

A few phone calls and a couple hours of primping later, Mandy eased her vintage sports car into the parking lot of a modest condo complex. As she turned off the engine, she threw her thanks out to her BFF Sandi whose father owned the local hardware store. Through her, Mandy had discovered where Javi lived. Glancing around, she spotted a brown pickup with his business name painted on the driver's door.

So, this was really happening. She sucked in a deep breath, leaned over to grab the cloth bag holding two bottles of her favorite pinot, and then climbed out. Until she actually rapped her knuckles on the door to number nine, she wasn't sure if she'd chicken out and turn tail. Didn't people always say the fantasy was better than the reality? She so didn't want that statement to be true about this hunk of a man.

The door swung open, and there he stood, bare-chested and barefooted, wearing cargo shorts low on his hips. Javi's eyes widened. "You came?"

"Not yet, but a girl can always hope." She stepped over the threshold and brushed her lips over his cheek, inhaling a fresh-scented cologne, then moved inside. The furnishings surprised her. She'd expected dark leather with heavy wood detail, but the caramel-colored plush sofa and matching recliner with light wood side tables gave the living room a homey look. The flat-screen TV hanging from the wall was paused on a soccer match. Peeking into the small kitchen, she didn't see much that spoke of his personal tastes.

"Uh, Mandy."

The hesitation in his voice served to bolster her courage. She would not allow him to back down from what he'd started in the barn. Sure, she'd egged him on. But the result was oh-so worth it. "Where would I find glasses?" Forcing a wide smile, she turned and lifted the bag. "I hope you drink wine."

"On occasion." He stepped toward the kitchen.

Unable to resist, she ogled the flex of his muscles as he walked and admired his loose-limbed stride. A single tattoo that looked military-related marked his left bicep. She couldn't wait to investigate the design. Hoping for a compliment on her floral sundress with the plunging neckline and ruffled hem, she gave a twirl like she was inspecting his condo. The cool air on her bare bottom sent a thrill through her. "I like your place."

Dual clinks sounded on the counter. "Nothing like the house at Wellington Acres."

Frowning, she set down the bag and reached inside for a

bottle. "Not every conversation we have has to highlight our differences."

Without a word, he lifted the wine bottle from her hand, stripped the foil, applied a corkscrew to pop the cork, and poured each glass half full. After handing her one, he lifted his glass in salute. "True, but finding commonalities might be harder."

This visit was not playing out as she hoped. Somehow, she'd thought he would have been thinking about the kiss as much as she had, and that by now, she'd be slumped over the back of his sofa with him pounding into her from behind. One of her top two favorite positions. To keep from complaining about that very situation, she gulped a big mouthful that dribbled along the sides of her mouth. Leaning forward, she tried to wipe away the drips before they landed on her dress.

A guttural groan sounded a moment before a muscled arm pulled her tight against a rock-hard body.

Javi's warm tongue lapped at both cheeks before he traced the faint lines down her neck, trailing open-mouthed kisses.

The heady sensation almost made her swoon, and she braced a hand on the counter. The other she caressed over his back, running fingertips along ridges and bulges of bunched muscles. In a couple of places, the skin was uneven and puckered. Her stomach clenched. Then her senses heightened as Javi's hand rubbed along her side, the tip of his thumb circling close to her breast. Her nipples pebbled against the dress fabric, and she couldn't resist rubbing the tight tips against his chest.

He chuckled. "Hey, slow down."

His breathy whisper tickled her neck, causing goose bumps to rise. She shook her head, running her hand into the thick hair at the back of his head. "Don't like slow."

Javi loosened his embrace until their gazes caught and held. "Tell me more."

Still running her fingers through his hair that had grown long enough to grab, she contemplated her answer. On purpose, she bit her lower lip just to watch the lust erupt and darken his eyes to obsidian. Her breath caught at knowing that hungry look was just for her. "I'd rather show you." But that wasn't what she really wanted. She wanted him to take charge and be the leader.

He loosened his hold and held out his arms at his sides, palms up. "Okay by me."

Scenarios of positions on various pieces of furniture flashed through her head, but each one appeared sluttier than the next. Her attitude might come off as balls to the wall, but she's never taken the sexual initiative. Flirting and innuendo had always stoked a man's libido to the point of no return. Then she'd gone along for the enjoyable ride.

Suddenly, she wanted an atmosphere of flickering candle-light, sexy music, and silky sheets. Javi did not look like a man who possessed any of those items. She glanced toward the hallway that must lead to his bedroom. Decision made. As secretly as she could, she sucked in a fortifying breath. Tossing a teasing look over her shoulder, she crooked a finger, and then moved in that direction, giving an extra swing to her hips. At the door she suspected was his, she paused and, dragging the hem of her skirt up to the point of her hip, she met his heated gaze. "Why are you back there?" For good measure, she ran her tongue around the inside of her lips. Then she turned the knob and pushed open the door —to a room with a weight bench and a rowing machine.

Smooth move, Mandy. Her confidence sagged a notch or two. Until she felt the heat radiating off Javi's body surround her from behind. For a big man, he moved like a silent cat.

"Looking for a workout?"

His voice had dropped about an octave, and the almost-growl created a shiver along her skin. "I'd hoped for one of a more personal nature." *Please take the hint.*

"Next door." His hand rested in the small of her back and pressed.

Still thrown by his subdued attitude, she stumbled forward and into a room with dimmed recessed lighting at the perimeter of the ceiling. A big bed on a pedestal occupied center stage with only a bedside lamp and nightstand as additional furnishings. Before she had a chance to look for pictures or personal items, she felt hot breath on the side of her neck.

"Don't know if I can wait for you to show me." He nipped her neck then soothed it with a long swipe of his tongue. "I've thought of having you here so many times."

The rasp of his warm tongue sent tingles from the bite straight to her core, heating her pussy. Her nipples pebbled, and she relished the tightening sensation. "Always nice to be welcomed." Unable to resist, she tilted her head, hoping for more attention.

Aligning his legs with hers, he walked her toward the bed, hands braced on her hips. Within inches of the mattress, he turned her to face him, caressed his hands along her cheeks, and his mouth devoured hers.

Mandy grabbed his shoulders and clung tight, over-whelmed by the assault of his tongue delving into her eager mouth. Moisture gathered along her throbbing folds, and she pressed her thighs together. At the cupping of his hand on her right breast, she couldn't stifle a low moan. Hadn't she always known they'd be good together? She arched her back to heighten the sensation.

Javi eased his free hand to her back and then lowered her until she lay on the bed, his hand continuing his sensual massage. "Fits just right." He braced himself above her.

Mandy ran her hands along the tight ridges of his shoulders, wishing she'd chosen a dress that opened down the front. She wanted to feel skin on skin…right now. Leaning upward, she planted kisses along his chest, loving the tickle of wiry hairs against her sensitive lips. She let her fingers trail down to his flat nipple and brushed quick strokes across it, testing what he liked.

His body stiffened for a second before he lowered himself to press against her body and bury his neck in the crook of her neck.

The hard ridge of his desire rocked against her belly, but not against the spot where she wanted it most. She ran her hand over the bulge, giving its girth a gentle squeeze. Feeling him drive into her grip pumped her satisfaction. Maybe she did know how to take the lead.

Javi nuzzled her neck then ran wet kisses along her collarbone.

Lost in the new sensation that raced her pulse, she lay limp and accepting, feeling the flush crawl along on her body as his attentions covered her exposed skin. His mouth was everywhere, titillating her senses like the first time she'd gone skinny dipping. How the water had touched all her secret places and initiated her in erogenous zones.

His fingers tugged at the straps and neckline of her dress until her breasts sprang free.

The warm capture of her nipple arched her off the mattress with a cry. Then she clamped her hands on his head to keep him there, reveling in how his suctioning mouth created electric pulls deep in her belly. Her response was like nothing she'd ever felt.

"So smooth. So lovely."

His words puffed along her skin, creating goose bumps, before her other breast received the same laving and sucking attention. Inching under the hem of her dress, callused hands stroked her legs. She scissored her thighs, heightening the pressure against her pulsing sex. The friction drove her wild, spiking her desire for more. "Mmm."

The double caress of thumbs on her inner thigh jolted her. She lifted her head and glanced to where Javi stood gazing at her bared crotch, his jaw clenched.

"No panties?" His eyebrow quirked. "What if I'd wanted to tear them off?"

Being stared at was unnerving. Sure, she'd taken the time to groom herself, but she'd much rather he be poised above her looking into her eyes as he pounded deep inside. Words failed her under his intense stare, and she could only rest her hand on the mattress, stretching as close as she could get.

Holding her gaze, he stroked her wet folds with a single finger, from the apex of her thighs toward her bottom and back. Then down the other side.

Her body tightened, anticipating the touch to the bud of nerves that waited.

Then he dropped lower and spread her knees wide.

Warm breath tickled her pussy only seconds before his hot tongue invaded, retracing the path his finger drew. With her feet dangling and nowhere to set them, she couldn't press against his mouth to let him know where she wanted his touch. Need spiraled with each stroke of his tongue as he moved it along her lips then into her channel. Mandy tweaked and pinched her nipples, savoring the burn in her delicate skin.

Then he hit the target, scraping her clit with the edge of his teeth before sucking it between his lips.

Mandy needed an anchor. A base to hold her as the sensations built. She needed Javi. Crunching her stomach, she rolled upward until she grasped his shoulders, fingers splayed. In this position, she rocked her hips and pushed against his mouth, kicking the tingles into a gallop. Ripples spread through her belly then contracted to one small knot held taut in suspension.

Javi licked her folds, flattened his tongue against her clit, and then inserted a finger.

With a cry, Mandy fell back onto the mattress, a prisoner to the masterful touch wringing every bit of her orgasm. Before she could catch her breath, he inserted another finger, stroked them deep, then fluttered a single one until he pressed on her G-spot. She spiraled into sensory overload and just responded on instinct—female to male. Her head thrashed, and her hands gripped the sheets until her muscles stopped twitching. She let out a long sigh. "As nice as I imagined."

Chuckling, Javi brushed soft kisses along her inner thighs, his hands stroking her hips. "You thought about this?"

Doubt crossed her thoughts. Had this been only her fantasy? "Haven't you?"

He dropped onto the mattress at her side, a broad hand settling on her belly. "Just teasing you, Mandy." He nuzzled his nose along the ridge of her shoulder. "I've thought of every kind of scenario possible." He propped his head on his upraised hand. "But this is the best, because it's in the flesh." With his free hand, he brushed at the strands of hair at her cheek.

Recovered enough that she could lie on her side to face him, she smiled. "I agree." She traced her fingertips along his arm and clasped his hand. "Now, get naked."

* * *

THE BOSSY TONE of her order revved his cock even harder, but reassured Javi that the Mandy he knew was back. For a second there, he hadn't known how to deal with the woman who seemed a bit lost before she went silent. Getting her off without immediately driving into her sweet body had taken control. A control that he barely held leashed as he smelled the tang of her arousal with each breath. "Same goes for you." He rolled to the side and jumped off the bed, then headed to his stash of condoms in the bathroom.

A quick splash of water cleaned his mouth and chin. He unhooked the button and dropped the zipper, letting the shorts pool at his feet before kicking them into a corner. Overhead, the air conditioner kicked on. Cool air circled his body, and he lingered a few seconds to drink it into his lungs and let it surround his heated balls and cock. If he had any hope of driving her to a third orgasm, he had to be in control.

Blood raced through his body like he was on high alert. He sauntered across the room, hiding a smile at the sight of Mandy's widening gaze. Damn, he wished he owned candles. Mandy's slender body with full luscious breasts deserved to be viewed in a golden glow. Her light brown bush trimmed into a lightning bolt was fitting. He tossed a handful of foil packets onto the nightstand before easing beside her and reaching out a hand to skim along her waist and hip.

So far, this encounter was nothing like he'd planned. He'd thought they'd come together like an explosion and burn each other out. But his first sight of the tentative look in her eyes made him change tactics. How had a one-night stand turned into wooing?

He tightened his hand on her hip, waiting to see if she'd get the hint. His reward was a smile, and Mandy wriggling closer. When her nipples grazed his chest, he bit back a curse, and his grip clamped. Maybe he wasn't as in control as he thought.

Her hand stroked his chest, and then she ran the backs of her knuckles over his belly, inching lower.

Blood pounded in his ears, and to distract her from her

intended goal, he used a finger to tweak her nipple then rolled it between his fingers. He waited for her reaction.

The quick inhalation also brought up her gaze to tangle with his.

Unable to resist the challenge he spotted in her arched eyebrow, he leaned forward and rimmed her lips with a slide of his tongue. Having it swallowed into the heat of her mouth made him suck in a breath, then he battled stroke for stroke, as he filled his hand with her soft flesh and massaged. Vaguely, he registered her other touches—on his chest, a nipple, his hip—but mostly he focused on restraining his desired movements to only the parry of his tongue. Right until the moment when her hand wrapped around his cock, and the master became the slave.

Groaning, he rolled to his back, accepting the sensations she created by soft strokes, hard tugs, tickling finger taps, and finally the warm heat of her tongue. The dream had been for so long held in his mind that with the reality, he almost gave in and fucked her mouth. Because he had to know how that felt, he flexed his hips once, and then again, savoring the tight suction of her mouth and the light scrape of her teeth as he eased lower.

But he wanted to be inside her. Blindly reaching to the nightstand, he grabbed a condom and ripped off the cover. He pressed a hand to her shoulder until she released him. Then he rolled on the sheath. "Top or bottom." His voice was no more than a growl.

Her eyes flashed, and she scooted back until she'd set herself up on hands and knees.

Shit, the woman was after more than a fuck, she was after his heart. Javi rolled to his knees and aligned himself behind her shapely ass. He gripped her left hip as he guided himself to the heat of her pussy, running the tip of his cock along her sex until he was sure she was ready again. Remembering her words in the kitchen about how she liked it, he flexed and entered her in one long stroke.

Her back arched, and she cried out his name.

A sound that imprinted on his soul. He withdrew, paused, and then speared her again, relishing the enveloping warmth and tight fit for just a second before he set a pounding rhythm. Thoughts of her flirty glances and accidental touches flicked through his mind, revving his excitement. His balls filled and tickled. He tried to slow the pace, but he was past the point of control. Close, so close. But he wasn't satisfied because he couldn't see her face.

Pulling out was one of the hardest things he'd done. He flipped her to her back, and then leaned down to embrace her, branding her with a hard kiss. After settling his ass onto the mattress, he dug his hands along her back and cupped her hips, then eased her up along his thighs until her pussy hovered over his erect dick.

"Oo, this looks interesting." Mandy smoothed her hands over his belly, dragged fingers over his nipples, until she leaned them on his shoulders as she lowered atop his cock. Then she circled her hips.

Heat shot to his groin, and he surged upward, filling her. The next strokes were wild and frenzied until he caught the push-pull of her moves, and they synchronized. "Look at me." He stopped until her eyelids opened and glassy-eyed blue gazed back. Then he stroked, lifting her several inches. Biting her lip, she circled her hips. Next, he eased down and she followed, driving her pussy into the wiry hairs of his groin, moaning as she moved.

The moan stole his resolve. He nibbled on her mouth, plunging in his tongue to taste more of her sweetness. When he couldn't breathe, he pressed his forehead to hers as he fucked her long, and deep, and with a feeling that caught him by surprise. Knowing he was close, he rubbed his thumb over her engorged clit. Feeling her body tighten, he stroked inside a few more times then hissed as his balls emptied.

He had no idea how long they stayed with limbs entwined. Finally, he eased them into a lying position so he could dispose of the condom. Slipping the sheet over her snoozing body, he climbed in behind her and pulled her close, nestling his nose into her musky-scented hair. Second or minutes or hours later, he felt the mattress shift, and she slipped away. He reached out to haul her back.

But Mandy stood at the side of the bed, pulling the sundress straps into place.

"Stay." Javi fought to keep demand from the single word.

"I can't."

Fear that this was just a one-time thing shot through him. "Got a curfew?"

"Early client meeting." Running a hand through her tousled hair, she shook her head and smiled. "I no longer live on the ranch. Now, you have to find me."

Meaning she had a job? Interesting new fact. He adjusted the pillow behind his head and let a grin spread his lips. So a future was a possibility. "You know I will."

Mandy made a moue of her lips then gave a saucy wink. "I'm counting on it."

IN THE HEAT OF THE MOMENT

M. MARIE

Lieutenant Crista de Marco's voice was civil as she called Detective Thomas Hale into her office, but that didn't stop the other detectives from flashing knowing grins in Tom's direction as he rose to answer their boss's summons.

"You're in for it now," his partner whispered with a cheeky grin.

Tom returned it boldly. "Yeah, what else is new?" He laughed. "She's always riding my ass," he called back to his friend, without thinking how his words may have carried until he stepped into the Lieutenant's office and saw the dark expression on her face.

"Shut the door behind you," she instructed in a quiet voice.

Tom swallowed hard. As he turned to pull the door closed, he caught the shocked looks on a few of his co-workers' faces. Tom could count the number of times the LT's door had been closed over the past five years on one hand. Lt. de Marco was a fierce, vocal woman, who never hesitated to reprimand her team when someone stepped out of line.

Normally, when the lieutenant wanted to chew one of them out, she started screaming before the guilty party had even stepped across the threshold into her office. Her subdued tone didn't match her stern expression, and the dichotomy was unnerving.

The door closed with a soft *click*. Tom turned and found Crista sitting behind her desk, staring. She was a tall woman, with a solid build, richly tanned skin, and short, slicked back, dark brown hair. At thirty-four, she was the youngest detective to make lieutenant in their district. Crista de Marco was focused, driven, and dedicated to her career. She was also clever and sharp in both her appearance and attitude. She had risen quickly since joining the Homicide Department. Although Tom joined the department two years before Crista, they had both earned their detective shields in the same year. Tom had been deliriously proud of himself, but Crista had only been motivated to push herself harder...

She watched Tom cross the room and sit without waiting for her to offer him a seat. She frowned at her subordinate as he crossed his arms over his broad chest. "You know why I called you in here, Tom."

Now her detective returned a frown. "You wanted evidence against the Tapparts. I brought it to you. And now, you're going to give me shit for following orders," he blurted before he could stop himself.

The vitriol wasn't unexpected, but it was a surprise when his boss didn't respond in a similar fashion.

In a flat tone, Lt. de Marco pointed out, "Your orders were to locate the suspect's new hideout and wait for the search warrant. Not barge in without permission and ransack the apartment."

"Ransack?" Tom exploded. "I found thousands of dollars' worth of stolen property, over three dozen stolen firearms, and enough drugs in the back bedroom to put away that scumbag for the rest of his life."

"Except he won't be going away for a single day now, because you didn't wait for a warrant!" Crista's voice shook with the effort to suppress her anger. "All the evidence you found is inadmissible, because it was obtained through an illegal search. *All of it!* We have nothing to keep him with now. We had to cut him loose this morning."

The lieutenant's voice was strained, and Tom could see her rage spreading in a red flush across her tan skin. His temper was still high, but it didn't rival hers. He wisely bit back his next response, but he couldn't hide the stubborn expression on his face.

Recognizing the look, Crista snapped, "Spit it out, Hale."

The detective huffed in frustration. "I was just doing my job."

"Your job is to follow protocol.

"I acted in the heat of the moment," Tom protested. "We had no time to wait for some judge to roll out of bed and give his approval. The suspect could have come back at any minute. I made the call—"

"You don't make those calls," his lieutenant cut him off loudly, giving up any attempts at reining in her anger. "You're a *detective*, Hale. You follow *my* orders, and if you aren't capable of doing that, then maybe we should see about having you demoted back to walking the beat."

His response exploded from him before he could hold it back. "You'd love that, wouldn't you? You've been on my case since you made lieutenant. You think you're better than me, just because you got promoted when Costos became captain, but we all know why you were picked to fill his position— and the reason's not because of how much you love protocols!"

The silence that fell after his tirade stretched. Tom could

easily imagine the shocked expressions on his eavesdropping buddies' faces outside their boss's office, but Crista's reaction was much harder to identify.

Clearly, she was angry; he had insulted her integrity, both as an officer and a woman, with his harsh and unfounded outburst. For such a proud, strong person, that kind of provocation would be difficult to ignore.

She was probably also embarrassed to know her other subordinates had likely overheard his comments. She had served her time as a detective with the rest of them under Costos, who was also no stranger to motivating his staff by loudly berating them. She had suffered through her share of his criticism, and she had to remember how thin these office walls really were.

She was unnervingly quiet now, and her face gave no hint of her true feelings. Tom fidgeted in his seat a moment, before attempting a gruff apology. "Look, I'm sorry, Cris—I mean, Lieutenant. That was out of line, and I apologize. I didn't mean what I said. No one really thinks that about you, either," he assured her.

She answered him with silence.

"Seriously, I'm sorry." He knew he was only making things worse, but the younger woman's lack of reaction was unsettling. He couldn't seem to stop talking. "I was just angry. I feel like you're always riding me harder than everyone else, and I really don't understand why you were promoted and I wasn't. I have more years of experience, and we have nearly the same number of collars." Her steady gaze gave him no comfort or answers. Tom sighed and looked away. "Look, sometimes I lose my temper in the heat of the moment. I'm sorry."

"Give me your badge."

Her voice was low but firm. Tom's eyes widened, and his mouth fell open. "What?"

"Now," she ordered. Her tone left no room for refusal.

Silently, Tom dropped his shield into her outstretched hand, and then watched as she balanced the badge on her open palm.

"I always imagined it would be heavier when I was growing up," she confessed in a thoughtful voice that made her companion even more uneasy. "A badge carries so much weight and responsibility, don't you agree?" Her gaze met his.

He knew she was waiting for a response, so he nodded mutely.

"Hmmm..." Rising to her feet, Crista slowly walked around her desk. "You don't seem very convinced, Tom, but that's not surprising, given your recent performance."

Her heels clicked sharply on the tiled floor with each step, and Tom's breath caught in his throat as she came to a stop directly in front of him. Silently, she lowered herself to sit on the edge of her desk and crossed her legs. In doing so, her skirt rose, revealing almost two inches of her smooth thighs. He struggled to keep his gaze off her lightly-tanned legs. Her words helped steer his focus back to the conversation, though.

"I'm starting to think a demotion isn't really what you need."

That came as a relief, but Tom couldn't help but groan over the only other option that came to mind. "Am I being suspended again?"

Lt. de Marco shook her head. "No. Suspensions don't seem to have a very lasting effect, either."

He swallowed. "Then... are you firing me?" he said, hating that she heard the tremble in his voice.

The intimidating woman considered him, her eyes narrowing. "I thought about it," she admitted, "but I have something else in mind."

The unexpected grin that spread across her face made his eyes widen. He was suddenly reminded of the way she used to smile during her first year in Homicide. They had often accompanied each other to the gym or the bar after completing a shift, depending on how their cases had unfolded that day.

They were both naturally athletic and competitive. Burning off stress over beers or weight training had been a welcome relief. They'd had a good chemistry. That they would hook up seemed inevitable, but when she made Lieutenant, Crista's ambitions and Tom's insecurities had pulled them apart before they could ever get together.

Still, his cock was twitching to life now as he remembered the way she used to grin right before she dominated him in any type of physical challenge. His gaze drifted again to her bare thighs. He regretted how quickly he had thrown away their friendship when she was promoted above him. Her power and confidence had always excited him so much...

Growing uncomfortably aroused with his wandering recollections, Tom glanced up and noticed Crista's smile had grown wider, as though she suspected where his thoughts were straying. Dropping his hands discreetly to his lap to hide any signs of his erection, he asked quietly, "What are you planning to do with me?"

She chuckled. "I'm going to teach you how to wait for permission before acting, even when you're in 'the heat of the moment.'"

"How—"

She cut off his next question with a shake of her head. Uncrossing her legs, she leaned forward and simply ordered, "Stand up."

Tom was on his feet before his mind had fully comprehended her words. He seemed surprised by his instinctive obedience, as well as by the flush of excitement racing through his body. He looked down to meet Christa's gaze. Her hands were on her hips, and her strong chin was pointed up as she watched him.

TOM'S COMPLACENCY surprised Crista as well. She had been uncertain if this course of action was the right way to deal with Tom, but his last reaction assured her that her instincts had been right. Emboldened by his obedience, her next command was issued immediately. "Take off your pants."

A heavy pause ensued, but then her detective slowly drew a deep breath and moved his hands to his belt. He unbuckled the leather and pulled it through the loops, then unfastened the button at the top of his dress pants. His zipper came open with a faintly audible, metallic *ziiiip*. He paused to wipe his sweaty palms on his hips and glanced at her.

Crista met his gaze coolly; her face was masked with a professional, closed expression that hid the excitement growing rapidly inside her. "Take them off," she said, her voice uninflected.

He obeyed. Tom roughly pushed his pants over his narrow hip bones and let the fabric drop to the floor. His cock was hard and visibly straining against the front of his boxers. Before she could comment, Tom hooked his thumbs on the band of his boxers and lowered that garment as well.

He then straightened, fully exposing his lower half. Tom might not know what her intentions were, but his body made it perfectly clear he was excited to find out. Crista caught a hint of his earlier cockiness in his shining eyes and frowned.

"Did I give you permission to take off your shorts?" she asked in a dangerously soft voice.

Tom's dark brown eyes widened slightly, and a faint flush began to climb up his neck. "I thought..."

Lt. de Marco's hand shot out and grasped her companion's stiff manhood before he could finish his sentence. He gasped loudly and jerked backwards, but her tight grip kept him in place. She gave him a little squeeze, just to make sure she had his full attention, before beginning her lesson. "You don't act without my permission."

"Yeah, yeah! I got it."

But Crista didn't loosen her hold. "Even if you *think* you know what I'll say, you wait until I give the order. Understood?"

Tom nodded quickly.

Crista held out her empty hand. "Give me your tie."

FOCUSING WAS hard with her strong hand wrapped around his cock, but Tom managed to pull the silk tie loose and handed it to her. She released her grip on his erection so she could stretch the tie between her hands. As she fingered the sleek fabric, she asked, "Do you have your cuffs with you?"

Tom' shaft twitched, drawing attention to the bead of pre-cum glistening on the tip of his penis as he pulled his state-issued handcuffs from the inner pocket of his jacket.

He offered them, but she shook her head. "Take off your coat and shirt, and then cuff your hands behind your back."

Tom's heart hammered in his chest as he complied with the first half of her request, but when he slid his shirt over his shoulders and felt the breeze from the overhead vent blow over his bare skin, he hesitated. "I didn't lock the door," he started. "Anyone could walk in..."

An amused smile tugged at Crista's full lips. "Do you really think anyone will interrupt us after the outburst you just made?" she asked, before staring pointedly at the handcuffs.

The metal was cold as he clamped them around his

wrists, and he felt a chill of anticipation pass through him.

Crista reached behind him to test the tightness of the restraints before gripping his cock again.

He exhaled loudly as she moved her hand slowly up and down his shaft, applying just enough pressure to make his erection swell to its full size. When he was fully aroused, she reached for the tie.

His breath shuddered as she made the first knot. The silk tie was smooth against the sensitive skin of his cock, but as she carefully bound his shaft from its base, working upwards, the pressure began to mount. As his lieutenant wrapped the fabric higher up his cock, the blood flow was restricted and his pleasure swelled.

She made a final knot and left a long section of the thin end of the tie dangling from the top, just below the head of his dick. She pulled on that loose end now, stretching his stiff erection downwards and making him moan loudly as the blood flow was restricted further.

"Oh *god*," he gasped. "I think I'm gonna—"

"No. You're not." Her voice was firm, as was her grip. "Not until I give you permission."

Tom started to protest, but a quick jerk on the tie cut off his complaints. Instead, he braced himself and distracted his thoughts from the hot, fierce pressure building up in his cock as Crista's hand encircled his penis once more and slowly rubbed him from base to tip. Combined with the tight pressure of the tie, Tom felt close to his limit.

The metal links of the handcuffs clinked loudly as Tom unconsciously tested the strength of the restraints. His body ached for more contact. Crista's touch was so agonizingly slow. "Please," he finally moaned, as her hand reached the top of his shaft and her fingers lingered lightly on the tip. He was dripping with arousal and desperate to climax. "Please, let me come."

Crista's thumb glided over his slit in a lazy circle. "Are you asking for my permission?"

"Yes!" he gasped, his voice cracking on the word.

Her other hand drifted between his legs to cup his balls, and her voice softly whispered, "What if I say no?"

"Please don't," he begged, thrusting his pelvis towards her, hopelessly.

She pulled away her hands from his cock.

He made a hoarse sound of anguish.

"If I say no?" she said slowly.

"Then I'll wait until you say yes," he promised, panting hard. She flashed him that grin he loved so much.

"You say that now, but how do I know you'll remember this lesson when you're caught up in the heat of the moment again?" she asked, throwing his earlier excuse back.

He was too overwhelmed by his arousal to vocalize a clear response. His expression must have given his boss all the answer she needed. Grinning, she gripped him tightly and pumped her left hand up and down his shaft.

Tom came with a groan so loud he knew his peers in the other room could hear him. The build up made the orgasm explode out, and with his cock so tightly bound, his semen shot across his abdomen.

His legs were trembling, and his arms ached from being restrained behind him, but any fatigue he felt was flushed instantly from his system when his lieutenant slid a warm palm across his upper chest.

A competitive gleam shone in her dark eyes as their gazes met, and his pulse quickened as she unfastened her own badge and set it down on the desk beside his.

"Go make sure the door is locked," she directed, as her hands hastily unbuttoned her blouse.

Tom wasted no time following his superior's order.

RENOVATING THE HEART

ROBIE MADISON

"**W**hat the fuck were you thinking?"

My two brothers said—shouted really, in perfect unison no less—when curiosity finally led them up the path from the main cottage to the Little Cabin to investigate the "unholy din." Their words. Their voices sounded judgmental as they exchanged glances that plainly said what *they* were thinking.

At forty-one, their little sister was, evidently, experiencing a midlife crisis.

I didn't bother to confirm or deny the allegation. Their big-brother attitude made it clear they weren't really interested in listening. Besides, I wasn't sure I could adequately put into words why I'd ripped out the walls to the studs.

That evening I received an invitation to a barbecue. Resistance was futile. I accepted with a modicum of grace. Letting those two believe they were doing me a big favor never paid.

My brothers cooked dinner and refused my offer to help clean up. I didn't protest. For all I knew, this would be my only midlife crisis, so I intended to take full advantage.

Beer bottle in hand, I could at least be considerate and not use a glass, I slouched in a chair at the table and ignored the glances my brothers were once again giving each other as they washed and dried the dishes. I appreciated the TLC, but I'd kick both their asses if they gave me any pity.

"What are you doing now that you're—" One brother started to ask, a plate and a dishtowel in his hands. He promptly shut up when he received an elbow in the ribs for his effort.

Okay, so my brothers, my parents, and the whole extended family were worried about me. Hell, *I* was worried about me. But no one wanted to utter, let alone talk about the seven-letter "D"-word.

Divorce.

My divorce. I repeatedly had to remind myself I needed to own it. Half of it, anyway.

"Mom and Dad will be back at the end of the month," my other brother said, without even bothering to turn around and look at me.

Message received. Our aging parents had decided to travel while they were still "go-go," but they hadn't transferred ownership of the summer compound to the three of us to see it destroyed. More importantly, while my brothers might be willing to feed me, neither of them was prepared to help me clean up my mess.

Divorce mess. Cabin mess.

Yes, I could see how my brothers might well conclude that my destructive madness this afternoon was a delayed response to my divorce, which had been granted earlier in the summer.

Now I'd been put on notice. I had a month to get my act together.

How? I wanted to ask but knew such a question was futile. I was the first person in my family to divorce. I was a trailblazer on a road I never thought I'd travel. I knew with absolute certainty my family loved me, but I could have done with a little less respecting of my personal space and a lot more reassurance that I hadn't just made the biggest mistake of my life.

I sat a little straighter, determined to look mature and responsible, even if I hadn't acted the part this afternoon. The end of my marriage might have demolished my heart, but that was no excuse to wreck a family heritage site. Our grandparents built the Little Cabin seventy-odd years ago, and while several upgrades had been done a few decades ago, even my brothers couldn't argue the place was due for a major renovation.

I was groping for a way to present this brilliant idea to my brothers, as though it had been my plan all along, when I realized I was staring at the perfect solution. On a square piece of paper, pinned to the fridge by four plastic, yellow magnet flowers, our mother had written in her neat hand, *Call Mr. Fix-It*. A phone number was dutifully printed underneath those momentous words.

Mr. Fix-It was, of course, not his real name, which was something prosaic like Smith or Jones. But that knowledge had been lost long ago when our mother created the nickname after an especially epic plumbing disaster forced the five of us to escape the main cottage for the cabin. As I remember it, my brothers pitched a tent near the parking lot, rather than bunk down like sardines in the small living room with me.

That night I slept in my old room at the main cottage. After my rampage, the Little Cabin was unfit for human habitation. The next morning, I followed my brothers up the hill to their cars and waved goodbye. They were heading back to Toronto and their homes, their families, and their jobs.

I tried, and failed, not to think about the fact that I currently had none of those things. The condo I'd shared with my ex had been sold. The proceeds divided quite civilly. No kids, so no custody battle, thank God. I'd even quit my job. Which sounded totally insane given the upheaval in my personal life, but then I'd worked with the person I'd been living with. The lines got too blurred, even for me.

If I was having a mid-life crisis, I was going full throttle.

I poured myself another cup of tea and phoned Mr. Fix-It.

Mrs. Fix-It called me dear and assured me someone would be right over.

WHICH WAS how I met Jeremy.

Not Mr. Fix-It, but one of his sons.

I had a lazy, summer memory of one or other of Mr. Fix-It's three sons trailing after him whenever he'd come out on a job. I didn't remember the grown-up Jeremy at all with his super-short brown hair and a neatly trimmed beard and mustache that made him look like he was in his mid-thirties, at best. But then my visits to the cottage had been sporadic in recent years.

He resembled his father enough to reassure me he was imbued with the Fix-It gene. He certainly looked the part in faded jeans held up by a pair of black suspenders that matched his T-shirt and his work boots. And he'd arrived in a large truck with a toolbox in the back, apparently ready to get to work.

I stuck out my hand. "Hi, I'm Victoria Carmichael."

With a shove, he slammed the door of his truck and stepped forward, right into my personal space.

His move forced me to look way up. He was barely six feet tall, but that meant he still towered over me. In the heels

I habitually wore to work, but had no use for at the cottage, I was five-five.

"Yeah, I know," he said.

His hand easily engulfed mine. Calloused fingers tickled my palm, but I didn't laugh, too fascinated by the slide of rough skin against smooth. Tendrils of heat licked at my wrist, and for an instant something very like desire stirred inside me. I couldn't be sure. It had been so damn long. Before I could grab hold of the sensation, he let me go.

"The Little Cabin, right?" He strode off in the correct direction.

A big clue his question had been rhetorical.

Bemused, I stood rooted to the spot.

What the hell had just happened? I'd always been more attracted to brains than beefcake. Metrosexual types with trendy glasses, sharp suits, and wiry bodies honed at a gym. But after spending months in absentia, my sex drive had other very intriguing ideas.

Then my brain kicked in, computed what he'd said, and I raced after Jeremy. When I'd called this morning, I'd told Mrs. Fix-It I was planning a reno, not that I'd started the process.

When I reached the cabin, he was standing with his arms crossed, surveying the interior. His brawny frame blocked the doorway. I didn't need to see inside. I already knew what the Little Cabin looked like in the rational light of a new day. The main living space was an unholy mess.

I crossed my arms, too, and took a look anyway.

Jeremy's biceps were freaking huge. I spent a full minute and a half indecently mesmerized by his well-muscled physique. I spent the subsequent thirty seconds estimating that both my hands would definitely not span one of his arms. Around minute number three, I faced the shameful yet tempting truth. I was ogling beefcake.

I'd experienced a case of insta-lust a time or two, maybe even three or four, while I'd been married. The fact that I'd been committed to someone else hadn't precluded me from looking and admiring. I may have scrutinized an especially fine male form. I may even have had a few stray daydreams. Both were perfectly healthy, legal activities. But never once had I converted thought to action.

This time, though, I was *not* married. This time, I could take my thoughts as far as I wanted.

I thought about Jeremy when we'd met at the compound's parking lot.

I'd been out of the dating game for a decade, but I was reasonably certain I wasn't the only one who had felt a flicker of interest back there.

Hello, he'd dropped my hand and left pretty damn fast.

Still, I was uncharacteristically unsure of my next move.

I actually liked having a plan. I liked structure. I liked being an organized person, thus creating the illusion I was in control. Recently, though, I'd done such an excellent job of deconstructing my life, I could no longer even imagine what a next move looked like.

"You do this?" Jeremy asked as he kicked aside a couple of wood panels with his steel-toed boot.

My random thoughts about seducing the handyman crashed along with the boards, creating a fresh pile of rubble. I ordered myself to ignore my hormones and stay focused on the job of renovating the cabin.

I looked up.

He looked down at me, frown lines creasing his forehead.

He was clearly waiting for an answer. I tried, and failed, not to notice his eyes were a deep sea green.

"As opposed to did I have help?" I asked, unable to stop the sarcasm from slipping into the words.

Defense was a lousy default strategy. That didn't mean I

was about to apologize for being capable. All it ever took was one stray comment, and I stepped into the ring. Ready to defend a woman's right to wield a crowbar or a sledgehammer or a—

He leaned in so close I could count the laugh lines around those amazing eyes. In the ten seconds before he opened his mouth, I wondered what it would take to make him laugh.

"Yeah, as *opposed to* did you have help doing all this over the weekend, because the cabin was in pristine condition when I was here Friday morning?"

His tone was surprisingly conversational given the attitude. But then I was the one who'd made assumptions. About him. About myself. Apparently, he hadn't been questioning my abilities at all.

He turned away, breaking whatever the hell spell he kept putting on me and walked along one of several pathways I'd created through the debris toward the other side of the room. About three quarters of the way, he stopped, pivoted, and used the toe of his boot to lift a sizable, jagged triangle of glass.

Mom had been talking about replacing the cracked mirror for years. Yesterday, I'd made an executive decision to speed the process along.

"You're in for seven years' bad luck," he said.

"Nine actually." I shrugged. "Though to be fair, the first two were half decent, so seven sounds about right."

Although I don't ascribe to superstitions, I was in no position to take one on.

"Half decent," he muttered as though testing the phrase. "As opposed to great, spectacular, love of your life?"

Jeremy, I was learning, was not a "Hi, how are you?" "Fine, thanks" kind of guy. When he asked a question, he seriously wanted an answer.

"Yeah, as opposed to good."

The simple, yet oh so complex truth. My marriage hadn't been terrible. It just hadn't been very good, either.

He moved his foot away, and the piece of mirror fell, perfectly intact, back onto the floor.

Figures.

"Here's to my seven years," he said.

Then he stomped on it. Hard.

A yelp of surprise whispered across my lips. Not because of the noise made by the glass shattering into a gazillion pieces. At least that was what I told myself. No, I was far more startled by what Jeremy had just admitted.

What I had admitted to him. I had just confessed more about my marriage to this man than I had to my family. I also had the distinct impression, because he was now staring at the wreckage in the kitchen and not me, that Jeremy's confession had been equally unexpected.

I stepped into the room, not quite sure what to say. I was sorry. Of course I was. Failing at a relationship, at love, didn't look good on the resume of life. It felt worse. Yet at the same time, a part of me was grateful for those few words.

They meant I wasn't the only one stumbling around trying to figure out how to move on.

"Stop. Don't move."

His voice was calm, clear, and commanding. I froze.

In three strides he was beside me. He grabbed my arm and tugged.

I stumbled and landed against his chest with a soft "oomph." A girly response for a woman in the midst of a midlife crisis, but then I'd always thought the phrase "he was built like a brick wall" a romance novel exaggeration. Apparently not.

"You may know how to rip out walls, but it's damn dangerous in here," he said.

He kicked out, dislodging another board only inches

from where I'd been standing. This one had a big-ass nail sticking out of it.

Up until now I'd held my own. Verbal sparring as fore-play. Game on. But just like that the tension in the room—between us—shifted abruptly, becoming far more intimate.

The heat of his hand on my skin where he gripped my arm. The brush of his fingers against my T-shirt, the slightest movement caressing my breast. The sharp ache deep in my core.

"You can let me go now," I said, pleased my voice sounded more or less normal.

I didn't care about the wannabe compliment or the nail. I wasn't being stupid or reckless. I simply did not need rescu-ing. Damsel in distress wasn't a role I wanted to play.

He released me.

Reluctantly, I thought. I knew he wouldn't step away. I didn't either.

"The cabin may have been tidy, but it was outdated by at least two decades," I said. "Why were you here Friday morning?"

My brothers hadn't said a word about maintenance work. I should have kicked both their asses. I was an equal partner. One who didn't need to be coddled.

"I've been looking after the place this year."

"Then you'll take on the reno job?"

A smile touched his lips. "I have to, or Dad will give me grief for ruining the Fix-It family reputation."

He didn't sound terribly grief stricken over the prospect.

"Ah, you read my mom's note on the fridge," I said, and like an idiot I smiled back.

My panties were wet. My face felt hot. My heart—my heart had only the most tenuous hold on hope it could heal.

I gestured toward the debris. "I did do all this myself. I'll help you clean it up."

He gave me the once-over, clearly assessing my attire.

Like him, I was dressed in a T-shirt and jeans. I was even wearing sensible footwear. A pair of old running shoes, though I would admit they were no match against a rusty nail.

Somehow, he found a pair of heavy duty work gloves that fit me.

I stood patiently and actually listened while he reviewed work safety rules.

When I'd first started my impetuous reno, I'd bashed a few holes into the walls, stood back to take a look at my handiwork, and decided it might be prudent not to destroy the furnishings and the kitchenware. Even though I'd been challenged to shove the furniture onto the deck and pack up the small kitchen, tearing apart the place had been a lot more fun than cleaning up the mess I'd made.

Relationship mess. Cabin mess. Maybe I'd invented a new form of therapy. If so, the work was hot, sweaty, and dirty. Not my usually thing, but the tangible act of throwing out crap was definitely very cathartic.

I dumped another load into the rear of Jeremy's truck. He'd backed it up close to the front door of the cabin for convenience. Then I pulled off one of the work gloves and tugged off the baseball cap I'd put on to keep my hair and the sun out of my face.

The day had turned humid, and I resented the heavy denim, the runners, even the T-shirt I wore seemed too much. As part of his onsite safety, Jeremy had regularly mandated breaks to rehydrate. I decided to call one and ducked around the side of the cabin to the deck where we'd stashed a big cooler filled with bottles of water.

I opened a fresh bottle, but instead of taking a drink, I dumped the contents over my head. Water cascaded through my hair and down the back of my neck and over my face. I closed my eyes and tipped my face toward the sun.

A shadow blocked the heat. I could sense this even with my eyes shut. And then his lips made contact with mine, cautiously at first, so as not to startle me. I barely noticed when the empty water bottle fell from my hand.

His mustache brushed lightly against my skin. This was a new experience, kissing a man with facial hair, but the second I started to analyze it, I ordered my brain to shut up, determined to give in to the moment and the sensations.

We stood there, not touching except where our mouths were locked together oh so innocently. Then his tongue ventured forth along the seam of my lips.

My heart was wary about taking the risk. But, my hormones didn't give a damn. I moaned, the reaction instinctive and primal, and I opened my mouth to tangle my tongue with his.

Blindly, I touched the soft cotton of his T-shirt and yanked. His laughter broke us apart, but I didn't care. I opened my eyes so I could watch his face.

He reached out and cupped my face in his hand. His thumb caressed my cheek, caught a stray drop of water, and brushed it away.

"You didn't need to pour a bottle of water over your head to cool down. We can go for a swim."

"Maybe later," I said, still determined to part him from his T-shirt.

His suspenders were impeding my progress. I slid them off his shoulders.

He obliged by tugging the tee free from his jeans and over his head.

"Later." He agreed and threw the shirt against the wall where it slid into a heap on top of one of the boxes containing kitchenware that I'd stacked against the side of the cabin.

I skimmed my hands across his chest and down his flat stomach to the faded denim waistband, fascinated by the soft, brown fur that covered his torso.

"Now who's the one in danger?" I asked, my fingers working their magic to undo the button on his fly.

He caught my wrists in his large hands, effectively preventing me from stripping him further.

"Two pieces of clothing to none," he said. "I need to even the odds."

No shirt. Check. But he still had on his jeans and—I glanced down. Ah, he wasn't wearing his work boots, which explained why I hadn't heard him approach until he kissed me. I toed off my running shoes and smiled up at him. His sea-green eyes turned stormy with amusement, and he shook his head ever so slightly.

He took two steps back, dragging me along, until he was leaning against the deck's railing. Another slight tug and I was trapped between his legs, his hard-on pressed against my abdomen. He bent low until his mouth brushed the shell of my ear.

I shivered at the intimacy he created with that one simple move.

"I want you," he said.

"Me, too," I said.

"Good, because I've been waiting the whole damn day for this."

"Me, too." I didn't understand how that was possible. I only knew it was true, and I didn't want this to stop.

These revelations did not distract Jeremy from his objective. Within seconds both my T-shirt and bra were off. Not that I particularly minded since that only meant more pleasure for me. He kissed my jawline until I arched my neck, willingly giving him access. His tongue licked the length of my collarbone, and I thought—I was certain—I begged for more.

The next several minutes were filled with awkward fumbling. Our appetites for each other were voracious. Tongues dueled. We were eager to learn the taste of each other's mouths and skin. I kissed his shoulder, breathing in his musky scent. Freed, my hands could finally investigate his magnificent muscles.

To kiss, to touch, and to keep our balance as we stripped each other, however, was a distinct challenge. I lost—or won, I wasn't quite sure which, when he took his mouth off my body long enough to shove my jeans to my ankles. Before I could return the favor, his hands grasped my waist and lifted me free of the restrictive material. An instant later, I found myself standing on top of the cooler facing the lake, not him.

I was panting and needy and slightly indignant I had once again failed and now lost my chance to unzip his pants.

His teeth clamped down on the base of my neck where it met my right shoulder, stilling any further protest. "Too much?" he whispered a second later, kissing the skin where it stung.

I shook my head. This type of aggression was new, too, but I couldn't summon even the feeblest of feminist rhetoric against such a blatantly barbaric act.

My hormones really didn't give a damn. My cunt was dripping wet.

In an effort to steady my precarious position, if not my emotions, I clutched the railing.

"More then?" He sounded amused and perhaps a little desperate.

A square foil packet appeared in my line of vision.

I choked on a laugh. The air around me barely stirred it was so heavy. I was only vaguely aware of the rustle of some animal in the foliage below and the sound of water lapping against the dock. It was the middle of the day, and I was stark naked on the deck with its fantastic view of the lake, bent over like some carnal offering to the gods of nature. And Jeremy.

"Yes, please."

He readied himself, and then his hand slid around my hip and down to cup my mound as though he needed to make sure I was wet. His finger found my clit, and I thrust up my ass. Seeking him, seeking more, I was so damn needy.

He added a second finger and slid down and deep inside me. His fingers pumped once, twice.

I sobbed when he withdrew to paint lazy squiggles along my abdomen, coating my skin with my juices. I shoved back, more insistent this time. That seemed to be the signal he was waiting for and, gripping my hips to steady us both, he plunged inside of me.

Delicious sensations bombarded me, and I clenched my secret inner muscles. Jeremy's grunt of satisfaction was encouraging. With great care and concentration, I crossed my ankles, which had the effect of tightening my vagina even more. He hissed his pleasure, yet somehow managed to slow his thrusts. At which point, he continued his leisurely exploration of my body.

One hand played with my breasts, tweaking my nipples into hard nubs. His other hand relentlessly teased my clit. And throughout, he couldn't seem to stop kissing me—my shoulders, my spine, well, most of it, and the super-sensitive and slightly ticklish spot behind my ear.

I shook my head, not sure I could take much more. And in the next breath told him what I would do with him if he stopped. The sensual overload left me literally trembling on the verge of orgasm.

And then, the instant before I was sure I would tip over

into oblivion, he stilled. I was about to scream in frustration when I heard it, the putt-putt-putt of an outboard motor heading along the shoreline toward us.

Holy crap! It was the middle of the day, and we were stark naked on the deck fucking like bunnies. Dazed and momentarily panicked, I let go of the railing. My rash move upset the perfect alignment of our bodies.

"Easy," Jeremy said as he pulled out of me.

I really did want to scream then. I would have fallen over —I'd forgotten my ankles were crossed—if Jeremy hadn't snaked his arm around my waist and caught me. I twisted round to face him.

"We—" I began.

"Haven't finished," he said. "Hang on."

I barely had time to settle my hands on his shoulders, before his hands skimmed across my bottom and hoisted me into his arms. Instinctively, I wrapped my legs around his waist.

"That's it," he said and slipped his cock back inside me.

Oh My God, I couldn't believe how good that felt. But while I was all for this new position, we were still stark naked on the deck, in full view of the lake, and with zero escape options. I thought longingly of the bedroom in the Little Cabin, which I'd left intact, but even though we'd spent the morning cleaning the place, it was now a bona fide construction zone.

I grinned at Jeremy. "The trail's downhill to the cottage. Nice and bouncy. This should be fun."

Even if we made the dash to the cottage, we'd be even more exposed than we were right this second.

"Smart ass," he said as he headed farther down the length of the deck.

In an instant, I understood his naughty plan. When I'd shoved the couch onto the deck, I'd positioned it with its back against the railings. Steps away from relative safety, we spotted the boat rounding the point.

Jeremy dove for cover. For an instant, we were flying through the air. He landed with a bounce on the cushions, pulling me down into his warm embrace.

His chest hairs tickled my already sensitive breasts. I slid my hands up the side of his face. Drawing closer for a soul kiss seemed the most natural thing to do. This time though our passion was lazy and slow.

His fingers made lazy patterns up and down my spine. His thrusts were shallow and teasing, and I kept my mouth on his for fear I'd cry out. I did whimper when his fingers teased their way past the crease in my ass.

I don't know how long we explored each other, rather frantic with need and yet incongruously content to hover on the edge of insanity.

He lifted his head and kissed my eyes, my forehead, my nose, and then whispered a single word, "Now."

I didn't know or care if it was a question or a command. I buried my head against his shoulder to stifle my cry as I came. His shout was loud in my ear, but I no longer cared if anyone heard.

Afterward, I was content to lie in his arms. The steady beat of his heart comforted me. As for my own heart—my heart felt full of plans for the future.

I decided I should winterize the cabin and ask old man Harrington if he'd plow this section of the cottage road. Then I'd have a place to live if I accepted a job I'd been offered in nearby Port Royal.

I hadn't realized I'd been talking aloud until the body beneath mine tensed. Of course, when he wasn't looking after vacation properties, Jeremy had a contracting business, a home, a life in Port Royal.

I sat up. "No strings and no obligations," I said, and I meant it.

"What if I want a few strings?" he asked.

He pulled me back down on top of him.

Intrigued by the possibilities, I went willingly.

What if...

FULL OF THE WILD LIFE

TRAY ELLIS

Lennox, Alaska
1989

Carrie Abaco stretched in bed. She pointed her toes and raised her arms. Something gently popped along her spine, and she relaxed again. Her body heat warmed a small section of the bed, keeping the early morning crispness at bay. When she'd pointed her toes, she'd discovered a colder patch beneath the blankets. The seasons shifted again, as they always did. The comparative warmth of the fleeting Alaskan summer ebbed away into an early fall.

She didn't mind the cooler bed in the summer. In fact, she appreciated not being sweltered all night long by the length of another body pressing so close to hers. As soon as summer waned, though, she longed for her absent bedmate. Keegan Porter kept the bed nice and warm, like a constantly blazing heat source, whom she could wrap her arms and legs around. The overly sultry summer bed-sharing, though, was the only downside she could count against having Keegan around all the time. Excepting that, she missed him terribly.

Carrie yawned and flipped away the covers. She rolled out of bed and eyed the calendar tacked to the wall. She'd placed a bevy of red stars, marked with a red felt tip pen, on today's date.

Keegan returned from the wilds for one week of vacation. Then he'd go back for another three-month surveying session before Alaskan winter would finally shut down the surveying operation. Spring would make it possible for people to tramp around in the wilderness again, but in the meantime, Keegan settled into her home for the winter. That late fall date had stars drawn in gold and silver on the calendar.

Usually Carrie pulled on jeans and a T-shirt and carried around a windbreaker to cut the occasional chill. Clothing needed to be functional and comfortable for work, not overly revealing. Carrie had a boyfriend, and she didn't need to attract unwanted attentions from other guys. Today, she yearned to look nicer. She wanted Keegan to remember why he returned to her, and perhaps why he should consider giving up his surveying job to stay in town.

She combed through her closet. She liked wearing pants, but those didn't show off her best asset. Her long, slim legs looked way better when she wore a skirt. A short cherry red skirt, with black flowers embroidered close to the hem, that stopped a few inches above her knees would pair well with a white cotton blouse cropped at her waist, giving her a trim figure. She pulled on the outfit and twirled in front of the full-length mirror on the inside of her closet door. Her honey-colored hair curled all around her face, and her dark hazel eyes took on a certain pizzazz with the red and white color combination that surprised her. She looked vibrant, and she liked it. She resembled a woman out of the fashion magazines. A blue jean jacket completed the ensemble and would keep her warm while she walked to work.

Carrie lived less than a quarter mile from the Elk Rack Lodge, which her mom and dad owned and operated. They'd bought out the previous owner ten years ago when her dad was compensated with insurance money for an injury received while out on a commercial fishing boat. Her two sisters helped sometimes, in between managing their growing families. A small, but competent, staff kept the Lodge running smoothly in all other aspects.

In her twenties, Carrie had rebelled against the family and living in Alaska. She'd gone to college down in the lower forty-eight and stayed there. She'd earned her degree in Hotel Management, and she'd also earned a broken heart and wasted-away bank account from the likes of one smarmy, quick-talking love 'em and leave 'em jerk. She'd slunk home, embarrassed and poor, and her family took her back as if no time had passed. It had taken a few years for her confidence to rebuild, and even longer for her desire for another partner to return.

Carrie didn't bother with breakfast or coffee in her own home. Plenty could be found at the lodge. She brushed her teeth and set off for work.

"Oh la la!" called out Amy, the desk clerk, when Carrie entered. "Look at you!" She stepped around the desk to look Carrie up and down and flash a thumbs-up. "Gorgeous."

Carrie liked Amy. They'd grown close since spending so much time together at the front desk. Amy was quite a bit younger, with a lot of aspirations and a very optimistic attitude that should get her where she wanted. Sometimes, Carrie envied Amy's positivity, but usually, she recognized its value and let it give her own mental status a buoyant boost.

Natalie popped into the foyer from the entrance to the kitchen where the continental breakfasts were prepared. "You do look extra nice," she said. Her dark hair swished past her face as she shook her head in confusion. A bulb seemed to go off in her head, and her brown eyes sparkled. "I bet I know what today is!"

"Me, too!" Amy hopped up and down and clapped her hands together.

Carrie didn't blush. Dating a man for six years meant everyone knew they were intimate. This wasn't an early romance. Carrie gave them both smiles. "Yes, Keegan comes in today." She brushed past Natalie into the kitchen area.

"What are your plans for tonight?" Natalie asked as she returned to clearing up the mess on the serving trays.

Continental breakfast had already been available for a few hours, and the guests tended to make a terrible mess. Carrie wondered if they were so sloppy in their own homes, or if they let themselves be messy because they knew someone else would clean up after them at the Lodge.

"I bought steaks and enormous potatoes for baking," Carrie said. "Sour cream, butter, and some chives I'll chop up. And an apple pie for dessert. We're staying in."

"Of course you are," Natalie said. She didn't add any twist or nuance to her words. She made it a commonsense statement. "Man's been eating nothing but sandwiches, jerky, dried fruit, and candy bars for weeks."

"And drinking and washing in bleach-sanitized water pumped up from the nearby river." Carrie stuck out her tongue in distaste. "Gross." Her reputation as a frontier sort of girl was always a bit shaky. She liked town plumbing and town water systems.

Carrie poured herself a cup of coffee from the carafe and doctored it liberally with cream and sugar. Then she picked up a lemon Danish and nibbled one edge. Lemon always seem to be left over. Everyone gobbled up the cheese, cherry, and strawberry Danishes first. Carrie didn't mind. She loved the sweet and sour lemon goo in the middle of the pastry.

Natalie chuckled. "Bless his adventurous heart. I surely

wouldn't want to be out there doing that job." She shuddered. "Too many bears and too many mosquitoes."

Carrie sipped at her coffee. "There are bears and mosquitoes here, too." Everyone kept their trash locked away until shortly before pick up, because audacious bears rambled wherever they pleased. No one could control the enormous swarms of mosquitoes.

"Yeah, I know. But not quite as many."

Carrie nodded. "The region is very primitive." *And dangerous*, she thought.

Keegan laughed off the danger, saying he'd easily passed the federal Bear Safety and Firearm Qualification course, and he got to carry around a sawed-off shotgun with special lead slug ammunition. Besides, nobody had been mauled in years. His job was perfectly safe, he'd told her numerous times.

His assurances didn't stop Carrie from having nightmares. When she wasn't dreaming about rampaging bears, she dreamed about horrible chainsaw mishaps.

Sobered from thinking about all the challenges Keegan faced on a daily basis, Carrie finished her breakfast and went to help Amy at the desk.

The morning rolled by slowly, and Carrie imagined she could hear the float plane roaring in every other minute, which she never could because the Lodge was too far away. Only tourists and general customers ambled in and out of the Lodge, although Carrie perked up every time someone entered. Her mom flitted by briefly, reminding her that Carrie and Keegan were invited to dinner later that week.

Carrie crouched behind the counter to organize loose papers and pens. Somehow, the lower shelves always got jumbled by the end of the day.

"Hey. When you're off work, can I walk you home?"

Carrie's heart hammered in her chest, and she jumped straight up.

Keegan stood at the desk, looking scruffy, tired, and very happy to be there.

"I'm done now," Carrie said. She bustled around the desk and rushed into Keegan's arms. He kissed and hugged her, and she kissed and hugged him back. He smelled freshly scrubbed. His bushy beard frazzled her chin, and she remembered how she had to get used to that every time he returned. Even though the lower half of his face was obscured by facial hair, his eyes remained the kindly blue she'd fallen in love with.

He looked just as he had three months ago when he'd left for another surveying season. Moderately tall, compact, strong, and wiry thin, he had the perfect build for thriving in the wilderness on modest amounts of food and never-ending amounts of exercise and effort.

"Have a nice afternoon," Amy called to them, her voice full of sunshine and glee.

Carrie waved at her, hardly turning her head. She and Keegan linked up hands, and Carrie grabbed her jean jacket with one free hand.

"How was your trip?" she asked as they strolled down the street, headed to her small house.

"Long," Keegan said. He pulsed his grip around her hand. "You look really nice."

"Thank you." Carrie glanced down to their hands. Even Keegan's fingernails were as clean as they'd ever been. Months out bushwhacking through understory nearly every day tended to leave them ragged and filthy, but he must have scrubbed them dutifully before coming to see her. The nails shined and only the barest hint of stain remained on his fingers and under his nails.

She unlocked the front door.

They stepped over the threshold. The moment the door closed behind them, Keegan's arms went around her.

"I've been waiting for this," he said, breathing the words against her neck. He kissed and nipped at the skin from the notch at her throat to the rounded end of her jaw line. "I missed you so much."

"I missed you, too." Carrie pulled him farther into the room. They stumbled together, Keegan not letting go, and collapsed onto her sofa.

Keegan paused, his gaze fastening on hers. "Are you still —" He let the words hang.

He'd never been good at voicing delicate issues.

"Yes," Carrie said, and then deliberately added more information so that there could be no miscommunication. "Still on birth control. And I haven't been sleeping around. You're the only one. You?"

Some women worked out in the wilderness as part of the surveying crews. Opportunities were available, if Keegan wanted to pursue them. Carrie's heart thumped in her chest. Cheating was always a sensitive topic. Her once-broken heart never did seem to entirely heal.

"Only you," Keegan promised. "I don't want anyone but you. You know that." He went back to licking her neck, but didn't remain there long. He rubbed his bearded face down the center line of her chest, his hands cupping along the sides.

It tickled, and she giggled.

He pulled at the blouse, searching for buttons or zippers. Confusion crossed his face. "How do I get this off?" he asked. "It's too nice for me to—"

Carrie wiggled her hands free from where he'd trapped them between their bodies. "Scoot off," she said.

He reluctantly moved away.

She quickly pulled the blouse over her head and deftly unfastened her bra.

Keegan tugged at the waistband of her skirt, finding the zipper and sliding it down.

Carrie shimmied and slid off her skirt and underwear.

"You, too," Carrie said.

Keegan yanked his jeans down and his shirt off. He didn't bother with underwear, so there was none to remove. He reached for her again, his hands clasping her solidly around the hips, the waist, traveling down to brush against her thighs. He leaned back down to capture her mouth in a long kiss.

With one hand, he touched her in all the right places, making stars appear before her eyes. Warmth spread all through her body, and she felt as if she were flying to pieces and being put back together again. Keegan moved into her, and they rocked together for what seemed like hours. He grunted and moaned, each sound a punctuation of exhilaration and effort.

Carrie thrilled to hear him, the noises a concrete reminder that they blended together like butter and honey. Jubilation rushed through her again, and she gasped, pushing at Keegan's chest. Her motion triggered something in him, because he grunted and every muscle in his body went rigid beneath her touch, and then sublimely soft.

With a mellow sigh, he curled around her.

She kissed him, shifted to a more comfortable position, and they fell asleep on the sofa.

A little while later, Carrie opened her eyes. Keegan remained asleep next to her. His face was placid, although his position on the sofa couldn't have been comfortable.

Oh, passion, thy name is a pulled back muscle. She didn't regret their inability to make it past the living room and to the bedroom. Three months was a long time to wait. She extricated herself from the sofa, stretched out her muscles from the cramped position, and spent a minute in the bathroom. She pulled on her most comfortable pair of sweatpants and shirt, and then went to the kitchen.

She prepared the potatoes first, washing them and wiping them dry. She slathered them with olive oil, salt, and pepper before wrapping them in foil and placing them in the preheated oven. The steaks she stared at for a moment.

Keegan enjoyed doing the cooking where steaks were concerned, it being some primal male activity that secured a man's position within the male hierarchy of manliness. Not that Keegan needed to worry about that. He trekked around the back country of Alaska, flying around in choppers, brandishing a chain saw, living in tents, and burying steel and copper monuments into the ground to delineate property line boundaries. Keegan had machismo activities down pat.

A soft noise alerted her that Keegan entered the kitchen. He'd pulled his jeans on, leaving his abdomen and arm muscles on view. Daily hard work gave him a chiseled, lean appearance. His brown hair was tousled, sticking up adorably and ridiculously on one side, advertising he needed a haircut badly. His beard seemed twice as voluminous as before. He looked at her, realizing after a moment what she was staring at.

He reached up to touch the bulk at his chin. "I can trim and shape it down," he offered. He wouldn't remove it completely. Getting such a healthy beard required more than a week, and he wouldn't want to return to work with his face exposed. The mosquitoes would have a feast.

"I like it," Carrie declared. She turned back to the steaks. "How do you want these done? And do you want to do it?"

Keegan slid in behind her, shadowing her posture, hugging her back to his front. "Sure," he said. Then he rumbled in her ear, "Marry me?"

Carrie stiffened.

"Please?" he asked. "I adore you. You adore me."

Carrie shook her head. Tears welled up in her eyes, and she resolutely tried to force them away. "No. Not with your job. You're always gone."

Keegan laughed, somewhat bitterly. "But you wait for me every three months anyway, and I spend all winter with you. How would being married be any different?"

Carrie twisted in his arms so they were face to face. "Because it would be. Because if we were married, your being away from me for half a year would be worse, feel worse."

Keegan nodded, his beautiful blue eyes very serious as he studied her. "Then, this'll be it."

"It?" Carrie tilted her head.

"I'm contracted for the last three months in the season, and then I'll find something else." He kissed her on the forehead.

Carrie frowned suspiciously. "Not salmon fishing?" A good portion of the jobs in Alaska took a person away from their family for some time. Out into the wilderness. Out onto the cold, fathomless ocean. Out where, sometimes, the person never came home again.

"I'll find something here." Keegan rubbed her shoulders with his hands. "I've got skills. Maybe I can put out my shingle as a handyman."

Carrie snorted. "You can start here at home. I have a whole list waiting. The downstairs toilet needs a new wax ring, it's leaking at the bottom. There's dry rot around the back door jamb. I can't get one of my bedroom windows to close all the way."

"I'll start tomorrow. If—" Keegan pulled a small box out of his jeans pocket. He'd offered it to her twice before, and each time she'd turned him down. Each time he'd been unable to give up his surveying work. In a state where the air was fresher than fresh, he'd loved living it rough and waking up to air so newly minted it sparkled.

Carrie took the small box. She knew it contained a ring with a small, precious diamond. The box fit in the palm of her hand. Keegan wasn't a wealthy man.

"I heard Lou Rogers say yesterday that he'd be looking for a new tour captain for his tourism business. Taking visitors out for short hikes. Sometimes longer ones." The box felt more substantial than ever in her hand.

"I guess I'll go see Lou Rogers tomorrow—before I fix that toilet." Keegan kissed her forehead again. "What do you think?"

Carrie fumbled with the box in her hand. Her breath hitched in her throat, and she felt like she couldn't quite get enough air. Inside the box, the ring sparkled. The diamond seemed larger than she remembered it, and far more beautiful. She tugged it free of its velvet perch. Tears were back in her eyes, but this time, she didn't fight them. A fat one rolled out of her right eye and slid down her cheek in the most inelegant way. Only by sheer will, she didn't blink, and the remainder of the watery tears stayed in her eyes. She sniffled, her nose going soggy even as her throat tightened up.

Keegan brushed away the tear with the tip of one finger.

The roughness of his fingertip reminded her again that he spent his time performing difficult, physical labor.

"Are you sure?" She found a tissue box nearby and wiped at her eyes and nose. She wouldn't let her emotions overwhelm her into making a mistake. "You won't regret giving it up? Come to resent me?"

Keegan shook his head. "Never. Time for a change. Lots of time to think when you're out in the middle of nowhere. I've had my fill of the wild life. I want to settle down, and I'm very serious." He gently rubbed his thumb across her cheek.

"I want to adopt a dog. I want to fix up your house. I want to spend my life with you."

Carrie took a deep breath. She didn't often hear Keegan speak so bluntly about these types of matters. That he did meant more than his words alone, he truly believed what he told her.

"Then, yes. I'll marry you." She slid the ring on her finger. It fit perfectly.

Keegan kissed her on the mouth, brushing her lips with his tongue, and promising a lifetime of passion and commitment.

"Thank you," he said. "I love you, Carrie."

Carrie held up her hand, getting used to the way her hand looked with the ring on. She liked it. "I love you, too, Keegan." She put her left hand on her hip. "Now, you have to prove it. Cook these steaks, and then I'll show you what needs fixing."

Keegan gave her a sloppy, faux salute. "It'll be my complete pleasure."

DELILAH DEVLIN

The hunters I work with all have cool, dangerous-sounding handles: Catch, Dagger, Bulldog. My first day on the job, Dagger nicknamed me Buttercup, and it stuck.

Catch, the hunter who'd founded this agency, decided he needed a bounty hunter with "soft" skills. Someone approachable, whom mamas and girlfriends could confide in. Not that he ever expected I'd have to do the "heavier" tasks, like break down a door or take a target to the ground. Bounty hunting's dangerous work, and not meant for faint-hearted dudes—or girls.

I felt lucky when they called me Buttercup, but mostly, they called me "the girl." Like this morning, when Catch handed out assignments and told Bulldog to take along the girl.

I didn't make a fuss. PC communications weren't part of any office handbook. I knew from day one I had to prove myself. Not that I'd gotten a chance, so far, to show them what I had. Being ex-military, and an ex-cop, didn't earn me any points. I guess it didn't help I was only five-feet-five and a hundred ten pounds soaking wet. Bulldog figured that with blonde hair and blue eyes, I looked more like a high school cheerleader—not a compliment, since he thought girls like that were stupid as hell.

Maybe I didn't help my cause with the way I dressed. Ever since they'd named me Buttercup, I'd done my best to dress the part. Sure, I wore denim, tees, and boots, just like them, but my pink T-shirt emblazoned with "Girl Power," and my purple-calico-lined jean jacket with lace inserts on the pockets, didn't exactly fit with their leather jackets and black tees sporting bike club slogans. The few times I hadn't been tied to a desk making phone calls to relatives to track low-lifes who'd skipped their court dates, I'd been relegated to staying in the truck while the guys did the dirty work.

Not so today, but only because we were going to reach out to Lenny Holcomb's mama to see if she wanted to keep her house, seeing as she'd offered her home as collateral when posting his bond.

Bulldog gave me the evil eye as we walked toward the small, clapboard house on the bad side of town. "Shit goes sideways," he said, "you stand back and let me handle it."

I offered him a non-committal nod. "Think Mrs. Holcomb will give you that much trouble?"

He snorted and skewered me a narrow-eyed glare.

"Ooh," I said in my best little-girl voice and gave an exaggerated shiver, hoping he'd trip over his big feet. Not that I had to pretend my reaction too much. Something about the big burly guy did it for me. His face was too manly to be handsome—square jaw, crooked nose, laser-sharp blue eyes. Thick, gold-brown hair dusted the collar of his jacket. His six-foot-four, heavily-muscled frame made me feel feminine and soft and all those other useless qualities I despised in "helpless" females. Go figure—the thought of those big, hard hands rasping over my skin made me tremble.

At Mrs. Holcomb's door, I knocked.

No response.

I knocked again. Still nothing.

Bulldog stepped to the left and peered into the window. "Don't think anyone's home. And since this is his address of record..." He backed up and raised a booted foot.

"Really want to knock down her door?" I pulled my lock-pick kit from my back pocket and knelt in front of the knob. A couple of twists of my tools, and the lock snicked. I turned the knob and quickly moved away from the door, giving way to Bulldog as he grumbled something under his breath about smartass women and strode inside.

Bulldog's big frame filled my view, so I was taken by surprise when he cussed and rushed toward a hallway.

A crash sounded in a distant room. Light from an open doorway in the back glared as he ran through it. I followed, watching as our target ran for the chain link fence and vaulted it.

Bulldog cussed again, placed a hand on the top of the fence, but when he swung over his big body, the thin metal running through the top caved, and he fell to the dirt.

I picked another spot farther down the fence, grabbed a post and swung over, landing on my booted feet and shooting down the alleyway.

Behind me, I heard grunts and more curses, and finally, "Dammit, Buttercup, wait for me!"

I wasn't waiting for shit. Lenny moved fast for a big boy. He was almost at the end of the alley. If I didn't catch him quickly, I'd lose sight of him, and we'd lose our paycheck. With my breaths coming fast and sweat trickling into my eyes, I sped up, reaching out with my fingertips to snatch a handful of his shirt. With the fabric in my fist, I drew back and swung him.

He went sideways, but he didn't go down. He twisted out

of my grasp and raised his fists, his eyes widening as he looked me up and down, an ugly sneer stretching across his equally ugly face.

He swung.

But I was ready, ducking beneath and coming up to drive my fists into his fat gut, then bouncing back to avoid the next wide swing.

When he didn't connect, his swing carried him forward, and he turned.

I rocketed to his back and wrapped my arm around his throat, grasping my fist to keep my arm in place, as he staggered then went to his knees, his fingers scratching my arms before reaching backward to pull my hair.

But he didn't get a hank. His body crashed forward, bringing me with him, because my arm was trapped beneath his thick neck.

Boots pounded the pavement then slowed.

"Buttercup, need a hand?"

I wheezed, trying to drag in a breath as his weight crushed me against the pavement. "Roll him so I can get back my arm."

Lenny's body rolled to his side.

Bulldog lowered his boot then bent to offer me a hand up. His gaze went to the thick scratches on my arms.

Blood ran in rivulets from the deep gouges.

"Goddammit." Bulldog's scowl was scary as he blew out a deep breath, and then reached behind his neck to pull his T-shirt over his head.

He tossed it at me.

All I could do was stare at the grayscale tattoos covering his shoulders and chest, disappearing into his jeans.

"Wrap this around your arm. You're gonna bleed all over my truck." Then he went down on one knee and locked cuffs around Lenny's fat wrists. When he stood, he kicked the low-life in the ass.

After we'd dropped Lenny at the jail, Bulldog remained silent as we drove.

My arm stung like hell, so I was fine with the quiet for the first while.

His expression was so dark, I didn't dare try to make small talk. When he missed the turnoff to the agency, I straightened and darted a glance his way. His narrowed gaze swung toward me, daring me to say a word. I sat back, my heart thudding hard inside my chest. Just how pissed was he?

Twenty minutes later, we pulled onto a gravel road. Once we passed the first curve, I saw a single-story house ahead. Gray stone and wood. A metal roof. He reached up to hit a button above his windshield, and a garage door rose.

So, this was his house. He'd brought me home. But would he cut me into tiny pieces and feed me to the Rottweiler jumping against the fence, or was he planning to read me the riot act in private, because he intended to yell and didn't want the world to hear?

I hoped for a third option. One where he pushed me face-down over the first piece of furniture we met and delivered his frustration in the sexiest way possible.

He pulled the SUV into the garage, hit the button to lower the door, and then turned to give me another glare. "Get the fuck inside."

I was tempted to chide him about his tone. Not his words. I wanted to be the fuck inside...fucking.

Without a word, I slipped out of the truck and headed to the wooden stairs leading into the house. I stepped inside a mud room then through another door and into the kitchen.

Bulldog entered behind me and closed the door.

His hands grasped my shoulders and turned me toward the table.

My heart stuttered—was this the bending over part? No, he pushed downward, forcing me into a chair.

"Unwrap your arm."

Disappointment turned the corners of my mouth downward. Slowly, because the shirt stuck to the bloody stripes, I peeled away the shirt while he headed toward the sink.

He ran water then pulled a washcloth from a drawer and wet it. Next, he strode back to the table, pulling out a chair to sit beside me. He laid the washcloth over my arm.

It was hot, and I winced.

"Got to soak the blood to loosen it," he said.

His voice was softer but no less growly, and my pulse raced.

When he wiped away the smears of blood, he shook his head. "Should have let him go, Buttercup."

I raised my chin. "Would you have?"

He grunted and completed his task, then stood, opened a cabinet above the stove, and pulled down a first aid kit. After he'd rubbed antiseptic gel over my wounds, he wrapped clean gauze around my arm and secured it with surgical tape.

"Thanks." I kept my eyes cast downward. "But I could have managed on my own."

"I know."

I lifted my head and found him studying me.

"You handled yourself well. I just didn't like you anywhere near that shithead."

"Oh." And because I was feeling off-kilter, his change in demeanor sending my insides swirling, I did what I always do when I feel a little afraid. I brazened it out, giving him a slow, seductive smile and a wink.

Instead of putting him back in his bad mood, his reaction to my taunt was a narrowing of his green eyes. He glanced at my mouth then shot out a hand and wrapped his fingers around the back of my neck to pull me toward him.

When his mouth slammed over mine, I gasped, giving him entry.

Bulldog might have been a big guy, but there was nothing lumbering or bearlike about his reactions. They were lightning fast. His tongue invaded my mouth, pushing past my teeth to stroke my tongue.

I gave a kitten-like mew, very un-me, and melted against him, my hand landing on his broad, bare chest, and my fingers tangling in his hair. Then he gripped my waist and slid me right off my chair onto his lap. Shock blasted through me at how much I liked the quick way he took charge.

He bent me backward, an arm around my shoulders. His free hand slipped between my legs and pushed against the damp denim, cupping me then squeezing my sex. "You're fucking wet, Buttercup," he rasped when he raised his head to let me breathe. Then slowly, daring me with his steady stare, he removed his hand from my crotch and cupped my breast through my clothing. "This okay with you?"

I managed a nod, and before I drew another breath, he went to his feet, with me in his arms, and strode through the house, past a living room filled with deep leather seating, down a hallway, and into a bedroom. His bed was enormous, an Alaska or a Wyoming-size King. He crawled onto the mattress on his knees and stepped toward the center before he set me down. Then he began stripping away my holster, my belt...my tee and bra...my shoes and pants. When the only thing I wore was a pair of bikini panties, he halted, backed off the bed, and began stripping off his own clothing, flinging each piece to the side while he kept his hungry stare on me.

But I wasn't any woman waiting on a man to decide what happened next. I lifted my bottom, scraped down my panties, and threw them at his face.

Magnificently nude, he leapt toward the bed, diving toward the middle.

I rolled away, and just had my feet on the floor, when his arms wrapped around my waist, and he pulled me back against his body. He sat on the edge of the mattress and bracketed my legs with his thick thighs, then smoothed his rough palms over my skin, starting at my breasts then moving down my belly to my pussy. I squirmed in his arms trying to turn, but he kept me faced away as he felt me up, sending tingles through me.

Again, he cupped my breasts, and I felt his tongue slide from the center of my back upward, following my spine. Goose bumps prickled on my skin. My breaths grew short. *Fuck, oh fuck.* I wanted him. "Bulldog," I said, shivering hard inside his embrace.

"Don't fight me, Buttercup. Don't move. Let me do you the way I have to."

He turned me until I faced him.

I stood with my arms at my sides as he raked my body with his gaze. His for the taking, because I wanted to be taken.

I couldn't resist dropping my gaze to his cock, so thick and straight, jerking against his belly to the beat of his heart.

"Fuck, oh fuck," I whispered and shivered hard again.

He reached to the side, slid open a drawer in the night-stand, and pulled out a condom. With his lips pulling back from his teeth, he cloaked himself, then scooted backward on the bed and patted the mattress beside him.

I crawled toward him then lay on my belly beside him, hiding my face against the coverlet, because I knew my expression would give away just how badly I wanted this. I rubbed on the mattress, because my skin burned and my nipples ached.

He kissed my shoulder and climbed over me, his weight

pressing me deep into the mattress as he fisted his hand in my hair and held me down, then slipped his legs, one at a time between mine, waiting for me to open to him.

When he rooted his cock between my legs, my breath shuddered out. His lower body scooped against me, rubbing against my ass as he teased me with the tip of his cock sliding between my slick folds.

His teeth dragged on my earlobe, and he whispered, "I'm gonna fuck you up, babe. Fuck hard and deep. You ready, Buttercup?"

I made a sound, half-laugh, half-sob. *Ready?* Never. But I quivered underneath him and strained to lift my ass, needing him to take me now.

With one hand still lodged in my hair, he lifted his hips and slid his free arm beneath my waist to raise my hips.

I braced on my knees, my belly barely off the bed, because that's all the room he gave me, and then he was rutting against me, pushing between my folds, quick in and out slides, penetrating only a couple of inches.

"Don't tease," I said, hissing when he tightened his fingers on my hair. My scalp stung, but the pain only made the tension winding inside my core tighten more. Already, my lips were clenching, releasing, trying to capture his cockhead as he wet it in the fluid drenching my sex.

"You want this," he whispered, pushing a little deeper then withdrawing.

Way past worrying about my pride, I whimpered. "Yes. Yes, please."

"One thing, babe. One thing before I give it to you. Promise me."

My pulse pounded in my ears. "Anything, just please, Bulldog..."

He nuzzled into the hair beside my ear. "Don't ever scare me like that again."

He pushed inside then rotated his hips, his fat head dragging around my entrance. "Promise."

"Anything."

"Mean it."

I could have lied and told him what he wanted to hear. And I was tempted, but lying wasn't in me. "I...can't." I wanted to cry. Wanted to shout. But his weight crushed me, making breathing hard.

He let go of my hair and moved away.

I pushed to my elbows, but I couldn't look behind me. I'd never been torn down like that, reduced to quivering and begging. Not by any man. "I should leave," I whispered.

The bed shifted beside me. He lay on his back beside me, an arm beneath his head, his gaze on the ceiling above.

I glanced down his body and noted with not a little disappointment that his cock was still rigid, so heavy it rested on his firm belly. "You had no right to ask me that," I said, staring at his dick and knowing my expression was shattered.

He tucked his thumb under my chin and turned my head to meet his gaze. "You'll make an old man of me."

"Then ask Catch to reassign me to ride with someone else," I said, my voice surly.

Frowning, he shook his head. "Doesn't solve a damn thing."

"You think I'm a problem to solve?" I pushed up to sit on my folded legs, not caring his glance roamed my nude body. "You're the one with the problem. I have a job I know I can do well. Do you have any idea what I've faced? Being a woman in the Army, now a hunter with a bunch of misogynists? You may call me Buttercup, but I'm not some delicate princess. I know you spent time in the sandbox. And you know damn well, I did, too. And I wasn't serving any damn coffee to some general in the Green Zone."

Bulldog's face tightened. "I know you're capable. That you can handle yourself, but shit…" His gaze went to the bandage on my arm. He shook his head and rubbed a hand over his face. "For that minute when I was picking myself up off the ground, and I lost sight of you…"

Again, he shook his head and speared me with a look so stark my ready retort dried on my lips.

"So, you were worried about me. Maybe tomorrow, I'll be worried about you. Sounds like we'll both lose some sleep."

He blinked. The corners of his mouth twitched. "We losing that sleep together?"

"Depends on you, shithead." I cupped my breasts and jiggled them. "You're the one who climbed off this."

"Come here."

I narrowed my gaze. "I'm not making any damn promises."

"And I'll learn to deal. But you'll have to get used to this—me working out my…*issues*, when you do something that hits me square in the gut."

I held still for a second, and then gave him a slow smile. "Maybe you shouldn't give me incentives to make sure you get *issues* to work out on my ass."

One wicked brow arched. "Does your ass feel neglected?"

Done with waiting for him to get over himself, I leaned back, braced on my hands, and stretched out my legs, spreading them to offer an unencumbered view of what his dick was still hard for. "Better get up inside me, Bulldog, or I'll see if Dagger needs a new partner."

With his abs flexing, he sat, then climbed over me, not stopping his upward crawl until his cock nudged my pussy. "You'll ride with me," he said, his voice hard. "Where I can keep an eye out."

"Show me why I should choose you," I whispered.

His chest jerked on a grunt. "Do you ever stop?"

I puckered my lips and blew him a kiss. "No. Can you deal with this mouth?"

His lips landed on mine, effectively proving he could, and very well, as he devoured my mouth.

With the way he chose to fight, the horny part of me hoped I'd never win an argument.

I raised my knees to bracket his hips then scraped my fingernails from his shoulders to his hard ass. Without raising his body to make room between us, he entered me with a slow roll of his hips.

My mouth went slack beneath his as I reveled in the way he filled me, his girth stretching my inner walls. When he was all the way inside, he lifted his head and nipped my nose and my chin. "Buttercup, for a girl with such a big mouth, your pussy's just a little thing."

I pinched his ass. "Not delicate. Move!"

He chuckled, his upper body jerking against mine.

Right then, I might have smiled, but he slipped his hands under my ass and began rocking against me, sliding in and out, while his body ground against mine, heating the skin of my breasts and belly.

I needed him to give me space to let me move, needed him to get on his knees so he could stroke me with deeper, longer thrusts. More than that, I needed my clit rubbed, or I'd never come. Frustrated, I glared upward.

His smile was sly. He knew he was driving me crazy.

I lifted my lips in a snarl. "You want something..."

"I do."

"You've already got me naked. You're already inside me."

"Baby, I just decided I want more."

I widened my glare and slipped a finger into the crease of his ass.

Again, showing surprising speed, he slipped his hands from beneath me, grabbed my arms, and moved them upward. "I want you to agree that when we're here, in this bed, you'll do whatever I want."

I shrugged. "Will whatever you want give me what I want?"

"Eventually."

I pursed my lips and frowned. "And what do you want right now?"

His gaze dropped to my mouth.

"I'm down with that," I said, my voice dropping to a husky whisper. Sure, it wouldn't have taken much to push me into an orgasm, a flick of a nail against my clit, but I was curious about he'd feel inside my mouth...for starters.

"I'm gonna pull out now, but I want you to stay still. Agreed?"

At my nod, he slid slowly from within me, then knelt beside me and rolled off his condom. "I'm clean, Buttercup," he said, fisting his shaft and giving it a long pull.

I liked seeing his big hand slide on his rigid cock. "Me, too. And on the pill. Just so you know." I swallowed then licked my lips because my mouth was drying up—likely because it had hung open so long as I'd stared at him fisting himself. Something about watching him pump his generous man-meat, the sight glorified by the background of his muscled body, covered in gray-and-black tattoos of skulls festooned with flowers and guns, made me feel very, very feminine.

Here in his bed, just as I'd agreed, I'd do anything he wanted so long as I could touch every inch of his skin...suck every inch of his hard cock...

He lay on his back and held his cock so it pointed at the ceiling. "Your mouth on me..."

I scrambled up to kneel by his side.

But he shook his head and held out his arms. "Your pussy on my mouth..."

Better and better. I angled my body around and slowly lifted a knee over his head. With his hands guiding me, I spread myself and lowered, then gasped as his mouth latched on my labia, sucking and nibbling on my folds.

He slid a hand over my ass and smacked it, reminding me of my task.

Braced on one hand, I used the other to grip him at the base and lowered my mouth to suck his head. I swirled my tongue around and around, learning the territory and sliding into his tiny slit.

His musky scent and taste made me hungrier, and I opened wide and glided downward, loving the feel of him sliding on my tongue as I went deep. When the cap touched the back of my throat, I swallowed, the action giving him a sexy caress that made him groan against my sex.

His fingers entered me. His tongue slid to my clit, slicking over it. Then fingers lifted the top of my folds, pulling away the hood protecting my swelling knot of nerves.

I opened my throat and sank deeper, giving him everything he could want, just so he'd keep doing what he was—tapping, rubbing, flicking—until my thighs and belly quivered.

Mouth stuffed, I breathed noisily through my nostrils, little whimpers escaping as he fingered me. When he sucked my clit, I gave a very muffled shout. He had me on the edge, but I wanted his permission, his encouragement, before I flew. I wanted to please him more than I wanted my own pleasure.

Bulldog released my clit and kissed it. Then he withdrew his fingers. "I want you on your hands and knees," he said, his voice rough and tight.

I came off him and trailed my tongue one last time up his shaft, then quickly crawled sideways, still faced away and waiting.

His hands gripped my ass and spread my cheeks. "Everything's red and wet," he rasped.

I sank my belly to lift my ass and braced my arms.

When he nudged my pussy, I bit my lower lip to still a cry. When he pushed inside, I arched deeper, waiting as he screwed slowly inside, swirling around and around, until his groin was snug against me.

I reached beneath me and gripped his balls, fondling the warm, heavy sac.

His thumbs slid into my crack and pressed on my tiny, puckered hole. "That ass is mine, Buttercup."

A promise I'd make him keep. "Yes."

Then he gripped the notches of my hips and strained inward. "This pussy is mine."

"Yes." I glanced sideways at the mirror above his dresser. I liked what I saw—every muscle of his body defined as he held himself there behind me. So big and ridiculously masculine.

Then there was no time to admire the picture we made—hard and soft, large and small—because he began to move, pushing me away as he withdrew, bringing me back with a snap as he thrust forward. Nothing gentle about his fucking. Hard, harsh—each muscular thrust rattling my teeth.

Slow, at first. Then faster. His cock tunneled, heating my core. Tension coiled deep inside me, making it hard to catch my breath. I grunted and moaned. Until I sobbed.

His balls banged against the top of my folds, each bounce a tease. But I didn't dare fiddle with my clit. That was his right. And I knew he'd take it when he was ready. Already, he'd proven he knew what I liked. What I needed.

My breasts quivered with his strokes, the tips hard as pebbles and aching. My pussy spasmed around him, my channel convulsed...wet...so wet, the sounds of his flesh hitting mine grew louder and sloppier.

When at last he shortened his thrusts and bent to reach around me, I tossed back my hair and stiffened, ready. *Now, now, now...*

He bent farther while he kept stroking and nuzzled the corner of my neck. "Now, baby. *Fuck, now.*"

He gave my engorged clit a twist.

I shattered, keening as he emptied himself inside me. The cry emitted long and thin.

Long moments later, I was still dragging air into my lungs and shivering.

Bulldog wrapped his arms around me, then bracing an arm on the bed, brought us both down, his cock still lodged inside me.

We lay on our sides, his hands caressing my breasts. The weight of his arm against my waist felt...right. Somehow comforting.

A kiss landed on my shoulder. "Fucking unbelievable," he whispered.

I grinned. Though my injured arm was beginning to throb and I was tired, I didn't want to sleep. I wanted to bask in the moment and catalog every sensation—the hot palms squeezing my tits, the waning thickness locking our bodies together, his large, bearish frame snuggled against my back. "Think you might want to do that again?" I asked, surprised that my voice sounded so girly, so needy. My heart tripped as I wondered whether I'd pressed for too much.

Bulldog bit my shoulder then eased away.

Without being told, I turned and rested my head on his arm. He pressed me closer until my breasts rested against his. Then he slid a hairy thigh between mine. Again, I was surrounded by his body.

His gaze was on the fingers that played with a nipple, where a thumb rubbed lazily across it. "We ride together. We sleep together."

I appreciated his simplistic speech. To the point. Reassuring. "I liked today," I said. "Everything about it."

"Even our argument?"

One side of my mouth twitched upward. "I like the way you ended it. But..." I waited until his gaze rose to lock with mine. "This doesn't mean I'll be so easy at work."

"Think you're easy?" he laughed. "My dick's a fucking nub."

I reached down and gripped his "nub." "And now, I have high expectations," I drawled as I gave it a gentle tug.

He grimaced. "I'd just as soon not let the other guys know."

I narrowed my eyes. "Because you're embarrassed?"

"No, because they'll be all over me, asking me how good you are in bed."

I gave his nub another, not-so-gentle tug. "What would you tell them?"

"I don't fuck and tell, babe, but if I did..." He flicked my nipple with a nail. "I'd tell them you're the best I've ever had."

I let go of his cock and snuggled closer to his chest. "Is that the truth?"

"I won't ever lie."

I guessed by his lowering eyebrows that he was waiting for me to respond in kind. "Don't go getting a big head," I said, sliding my gaze away, because truth-time made me uncomfortable. I rubbed my palm over his heart and thought about what I wanted to say. Something to tell him just how pleased I was with him as a lover, but something that would also tell him that this, for me, hadn't just been about fucking. Somewhere along the way, I'd started feeling something... more. "I'd like to try this, Bulldog."

"Chris."

I blinked.

"Just because I want you to say my name doesn't mean I'll stop calling you Buttercup."

I pressed my lips together to keep from grinning. He'd saved me from getting all mushy, but at the same time, he'd told me—with just one word, his name—that he wanted to be closer, too. "Chris." Taking a deep breath, I finally met his gaze.

He was smiling.

Maybe it was a bit smirky, but he'd earned the right to feel proud of himself.

I inched my thigh upward until I nudged his balls. Then I arched a brow in challenge.

Bulldog growled deep in his chest and rolled over me, trapping me with his weight. "Sure you can take more?"

"Again," I said breathlessly. "Not delicate."

* * *

A WEEK LATER, we pulled into a far corner of a parking lot outside a biker bar that Sparky Leonard's ex-girlfriend named as his favorite haunt.

"His bike's here, all right," Bulldog muttered as he stared down the long line of bikes parked in front of the bar.

"And you know that, how?"

He shrugged. "I ride with his club sometimes."

I frowned, trying to see inside the window, but we were too far away and the glass proved too dirty. "They know where you work?"

"I might have mentioned it."

I shook my head. "Then you can't go in first. Everyone will know straight away why you're there."

Sparky had failed to show up for his regularly scheduled drug test. Our job was to deliver him straight to jail.

"Not how this works, Buttercup."

"So you keep saying." I didn't glance his way as I took off my jacket then wrestled under my shirt to remove my bra. I pulled the band from my ponytail and shook my hair around my shoulders. Then I opened my jeans and tucked in the tee, tightly enough the tips of my boobs were clearly visible.

"What are you doing?"

I removed my holster and stuffed my weapon in the glove box. Then I shoved handcuffs in the back pocket of my jeans. "Give me a couple of minutes before you come inside. I'll get close to him."

He reached out and wrapped his fingers around my upper arm.

I stared down at his hand then lifted my head to give him a steely glare.

Only he didn't begin reading me the riot act, telling me how this would go down—me waiting in the truck while he took down the bad guy. Instead, he pulled my upper body over the console between us and kissed me silly.

When he released me, he gave me a wink. "Two minutes. Tops."

I touched my puffy lips as I headed inside, sure everyone there could tell how turned on I was. Sure enough, my chest got whistles.

Sparky was sitting at the bar, his thinning red hair peeking out from beneath the blue bandana he wore Axl-Rose style around his head. As I approached, his gaze locked on my chest.

I paused beside him and leaned over the arm he held extended toward his beer, making sure my breast brushed his skin as I pretended to seek the bartender's attention.

"Hey, sweet thing," he said, his gaze going from my boobs to my eyes.

"Hey, yourself." I gave him a slow wink.

He cleared his throat and sat straighter. "Can I get you a drink?"

I leaned closer, trying not to wrinkle my nose at the smell of stale sweat. "No, but you can place your arms behind you."

"I can?" he asked, his gaze falling again to my tits as I rubbed them on his chest then on his arm as I circled behind him. Then I reached into my back pocket, pulled out the cuffs, deftly slapped them open, and clicked one around his wrist.

"Baby, you don't have to do that," he whined. "I woulda said yes."

Around him, laughter started as his buddies figured out quicker than he did that he wasn't about to get lucky. Maybe they knew because Bulldog was making a beeline toward me, his gaze smoldering.

Had he seen me cozy up to Sparky?

I grabbed Sparky's other wrist and pulled it back. The second cuff secure, I pushed him off the stool. "Time to go, baby."

Bulldog growled and gripped Sparky's upper arm, yanking him away.

As I followed the two men, I swung my hips, grinning as whistles followed me out the door.

After Bulldog helped Sparky into the back seat of the SUV, he slammed the door then rounded on me. His hands shot out and gripped my hips to pull me against his body.

The kiss that landed on my mouth ground my lips against my teeth, but I didn't mind. I slid a hand over the front of his jeans.

He jerked back and handed me the keys. "Drive."

He never let me drive, but I got it. He didn't want my unfettered boobs anywhere near Sparky's person. I sauntered to the driver's door and let myself in. Then I adjusted the seat and mirror, dipping it low enough I could lock gazes with my man.

"Bulldog, she's yours?" Sparky asked, his voice a tinny whine.

"All mine."

"Damn. Are her tits for real?"

"Sparky—" Bulldog gritted out. "You want to keep your teeth, you won't mention my girl's tits again."

The rest of the drive was made in silence. Bulldog insisted I remain in the car while he took care of Sparky and the paperwork inside the jail. I figured he didn't want anyone else seeing my assets bounce.

When he returned, he eyed me through the windshield, and I quickly climbed over the console into the passenger seat. Before my butt hit the leather, he slammed the door.

Five minutes later, he pulled into a small gas station and escorted me straight into the restroom in the back. Inside five seconds, he had my jeans around my knees. Then he bent me over in front of the sink and fucked me.

After we both came hard, we bought sodas and took a more leisurely route to the agency with our hands clasped atop the console.

"That was fun." I rolled my head on the headrest to glance at his profile. Bumpy nose, heavy brows, square chin. All manly muscle. I sighed.

"Next time," he said, lowering his voice into that gravely growl I was coming to love, "don't give me a hard-on before we make the grab."

I huffed a breath. I wasn't making a promise I couldn't keep.

MR. BIG

SUKIE CHAPIN

Thanks to my thrice-wrecked '96 Taurus with a botched engine rebuild, I'm a master at looking cool and tough on all varieties of roadsides. This time, my POS car kicks it on a deserted country road. I'm knee deep in grass and burs, definitely not imagining the bushes rustling around me in a definitively sinister way. Yeah, no Texas-Chainsaw-Massacre thoughts running through my mind.

Lights appear in the inky darkness, and I shield my eyes. I also say a little prayer. "Please God, let this be Gabe and not a man with a chainsaw. And if it is a man with a chainsaw, I'm really sorry I stole that Mounds in sixth grade. Amen." And although I'm pretty sure I've never had a prayer answered, the familiar black tow-truck stops in front of my hunk-of-junk. Hey, there's a first time for everything.

The door opens and a muscular arm appears, familiar tattoos snaking up the tanned skin and disappearing under the rolled-up sleeve of a flannel shirt. Boots hit the ground and kick up dust, and his smile does the same, stirring the motes in my long-forgotten libido.

Okay, okay. No sense pretending. I, Daisy Mays, have a teeny-tiny crush on my mechanic.

His hair is standing up in all directions. He always has that sexy-tousled look, like he just finished doing something manly and sweaty. I like it. But that smile, man. That smile with those deep dimples and the little bit of scruff. *Unf!* It's not fair, really. I can't fight a smile like that; it's pussy-kryptonite.

"Again?" he says, grinning and pulling tools from the backseat.

I watch his arms flex and feel a little tingle between my legs. Crap. "Jesus, Gabe, I'm *so* sorry." I feel horrible for dragging him out past midnight on a Wednesday.

He chuckles and waves me off. "It ain't no thing, Daisy. Couldn't leave you stranded, could I?"

He pops my hood, and it's magic time. He tells me to turn this, pump that, but Wynona just sputters, and then noxious smoke billows out around Gabe's head.

He slams the hood and swipes grime off his face with his sleeve.

I get a peek of lean belly. The irrational urge to lick him there trickles through me, but I shove it away. This is serious business. My bank account is riding close to zero, and I owe tuition.

"Sorry, sweetheart, got to tow it."

And to really seal the deal of my absolute shit-luck, Gabe's announcement is punctuated by a giant clap of thunder; the sky opens up, and God rains down his tears of disappointment for my life. It pours. Steam rises off the pavement, and the smell of wet cement and crushed grass fills the air.

I climb from the driver's seat and kick the piece of crap, not caring that rain pours into my shoes and my mascara streams down my face.

"Hey, hey. Be kind to Wynona, and she'll be kind to you,"

Gabe says over the sound of rain pinging against metal. He pats Wynona's hood.

"Yeah, well, she's not kind to me. She's evil and wants to ruin my life."

He chuckles and gets to work hooking her up. "Get in the truck," he yells, but I shake my head, and he pins me with a withering look.

I'm not sitting in his warm, dry truck while he gets drenched. Besides, watching him is a nice distraction. Nice enough that I don't even mind the rain so much. Damn, his ass is incredible. It fills out his faded Levi's, and I fight the impulse to touch it.

And now, his soaked pearl-snap is clinging to his back and arms, and honest to God, the picture is pornographic. He's like something out of some filthy video. Any moment now he'll start popping buttons, maybe chug some water, pour it on his head, then shake his hair so all the droplets fly.

I shake my own head.

I'm not usually a cat in heat, but something about Gabe gets me going. Maybe it's how gruff and no-nonsense he is, or it's that body or the fact that he's rescued me exactly twelve times in four months. Whatever the reason, I've got it bad.

"Please get in the truck," he hollers again, this time with more conviction.

Lightning blazes across the sky, illuminating him in a way that should be illegal. People shouldn't look that good wet. "No thanks," I yell back.

He makes a frustrated sound. "Then get what you need out of Wynona before I load her up."

That he remembers my car's name is pretty damn cute. I might be a little flattered. I might try to read too much into it, too. I bat that away and open Wynona's trunk.

"What's all this? Making a break for the border?" Gabe

asks, appearing beside me and pointing at my collection of bags.

I don't want to tell him I have four suitcases of high-end sex toys. I really don't. "Work stuff." Hey, sex-toy-seller is too a real job. It pays for grad school, and that's what counts.

"Heavy," he says, grabbing bags.

"Paperwork."

He gives me a funny look, his handsome face kind of squinched up, one dimple super-pronounced while the other disappears altogether. His eyes are warm brown, but in the dim light of the roadside, they look black and deep, but I know they're smiling.

He finishes loading Wynona, and then turns to me, my keys in his hand. "Here," he says and sends them sailing in my direction. "Grab your house key…"

But the rest of his words die on his lips because somehow, out here in the middle of butt-fuck-Egypt, Texas, a sewer grate just happens to be in the road, and the flying keys bounce off my open palm and directly into the bottomless pit. We both stare at the spot that just swallowed my hope.

"Well," he says, hands on his hips. "That happened."

"Son of a mother."

I hit my knees, prying up the grate. Gabe's beside me, and we lug off the cover and peer into nothingness. He shines a light down there, ever the Boy Scout, but the water rushes so fast that I can't see a thing.

I sink back on my heels, defeated. Gabe heaves the grate back into place and stands. I look up at him, utterly spent, soaked to the bone, broke, exhausted, and in need of some alcohol, an orgasm, and a warm bed, not necessarily in that order.

He holds out his big, warm hands, and I place my smaller, cold ones in his. Lightning streaks across the sky, and I catch a glimpse of his face. Empathy and a heaping tablespoon of knight-in-shining-armor, all dressed down in threadbare jeans and oil-stained boots.

He pulls me to my feet, and my shoes squelch their way to his truck. He opens the door for me like he's a gentlemen and we're on a date to a nice restaurant, instead of drenched and screwed on the side of the road. When he starts the car, the last strains of my favorite song boom from his speakers, and I lay my head against the headrest.

"We'll figure it out," he says, his deep voice comforting.

I chuckle, no real humor behind it. "I don't have a spare to my house. Or car."

He pats my knee.

Despite everything else, I feel the touch in other, more intimate places.

"We'll figure it out," he says again, then pulls a beat-up sweatshirt from the back seat and lays it in my lap.

"No, no," I say. "You're cold, too." I push it into his lap, but he plops it back in mine. Now it's smudged with grease and rain. His hands are always a little stained with oil, and for some reason, that's just as hot as everything else about him. He *fixes* things. With those hands. Those talented, talented hands that take broken parts and make them okay.

"Put it on, Daisy," he says, his tone not inviting any resistance.

But of course I resist. "No, you." He pins me with a look that roots me to the spot. And, oh man, spots respond.

"Put it on, now. You're freezing, and I can see…everything." He makes a swirling gesture with his hand around the vicinity of my breasts. "And it's distracting me."

I glance down, and indeed, my white shirt isn't leaving much to the imagination.

"A lot," he adds for emphasis.

I sigh and take the sweatshirt. "Alrighty, then." I pull it over my head. The shirt's warm and smells like him.

He's quiet as he drives, listening to the radio, sometimes humming along. He doesn't seem to want to talk.

Instead, I think he's giving prickly-me some time to de-prickle. And it's working. All I'm thinking about is that he was distracted by my breasts. Gabe. Distracted. By my breasts. "Were you still at the garage this late?" I ask after a few miles.

"Technically." He glances at me, and in the dim light of the passing street-lamps, he looks dark and dangerous. But I know better. "I live over the shop."

"Can you hear the garage phone from upstairs?"

He shakes his head and purses his lips, like he's about to share something he's not sure he should. "You didn't call the garage."

"But that's the number—"

Then it clicks.

"Ooooh," I say, letting the end trail off and down the road with all my assumptions.

"Ooooh," he says back in the same tone, nodding.

"You gave me your cell phone number? Why?"

Gabe shrugs those broad shoulders, and I itch to touch them. "Because I wanted to."

I'm quiet, mulling over that little nugget. But I can't make it add up. Gabriel Torres is that hero from romance novels who rides a Harley and breaks girls' hearts with his penis. He's the type of guy who goes for Ginger.

And I'm most definitely Mary Ann.

"How's the thesis?" he asks, yanking me back to *now*.

"Thesis?" I ask, my brain momentarily overloaded with paradigm shift and lust. "Oh, yeah, that. It's good. Almost done."

"Robert Frost treating you right?"

He remembered, and I'm doing that reading-too-much-into-it deal again. "Yeah. My one true love." I wait a beat then ask, "How's your niece? Did they put tubes in her ears?"

He grins, all those dimples again, like crack but for faces. "She's good. They didn't have to do the tubes."

"Your brother getting to see her more?" His relationship with his brother and his family is complicated. Lots of back and forth, and it tore Gabe up.

He tilts his head a little and raises his brows. "Actually, he and his wife are back together, if you can believe it."

"After all the drama? Really?"

"Yeah," he says, nodding. "But they're really happy this time. Them being happy is good for Tatiana."

"I'm glad to hear that." I never had a family unit like that. Mom's back in Missouri, and I've been on my own since I was eighteen. Moving from boyfriend to boyfriend, she wasn't the type to settle down and raise kids. I try my damnedest to be nothing like her. Her behavior made me careful and jaded.

"How's your mom?" Gabe asks, like he's reading my damn mind.

"She's okay. Broke up with Billy, but there's somebody new. Says she's moving to Tampa with the new guy."

Gabe nods.

I'm hit with the fact that he knows more about my life than my closest friends. Hell, I've spent more time in his truck or garage than I have with anyone else in ages. And, for some reason, I tell him stuff. I chalk it up to the silly crush. My libido must trigger some hormone that loosens my tongue. Yeah, that's it.

"Daisy?" The way he asks, I know I'm not going to want to answer.

"Huh?"

"What's really in those suitcases?"

I sigh, because why the hell not? "Sex toys. Lots and lots

of sex toys." Gabe laughs because he thinks I'm joking, and I really wish I was. Selling dildos and vibrators to drunk, cackling, grabby women isn't the most dignified career.

When I don't join in, he sobers. "Oh. Really?"

"Yep. I sell sex toys." I pump my fist weakly. "Woo-hoo."

"Do you test them out?" He realizes the can of worms he's opened just as the first wriggly pink head appears over the rim and tries to smash the lid back on. "And *that* is none of my business."

I shrug. What the hell do I have to lose? He's already admitted to looking at my boobs and giving me his number. Lord knows, I want him more than I've ever wanted anyone in my life. Might as well discuss sex toys. "Some of them."

"What's your best seller?"

"Hands down, Mr. Big."

Laughter explodes. "Mr. Big? What the hell is that? Wait, I don't want to know."

I laugh too, now. "Oh, sure you do. Mr. Big is the Rolls-Royce of dildos. Nine inches of anatomically correct purple pleasure. Made of easy-to-clean silicone and manufactured with a suction cup for shower play and a curved shaft for g-spot stimulation. He's also grape flavored and ribbed for your pleasure." I finish my sales schpeal with a cheesy grin.

Gabe bites his lip to keep from laughing. "Don't tell me anymore. I don't need to know," he says, and then melts into hilarity.

I shrug. "Suit yourself, but you're missing out."

He maneuvers the subject back to a safe-zone, my classes, and we chat for the remainder of the drive.

"So you can't get into your house?" he asks as he pulls into the garage.

"Nope," I say, popping the 'p.'

He cuts the engine and turns to me. "You take my bed. I'll crash on the couch. We'll figure out the rest tomorrow."

Sounds simple enough. Simple and dangerous, but hell, who am I to complain? Not like I have anyplace else to go. I nod and unbuckle.

The garage smells of oil and concrete as I follow Gabe to a narrow stairwell, my bags banging against the walls. At the top, he swings open the door and waves me in.

His apartment is small but neat—an efficiency with a bed against one wall and kitchen against the other. In the middle floats a small island of low bookshelves covered in rows of books. Paperback, hardback, graphic novels— they're all represented. A small, breathless "Wow" escapes my lips.

Gabe crosses to the kitchen and grabs a tea kettle of all things.

I laugh. I can't help it.

"What? My books?" he asks.

"No. I mean, yes. I didn't expect that. But the tea kettle is what really did me in."

He shrugs those big shoulders and grins, not the least bit bothered by my poking. "I like tea."

I nod and take a look around the place. Nothing feminine here. Black leather sofa, dark furniture, big-ass TV.

"Want some?" he asks.

I turn, finding him watching me. "Sure."

"Wanna grab a shower while it boils?"

"Sure," I say again, but what I really want is something else. But how to make that happen…

I drop my bag, and when it hits the tile floor, the cheap latch pops open and out tumbles none other than Mr. Big himself, in all his phallic glory.

Well, that's one way to do it.

Gabe makes a small sound that might be a laugh but could just as easily be a sound of horror. Who really knows? Despite my comfort level with fondling these devices of female pleasure in front of strangers, my cheeks heat. This is different. Gabe is different.

I stoop and shove the purple-pussy-eater back in my bag and stand, clearing my throat. I force my gaze to meet his, and he's trying to keep it together, to not laugh. But he can't really help it, and now I can feel the heat of my flush in my ears and neck. *Jesus.* "Yeah, so, about that shower. Cold, right?" I say.

He laughs harder. "Wanna bring Mr. Big?" he asks, gesturing to my bag and its weapons-of-pussy-destruction.

"I'm good, thanks." I slink behind him to the bathroom, face aflame.

Gabe starts the water, places a clean towel on the sink, and tests the temperature.

Pretty damn cute. I pull off the sweatshirt, and Gabe watches, his gaze eating me up for a fleeting moment before his gentlemanliness takes the wheel again. He's staring at me, and I'm staring at him and all I can think is *kiss-me-kiss-me-kiss-me.*

But then the kettle whistles, and he backs out of the bathroom. "Shampoo's in the shower. Yell if you need anything." And he disappears, closing the door behind him.

I make quick work of my hair and washing, avoiding the urge to let my fingers linger between my legs. I'm excited. More so than I've been in...forever. When I'm finished, I wrap the towel around myself.

The bathroom door makes a soft snick sound as I open it, and Gabe looks my way. His gaze travels over my bare shoulders and the knot I've made in the towel over my breasts. It lingers there, then shimmies down my body, over my hips and bare thighs. He clears his throat and looks away, but his gaze skates back to me. "Clean clothes are by the door."

Then he turns back to the stove like he can pretend he didn't just check me out. Like he can pretend that there isn't enough sexual tension in his apartment to blow the place to bits. I don't reach for the clothes.

He notices.

"You should put those on, Daisy. It's cold." He keeps his gaze trained on the tea.

I still don't touch the clothes. Instead, I move toward him.

"Daisy, honey, for the love of God, put on the clothes."

He sounds so exasperated with me, and I love the way "honey" drips off his tongue like the sweet syrup itself, thick and warm and sticky. Hearing it makes me want him more, this man who keeps rescuing me. The one I tell things that nobody else knows. The one who fixes broken things and has a house full of books and remembers that I'm working on my thesis, because I want to write, too.

I'm behind him now, close enough that I can touch him. He's in a T-shirt and pajama pants, but I want him to be in nothing. "Gabe," I say.

But he shakes his head. "Daisy, if I turn around and you're standing there in a towel..."

But he doesn't finish the thought. I fill in all kinds of things like, "I'll ravage you," and "I'll have to bend you over my knee and spank you," and even, "You'll really, really like what comes next," because I'm about 115% sure that I will. Whatever it is, I'll like it because I can read it in the lines of his body and the way he shifts his weight like maybe, just maybe, he's trying to relieve some pressure in his pants.

"If you turn around and I'm standing here in a towel, what?"

He makes an impatient sound and runs a rough hand through his hair. "You realize what you're doing, right?"

I step closer so my breasts brush his back, and he sucks in a breath. "Mmm-hmmm," I say.

My fingertips find the hem of his T-shirt, and I lift it and trace the line of hair that trails from his chest to his—"

Gabe whirls in my arms, and his lips touch mine.

This kiss is so, so damn sweet. All I can think is *finally* and *hallelujah*. He doesn't finesse, with polite lips and delicate tongue; he takes, grabbing a fistful of hair and guiding my head where he wants it. I open to him, moan when his tongue brushes mine and his hand finds its way inside the towel. All it does is rest on my back to pull me closer, but it feels like much more. Like a tongue or a cock inside me or, at the very least, a rude finger someplace it definitely doesn't belong among polite society.

My arms twine around his neck, my fingers in that dark, messy hair, and he crushes me against his chest. We're frantic, hands and mouths mauling every inch of each other. My towel is gone, lost to some struggle around the kitchen table, and Gabe's shirt fell someplace in the vicinity of the couch. It's full on sex-war, and we're doing our damnedest to achieve world domination.

My thighs hit mattress, and then we're both falling into the softness. His skin is warm, almost hot, against my breasts, and I moan and sigh and wriggle to get closer. Gabe echoes my sentiments and kicks free of his pajamas, until I feel his hard thighs against mine.

"Oh God," I say, spreading my legs so his weight settles there. If I rock my hips just a bit—

But then Gabe grinds against me.

I see stars and moons and heavenly bodies singing the Body Electric.

"Good?" he asks and does it again.

My eyes roll back in my head as his lips caress my neck, nipping and kissing along the vulnerable flesh. Fingers grasp my nipple, rolling, and elicit a shudder and a moan, everything low in my belly pooling hot and liquid.

Gabe's back is hard under my exploring hands, muscles pinched to peaks. I want to see him, to feel every inch, and remember every second in case I never get another chance. He feels solid and reassuring. Like his strength, the heft of him alone, could solve half my problems. The thought's ridiculous, I know. But it doesn't change the fact I feel safe and more okay than I've felt in a very long time. "You're big," I say.

"Uh-huh."

"Do you lift?"

"Uh-huh."

"Why'd you never tell me?"

He raises his head and gives me a look. His brows are raised, but he's fighting a smile. "Daisy." The *come on* is implied.

"Right," I say. "Back to work."

He smirks as I push his head to my breast. His lips surround my nipple, and I cry out.

"Oh, God," I say again.

When he looks up at me, a smug but adorable grin spreads over his face, and those dimples make this sex scene into a four-way. "Gabe," he says.

"Huh?"

"My name, sweetheart. I'd like to hear it on your lips. *God*'s okay, but *Gabe*'s better."

I push his shoulder but grin back. "Smug-ass," I say, then lean up to kiss his dimples. "These are adorably hot."

He indulges me, chuckling and letting me kiss all over his face like an over-stimulated puppy. I definitely tongue one at one point, and he doesn't even flinch, instead sliding a hand down my body, through my curls, parting my lips, and finding my clit.

I suck in a sharp breath as he circles the bundle of nerves, and my head lolls against the bed. I'm incapacitated by his sex magic. His fixing hands. I'm going to have an orgasm, and we've barely just begun.

He switches things up, slips a finger inside me, then another, curls them until they're doing the exact right thing to make me come. "Oh, God, Gabe," I say, my legs shaking.

He presses a thumb to my clit, and I tip right over the edge into orgasmville. My mind goes blank, and the whole world spins on the axis of contracting muscles and delicious brain chemicals.

Gabe's lips are on my neck when I'm finally sentient enough to realize where I am. He's nuzzling me, and his lips and tongue feel better than the orgasm. His big hand strokes the curve of my back, holding me tight to him like I'm something to hold onto.

His lips find mine, and although I'm usually a one-and-done kind of girl, the hunger grows immediately.

"Daisy?"

"Mmm-hmm." He's nuzzling my neck again, except now he's biting, and it's sending shivers all over me.

"Go get Mr. Big."

I freeze, my hand on his tight butt cheek. There's very little 'asking' going on here. It's mostly commands, and I have to say, it's working remarkably well. I climb from the bed on Jell-O-legs, loving the way Gabe's gaze feels on my skin as I walk to my suitcases.

I turn, a brand-new-in-the-box Mr. Big in my hand, and all the breath rushes from my lungs. Naked Gabe does that to me. He's gorgeous—long, lean lines of muscle, tanned skin, and dark hair—all culminating in a masterpiece, something born from Michelangelo's chisel, but better, because he's flesh and blood. And most of that flesh and blood has accumulated between his legs.

The man has a monster cock. I glance at poor Mr. Big in my hand. The hunk of purple silicone doesn't have a thing on Gabe.

A slow smile spreads across his face at my reaction, and

as if to make sure I know it's reciprocal, he lets his greedy gaze travel over my body, stopping at my breasts in a bold display of male approval. His hand travels south, and he grasps his cock in that tanned, oil-stained fist and gives it a slow pump as he drinks in the rest of me.

And good God, I've never seen anything like it. I scramble onto the bed, and Gabe tears open the package just as I lunge for *his* package. My lips slide over the thick head of his cock, and he hisses a breath, his fingers tangling in my hair. He tastes like salt and decadence. I open my mouth and take more, wanting to feel him, measure him with my lips, taste the salt-tang of his pre-cum on my tongue.

The bed shifts, and Gabe curls around me. A small maneuver and we'd be sixty-nining. A tremor runs through me at the thought.

But instead, I feel something that definitely isn't a finger or a tongue. I freeze, not that I should be surprised, but now my situation seems surreal. Mr. Big himself is using Mr. Big on me.

Gabe works slowly, stretching me little by little. The walls of my pussy resist the intrusion, but Gabe is far more patient than I am. The combined effect of his cock in my mouth and Mr. Big inside me is intoxicating, and I push back and swallow more.

He massages my clit, Mr. Big slips farther inside, and I moan. And that's his cue. Gabe fucks me with the dildo, each stroke sliding heavy against my sensitive g-spot. I suck harder, bobbing my head and using my tongue in an effort to distract myself from the impending orgasm, but it's hopeless.

I come again, arching off of Gabe's erection and crying out. I collapse onto the sheets, my legs shaking, and then Gabe is over me, flipping me onto my back and kissing every inch of my face. I smile up at him, loopy and spent.

"Christ, that was hot, Daisy," he says between kisses.

Put a fork in me, I'm done. I can't even lift my head, but I can feel Gabe's hard, patient cock pressing against my thigh, and I'm not leaving this apartment anything but bow-legged.

Gabe is propped on his elbows over me, and I reach between us to fist him. He's slick from my mouth, and my hand glides up and down his rigid length. "Damn, man, I had no idea," I say.

"Me either," he says, but he's not looking at my body when he says it. No, he's looking at my face, mostly into my eyes, when the words leave his mouth.

My heart does a terrifying squeeze inside my chest.

He kisses my forehead tenderly and then the tip of my nose.

I feel fluttery inside. When I pump my fist again, Gabe groans and pushes into my grip. And how could I deny him? I shimmy my hips in his direction, and he moans.

A big hand brushes the tangled hair from my face. "Fuck, Daisy, I want this. No, need this. I need you."

And those words are scary as hell and the most perfect pillow talk I've ever heard.

He rolls on a condom, moves between my thighs, and guides his cock to my eager pussy. I say eager because that's exactly what it is. As soon as he tells me how much he wants me, needs me, I'm ready for him again. His thrusts are slow and careful, but I wriggle under him as he parts the delicate and abused flesh. Even through the discomfort, there's something exquisite about how thoroughly he takes me.

His mouth covers mine, and I sigh into the kiss, moving my hips in a restless, greedy way. I can't believe it, but I might come again. He holds my face in his hands and kisses me all over, and sometimes he just looks into my eyes. My fingers draw words on his back. Words like good and tomorrow and future. I don't even know why I do it, what possesses me, but I have this need to capture the moment, and words do that for me.

Gabe speeds his thrusts, and now his pelvis is rubbing my clit, and his cock is stroking, stroking inside me, and it's like hanging at the tippy-top of a rollercoaster.

I cry out his name as an orgasm takes me by surprise. It's a gentle roll this time, although no less intense. With each thrust, Gabe encourages it to start fresh until I really can't take any more, and tears leak from the corners of my eyes.

"Fuck, Daisy," he gasps.

I know he's feeling the same thing I am, the unrelenting squeeze of my body's pleasure. And other things, too. Things that need to be looked at, turned over, and discussed.

He kisses away the tears then speeds through a flurry of sloppy thrusts, face hidden in my neck. With a soft grunt, he stills, and I feel his cock jerk.

The mattress trembles as he collapses then drags me to him, so we're a tangle of hair and arms and legs and sheets. Our bodies, slick with sweat, stick together, but the feeling is amazing. And right.

Gabe kisses the top of my head over and over, and his fingers trace my backbone, the length of my arm, down my hip. "I have something for you," he says after a while, and then leaves me to rummage in his nightstand.

I miss the feel of him against me, and my fingers itch to pull him back. "Really?" I ask, surprised.

He drops a tattered old book on my bare belly, the spine broken and the cover stained.

I adore old books, the feel, the smell, the way the pages are soft under my fingertips. I told him that once. I lift the book, flip carefully to the cover page, that incredible aroma of old book wafting from the tatty pages.

Robert Frost.

First Edition.

Tears sting the backs of my eyes. *No way.*

"Do you like it?"

"Oh my God."

"Gabe," he teases and swats my thigh.

"It's perfect. Thank you," I say, looking into the eyes of the man who's quickly teaching me that maybe *careful* and *jaded* aren't the best things to be.

"I know we did this backwards, Daisy, but let me take you on a date. Let's see what this is between us, because it's something," he says.

And how could I say *no* to my very own, real-life Mr. Big?

Adele Downs is the best-selling, award-winning author of more than twenty romance titles, including those written under another pen name, and a former journalist with hundreds of articles to her credit. When not writing in her home office in rural Pennsylvania, she can be found reading a book on the nearest beach, taking photographs, or riding in her convertible.

website | facebook | twitter

Belinda LaPage lives in Sydney, Australia, and one day hopes to write for a living. She likes stories more than words, journeys more than destinations, and numbers more than anything they count. When not writing, she enjoys reading, Sydney beaches, time with friends, and buying the wrong shoes.

facebook | website | twitter

Elle James spent twenty years livin' and lovin' in South Texas, ranching horses, cattle, goats, ostriches and emus. A former IT professional, Elle happily writes full-time, penning adventures that keep her readers begging for more. When she's not writing, she's traveling, snow-skiing, boating, or riding her ATV, concocting new stories.

website | facebook | newsletter

Jennifer Kacey is a writer, mother, and business owner in the great state of Texas. She sings in the shower, plays piano in her dreams, and has to have a different color of nail polish every week. Best advice she's ever been given? Find the real you and never settle for anything less.

webpage | facebook | twitter

Kalissa Wayne spends time in multiple universes, this is the blessing and curse of having a creative mind. She does her best to balance the real world and the creative one, but has a lot of help from her loving husband of 17+ years. She hopes you enjoy her story as much as she did writing it!

facebook | amazon

Kris Norris is an author, single mother, and slave to chaos. Kris is a jack-of-all trades who's endlessly searching for her ever-elusive clone. She loves writing heroines who kick ass, heroes who are larger than life, and stories that keep you on the edge of your seat. Life's an adventure…go find yours.

Layla Chase, on a dare, dove into exploring the steamier side of romance and discovered characters, both contemporary and historical, from all walks of life whose stories needed to be told. Layla lives in southern California with her soul-mate husband and two beloved dogs.

M. Marie lives in the heart of downtown Toronto, and is both an erotica writer and enthusiast. She finds the experience of writing erotica challenging, but also exciting, as it pushes boundaries she didn't even realize she had. Her stories and poetry are available in a number of anthologies.

Megan Mitcham is a *USA Today* bestselling author who pens sizzling suspense novels that whisk you across the globe, wedge your heart in your throat, make your hands sweat and your naughty bits tingle. Check out her special forces heroes in the Base Branch Series.

Mia Hopkins writes lush romances starring fun, sexy characters who love to get down and dirty. She's a sucker for working class heroes, brainy heroines, and wisecracking best friends. Mia lives in Los Angeles with her roguish husband and two waggish dogs.

website | twitter | facebook

N.J. Walters is a *New York Times* and *USA Today* bestselling author who has always been a voracious reader, and now she spends her days writing novels of her own. Vampires, werewolves, dragons, time-travelers, seductive handymen, and next-door neighbors with smoldering good looks—all vie for her attention. It's a tough life, but someone's got to live it.

website | facebook | twitter

Robie Madison pursues her own adventures traveling around the world. When she's at home, she writes about men and women who aren't afraid to take risks for love. When she's not traveling or writing, she can often be found teaching writing courses online.

Sukie Chapin has been a military wife, world traveler, almost-groupie, and preschool teacher. Naturally, the next logical step was writing erotic romance. She lives in Texas where she can be found reading, writing, mommying, and making a homemade chocolate pudding that will make you want to slap your mama.

website | newsletter | facebook

Susan Saxx writes sexy, heartwarming romances. Her REAL MEN series focuses on a band of Canadian military reservists and the strong women they fall in love with. Meet the cowboy, the ex-hockey player and more at her website, and join her mailing list for exclusive teaser stories and release updates!

website | twitter | facebook

Tray Ellis never learned to whistle and her home is rarely organized, but that just leaves more time for writing, which she adores. Gentle twirls of fate are her specialty and when she writes, she aims for quiet humor and a satisfying ending.

twitter | blog | facebook

Delilah Devlin is a *New York Times* and *USA Today* best-selling author of erotica and erotic romance. She has published over a hundred eighty stories in multiple genres and lengths, and is published by Atria/Strebor, Avon, Berkley, Black Lace, Cleis Press, Ellora's Cave, Grand Central, Harlequin Spice, HarperCollins: Mischief, Kensington, Kindle, Kindle Worlds, Montlake, Running Press, and Samhain Publishing.

Her short stories have appeared in multiple Cleis Press collections, including *Lesbian Cowboys, Girl Crush, Fairy Tale Lust, Lesbian Lust, Passion, Lesbian Cops, Dream Lover, Carnal Machines, Best Erotic Romance (2012), Suite Encounters, Girl Fever, Girls Who Score, Duty and Desire, Best Lesbian Romance of 2013,* and the upcoming *On Fire.* For Cleis Press, she edited *Girls Who Bite, She Shifters, Cowboy Lust, Smokin' Hot Firemen, High Octane Heroes, Cowboy Heat, Hot Highlanders and Wild Warriors,* and *Sex Objects.* She also edited *Conquests: An Anthology of Smoldering Viking Romance* and *Rogues: A Boys Behaving Badly Anthology.*

website | facebook | twitter

ROGUES

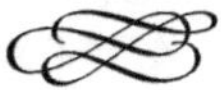

BOYS BEHAVING BADLY BOOK #1

EDITED BY
DELILAH DEVLIN

New York Times & USA Today

Bestselling Author

Rogues
A BOYS BEHAVING BADLY ANTHOLOGY #1
EDITED BY DELILAH DEVLIN
NEW YORK TIMES BESTSELLING AUTHOR

CONTENTS OF ROGUES

Her Heart's Tomb - Jennifer Kacey
Opals – Axa Lee
The Highwayman's Treasure by Emma Jay
Swindled by Megan Mitcham
Plunder by Delilah Night
The Heat by Mia Hopkins
The Highwayman Came Riding by Erzabet Bishop
Queen High by Cela Winter
Lady of the House by T.G. Haynes
Billionaire and the Jewel Thief by Elle James
An Eye for Love by Cynthia Young
Roguishly Handsome and Other Superhero Problems by Tray Ellis
Glass Slippers, Hardly Worn by Bibi Rizer
Rogue's Heart by Delilah Devlin

Rogues

ABOUT ROGUES

Rogues! Even the word conjures a special sort of hero—a playful bad boy with a heart of gold—at least when it comes to his lady love. This volume is filled with the Jack Sparrows of old—pirates sailing the high seas, Regency-era highway men, modern day jewel thieves, like Cary Grant in *To Catch a Thief*—men doing bad things, bending or breaking the law, but in a very sexy way. With thirteen stories sure to satisfy the reader who craves that ultimate bad boy, prepare to have your heart stolen!

Rogues

www.ingramcontent.com/pod-product-compliance
Lightning Source LLC
Chambersburg PA
CBHW060949120726
47910CB00002B/549